THE DENVER CEREAL

For Heather—

You are a blessing!

May every new beginning

bring you love!

Claudia Hall Christian

ALSO BY CLAUDIA HALL CHRISTIAN

THE DENVER CEREAL

Claudia Hall Christian

Cook Street Publishing
Denver, CO

ISBN (*13 digits*) : 978-0-9822746-4-4
(*10 digits*) : 0-9822746-4-5
Library of Congress : 2009909009

PUBLISHER'S NOTE:

This is a work of fiction. Names, characters, places and incidents either are the
product of the author's imagination or are used fictitiously.

Second edition © September, 2009
Cook Street Publishing
PO Box 18217
Denver, CO 80218

For the Silent Partner,
who talks a lot.

September, 2009

Dear Reader,

When we published Denver Cereal, I wanted to follow in the tradition and style of the masters of serial fiction. I combined the living chapters from the website with the original drafts of the chapters and we did light copyediting.

Our first comments? "Great book, but what's up with the copyediting?" Jennifer Riley, one of our content editors for the Fey series, called to say that there were "big problems with Denver Cereal."

Oops.

Over the course of the next eight months, a number of people offered their time, energy and attention for copy editing. When the opportunity arrived to create a second edition of Denver Cereal, I asked them people if they might help out.

We created a secure wiki and asked them to change what they felt needed to be changed. The site included discussion page to talk through specific issues and a page for people to introduce themselves.

The results are amazing.

With great apologies to Charles Dickens and the rest, Cook Street Publishing presents the second edition of the Denver Cereal. For all their hard work, special thanks goes to Jennifer Riley, Angeles Winesett, La Shae Dorsey, and Payson Cooper. I am also grateful to Susan Parker and Tessa Bartz who helped bring the project along.

Denver Cereal is a labor of love. I cannot thank everyone involved in this project enough. I am also particularly grateful for you, the reader. Without you, Denver Cereal would not have come this far.

Warmly,

Claudia Hall Christian

CHAPTER ONE
JILL

"You cannot be serious," Megan said to Jill.

Jill's hazel eyes shifted to catch Megan's reflection in the full length mirror. Jill nodded then smiled at Megan's sour face. Jill zipped the back of her tight black leather skirt and tugged at the starched white shirt. Reaching behind her, Jill took a white vest from Megan.

"Turn around," Megan said.

Jill turned so Megan could help her button the vest.

"It's tight but..." Megan buttoned the top button in the white shirt.

Jill turned back to the mirror to evaluate. At twenty five years old, post one baby, she was still round and flat in all the right places. Leaning around the Colorado Rockies sticker on the mirror, she checked for mascara smudges.

"You are not going," Megan said.

"I'm going," Jill replied.

Jill wandered into her bedroom looking for the matching black pump to the four inch heel she held in her hand. Her head was under the bed when Megan said:

"He only invited you as a courtesy."

Jill grabbed the pump from under the middle of the bed.

"I have an invitation. I'm going," Jill said. "I want Trevor McGuinsey to see what he's missing."

"He's not going to see any farther than his fiancé's father's wallet."

Before Jill could put the shoes on her feet, Megan snatched them from her hand.

Jill looked Megan in the eye. "You are not helping, sis."

"I don't have any intention of helping my little sister make a complete fool out of herself."

Turning the shoes back and forth, Megan shook her head at the worn, dry Salvation Army found shoes. She peered at the point of the heel. At least the plastic wasn't showing yet.

"Pllleeezzzzeee," Jill begged.

Megan dropped the shoes in resignation. Why fight it? She could never resist Jill.

"Wear your boots," Megan said. "If you want my help, don't just bring the boots. Wear them."

Jill's eyes grew wide. She trotted into her bedroom closet and pulled out the boots, those beautiful boots. Holding the boots against her chest, Jill drew in the smell of the butter soft black leather from the thigh-high five-inch stiletto heel boots. They smelled like love, luck and happiness.

Trevor bought these boots at the Mile High Flea Market. They were three hundred dollars cash, more money than they had seen in six months, and so worth it. They had a good time in these boots. Trevor used to tell people that Katy was conceived with these boots. They were lucky boots. She used to tease him that they were his 'get lucky' boots.

Of course, she was wearing these boots, languishing in post coital bliss, when he told her. Pressing the divorce papers across the crumpled covers, he asked her to sign. He had met a rich girl. She was going to pay for law school at Denver University. He was doing it for Katy. Certainly Jill would understand.

But Jill never understood.

Oh, she signed the papers then scrubbed the remnants of him from her body, her apartment, and her life. When he returned, his things were waiting for him in the hall and the locks were changed. With Jill sobbing on the other side, he screamed, "I don't love the rich girl," and pounded on the cheap hollow core apartment door for an hour. Trevor only left because the apartment manager said he would call the police.

"Now, how's that gonna look to the rich girl, Trevor?" the apartment manager sneered.

Tonight, Trevor was to be officially engaged to the rich girl at a black tie affair.

Returning to the mirror, Jill saw that Megan was right. The boots looked great.

"Let me get the tie." Megan tied a black bow tie around Jill's neck. "You have the jacket with tails?"

"Mike's bringing it when he picks me up in the limo," Jill said.

"Do you want me to come?" Megan asked.

"I can do this, Meg," Jill said. "Steve's working security. If I need to get out fast, he'll be there."

"Mike and Steve are both in on this? What about Candy?"

"She's working the bar. I'm sorry, sis. They didn't tell you because they thought you would be mad."

Megan shook her head. Of course their brothers and sister were in on this. No one but Megan saw that Jill was making a fool out of herself. But Jill always made a fool of herself over Trevor.

"He's my soul mate," Jill pleaded when she needed Megan's signature on their marriage license. Sixteen years old and in love. Now twenty-five years old and heart crushed.

The apartment door opened to their brother Mike. Megan smiled at the worry on his face. At least she wasn't the only one who was worried. Mike's face shifted to a smile for Jill.

"Here you go, Jilly," Mike said. "I brought three."

One at a time, Jill tried on the black tux jackets with peak lapels and tails. She selected the one Mike thought made her look the sexiest.

Jill gave herself an 'I can do this' nod in the mirror.

She clutched Megan in a hug. With tears in her eyes, Megan released Jill.

"Love you, sis," Megan said then closed the apartment door.

Mike escorted Jill through the crowd of neighbors. Everyone wanted to cheer Jill on today. One last, 'Make us proud,' and Mike closed the door to the front seat of the limo. Slipping behind the wheel, Mike told her that Steve, their middle brother, said the guests had all arrived.

Jill would be the last one to show.

With a nod of his head, Mike started the limo. They turned down Thirteenth Avenue to make their way through the slow Friday afternoon traffic. Never one for conversation, Mike was relieved when Jill turned on the radio. They drove in silence to the Seawell Ballroom, Denver's Grand Ballroom, the place where her soul mate was announcing his step up in life.

When he turned onto Speer Boulevard, Jill closed her eyes to review. Her best friend, Sandy, squeezed her in between paying clients. Talking non-stop about 'That Prick Trevor,' Sandy colored, curled and primped Jill's hair until her hair fell in beautiful honey blonde waves.

She spent an hour at the MAC counter in the Cherry Creek Mall where Heather worked. Heather tried this mascara and that shadow. Careful not to mess up her hair, Jill washed her face at least three times before Heather was satisfied with her makeup. Leaving the shop, Heather pressed a bottle with the last drops of her favorite French perfume into Jill's hand.

"Don't cry. Don't cry. Don't cry," Heather said. "You'll ruin your make up."

Jill borrowed the vest and tie from Jack, her next door neighbor. The vest was part of Jack's uniform as a valet at the Brown Palace. She touched the vest as if to insure it wouldn't get stained. She promised Jack.

Tanesha arrived at the apartment just before Megan. She assured Jill the Italian bra and matching panties were on sale. When Jill went to put them on, she saw the tags. A hundred dollars! A piece! On sale!

Knowing she had been caught, Tanesha shrugged, "Once in your life, you deserve something beautiful. Especially today."

Megan came in when they were hugging and it was back to the business of getting dressed. Her stockings were sheer, black and beautiful. Jill was certain she had never worn such beautiful undergarments.

I wonder what Trev's gonna...

She bit her lip to keep from finishing the thought. She wasn't out of the habit of thinking of Trevor as her love, her life. Maybe tonight would do the trick.

Jill jerked back to the present when Mike touched her leg.

"You better get in the back, sis," Mike said. He pulled the limo to the curb at Colfax Boulevard.

Jill went to the back of the limo where she found a single long stem white rose with a red ribbon around it. She caught her brother's eye in the rear view mirror.

"I thought you could strangle him with the ribbon."

"Thanks Mikey."

At least people loved her. All of her low life friends - that's what Trevor called them now, 'her low life friends' - pulled this off. They waited the tables at the event, tended bar, played in the band, provided security and helped her get ready. They all wanted to show Trevor that he may be moving to an ivory tower, but it's friends that make a life.

"Ready?" Mike said. He extended a hand to help her out of the back of the limo.

Jill nodded then kissed his cheek.

"Love you sis," Mike said. "I'll be here 'til it's over."

"Oh Mikey, what about work?"

"The boss said you can have the limo and me all night. He thinks Trevor is a world class jerk."

"Don't kiss him again," their brother Steve said taking her arm. "Remember, high class women don't fraternize with the help."

Jill took Steve's arm. "Please thank Leslie for taking care of Katy tonight."

"We love her," Steve said. "It's easy. Now go in there and make us proud."

Clutching her long stemmed rose, Jill took the escalator up toward the ballroom. Her heart pounded in her chest and her pulse thumped in her ears. If she wasn't riding an escalator, she would have certainly run back to the limo. She shifted her feet back and forth on the step.

"I can do this," she reminded herself when she reached the top.

Letting out a breath, Jill waited for security to notice her.

CHAPTER TWO
AT THE SEAWELL BALLROOM

Letting out a breath, Jill waited for security to notice her. When the man turned, she smiled. It was her brother Steve's best friend, David.

"God damn, you look good," David said. "You should see the prunes inside."

She smiled and turned to look at the crowded room. She had never been in a room where she knew no one. As she watched, her sister's best friend floated by with a tray of hors d' oeuvres. Well, almost no one.

"Go find Candy," David said. "She's waiting for you behind the main bar."

Crossing the room, Jill felt every eyeball evaluate her. Out of the corner of her eye, she saw men stare while women shifted away. She chucked to herself over the men's lust filled looks. A hand brushed her arm and another friend walked by with a tray of hors d' oeuvres.

Catching a glimpse of Candy, Jill stepped to the bar. With the bar pressed against her ribs, she recited her purpose in her head:

"Show him what he's missing; just show him what he's missing; that's all, just show him what he's missing."

Jill was seconds into her mantra trance when she felt the warmth of a man standing next to her. His eyes were focused on her face.

"Hi," he said.

Jill looked over at him, then back to the bar. She had practiced this for weeks. Sophisticated women are unfriendly. Don't smile. Don't be nice. Don't be your effervescent self.

"I thought I knew everyone on the guest list," he said. "But I do not remember an invitation to the most beautiful woman I've ever seen in my entire life."

Jill couldn't help herself. She started laughing.

Wrinkling her nose, she asked, "Is that a pick up line?"

"Pretty pathetic, eh? I'm Jacob," he said.

"Jill." She held her hand out and he shook it.

"Jill as in 'baby mommy' Jill?" Jacob asked.

"I'm not sure what you're asking," Jill said.

"My sister is marrying this guy, Trevor? He has a baby with a woman named Jill. Some one night stand thing. He says she's a total bitch...."

Candy flew across the back of the bar to Jill. "Sir, can I get you something to drink?"

"I'll have whatever she's drinking," Jacob said pointing to Jill.

"She's not drinking. Bitch whores tend not to drink at social functions." Candy's voice was saccharin sweet but the temperature dropped with her icy smile and cold eyes.

"I didn't say that," Jacob said.

"I heard what you said..."

"Candy!" Jill said through her teeth. "I'm sorry. I'm the baby of the family and my sister is very protective of me."

"What are you drinking?" Candy asked.

"Uh, whiskey neat. Whatever you have," Jacob said.

Jill turned away from Jacob and stared at the back of the bar. She felt her face flush with heat. Trevor, who begged her to have a baby, now told people Katy was a one night stand. An accident. And she was the bitch? Oh I just don't belong.

"Listen." Jacob touched her arm. "I meant what I said."

"About me being a total bitch? Or the one night stand thing?"

Jill imitated Candy's sweet tone. She hadn't thought Trevor could hurt her more. Between the stiletto heels and the sick feeling in her stomach, Jill had to clutch the bar to remain standing.

"That you are absolutely the most beautiful woman I have ever seen in my entire life," Jacob said.

Jill's head jerked to look at him. "What?"

"Here's your drink. Now buzz off." Candy slapped the whiskey down in front of Jacob.

"Listen..." Jacob started but Candy raised her hand in the air. Within moments, a friend wedged between Jill and Jacob. Candy put her hand on Jill's arm to lead Jill toward the end of the bar. Jill glanced back to see Jacob stuck in place by a tray of hors d' oeuvres and a hostile server.

"You look great," Candy whispered. "The boots are genius."

"Meg's idea." Jill passed the rose to Candy. "I don't belong here, sis. I should go home. Did you hear what he said about Katy?"

"Jill, that man begged you for a child. You guys argued about it for years. He's just..." Candy said. She squinted her brown eyes then released them wide. "I knew the moment you entered."

"How?"

"Every male eye turned to watch you walk across the room," Candy said. "This outfit is sheer brilliance."

"The invitation said, 'black tie.'" Jill beamed at her sister.

"Watch out, here comes the bride." Candy raised her arm again.

"I'm sorry," the tiny blonde rich girl said. Her straight gleaming white teeth matched her perfectly sculpted nose and eyebrows. Her blue eyes, enhanced with blue contacts, shot daggers of hate. "This is a private party."

"I... I was invited," Jill said. "I..."

"I don't remember you on the guest list. And I should know. This is MY engagement party."

Just then a server bumped into the bride-to-be, spilling a full tray of red wine down the rich girl's ivory silk dress.

"I'm so sorry," Megan's husband Tim said. "I didn't see you there. Oh my God..."

Jill watched Tim scamper to get a towel. To keep from laughing, Jill coughed into her hand. The rich girl screamed at Tim then at Candy. When her father came over, she screamed at him only to collapse sobbing into her mother's arms. Her mother led the tiny woman away to change.

"This is the most fun I've had at a family gathering in at least a decade," Jacob said.

"I assume he was a friend of yours."

"Brother-in-law," Jill said.

"She had it coming," Jacob said. "She knows exactly who you are."

Jill shrugged. When she turned to look at the party, she saw a variety of male eyes looking in her direction.

"Would you like to dance?" Jacob asked. He nodded toward the dance floor where couples danced a perfect waltz.

"I don't know how," she replied.

"Just follow me," Jacob said. He set his glass down on the bar. "I'm this close to you. I'm not going to let you go."

He put his hand on her arm and was confronted with another server holding a tray of drinks.

"It's all right, Christy," Jill said. "He just wants to dance."

Christy scowled at Jacob then looked him up and down. "Be nice."

"Yes ma'am," Jacob laughed.

Holding Jill's hand, he led her to the dance floor. He situated her hands then whispered instructions into her ear. After a few missteps, she fell into the simple rhythm of the dance and the closeness of this man. For the first time in a long time, she felt, well not exactly happy, but a tiny bit of delight.

"You are a wonderful dancer," Jacob said.

"Not really," Jill replied. "I just know how to follow what you're doing."

Jacob laughed. "That's most of the work."

"It's not hard to follow," Jill said.

"Do you dance?" Jacob asked.

"I like to dance... oh you mean for a living? You think I'm a stripper?!?"

Jacob laughed.

"Why is that funny?" Jill asked. Dropping her arms, she stopped moving. "I'd like to sit down now."

"Please don't. I laughed because I suck at this small talk crap, particularly with a beautiful woman. I rehearse what I'm going to say, you know, in my head? But it sounds awful when it comes out."

"Oh. I do that sometimes if I'm nervous. Are you nervous?"

"Yes, I'm nervous."

"Why?"

"Well, if I blow this, someone might kill me," Jacob laughed.

They danced in silence for a while. Listening to the music, Jill enjoyed the liquid pleasure of movement in the arms of this man. She'd only been this close to Trevor. She sighed a little as her body warmed in response to him. God, he even smells good.

"Is your wife here?" Jill asked.

"I don't have a wife," Jacob said.

"How come?" Jill asked.

"It's shocking. I know. I am smooth with the ladies," Jacob laughed.

She pulled back to see if he was serious. He winked at her and she returned to looking over his shoulder.

"Actually, I fell in love with a woman then found out she was married."

"Oh, did that stop you?"

"Yes, it stopped me," he said.

"Why? I thought that's how you people did things."

"You people?"

"Rich people," Jill replied.

Jacob laughed. He's funny too. Jill sighed, melting a little closer to his warmth, his strength. She nodded at the guitar player in the band when he winked at her.

"Is she here?" Jill asked.

"Who?"

"The girl you fell in love with."

"Yes, she's here," Jacob said.

"Where?"

Jacob pulled back a bit to look at Jill. His eyes puzzled for a moment. Seeing her sincerity, he made a vague movement in the direction of a crowded corner of the room.

Jill waited until they were in full view of that side of the room, then gave him a soft, lingering kiss.

Pulling back, she whispered, "So she knows what she's missing."

Jacob blinked, his eyebrows moving as if he was trying to work it out, then he laughed.

"What would it take for you to kiss me again?"

"You mean kiss you for real?" Jill's voice held her surprise. "You don't even know me."

"Actually," Jacob said. "You wait tables at Pete's. I play midnight hockey and our team goes to Pete's after the game. I've been there every Sunday morning… gosh, for years."

Jill wasn't sure how to respond. She had no memory of this man. Sunday mornings were always crazy. The bars close at two and Pete's Kitchen filled to the brim with drunken happy people. She slung coffee, pancakes and eggs until four in the morning every Thursday, Friday and Saturday night. She made great money, and right now money took precedence over everything, especially handsome men.

Looking over his shoulder, she saw Trevor's dark eyes, so like Katy's, follow them on the floor. As she watched, the tiny blonde rich girl, dressed in another ivory silk gown, took his elbow and guided him toward a group of elderly couples.

"I work in an office during the week. Secretary. But Pete's is an oasis for me," she said finally. "I've worked there as long as I've worked. I've got friends there. That probably doesn't mean much to you since they're low class friends."

"Friends in low places?" Jacob asked.

"What does that mean?"

"It's a country song."

"I don't listen to country," she replied.

As they twirled around the room, Jill watched the people. That woman's shoes cost more than a month of Katy's day care. Jill nodded slightly. Trevor was right to choose this life over scraping by every month.

"May I cut in?" Trevor said to Jacob. Jill bristled at the sound of his voice.

"It's up to the lady." Jacob pulled back from Jill. His eyes searched Jill's terrified face. "Yeah, I don't think so."

Jacob took Jill's hand and walked her off the dance floor. Picking up two glasses of champagne from another server, he led her to an empty table. He helped her into her seat then sat down beside her. She took a sip of champagne.

"Will you kiss me again?" Jacob asked

Jill blushed.

"I thought you'd be so overwhelmed with gratitude that you couldn't help but kiss me again," he laughed then took a sip from his glass.

"Why are you uncomfortable around women?" Jill asked.

"I'm not around them much," Jacob said. "My sister lives in California and our mother died when I was in high school. I work in construction so I'm around men all day long."

"You mean you own a construction company?"

"I'm a carpenter by trade, like my father was," Jacob said. "But yes, I help my father manage his construction company."

"What about these sisters?" Jill gestured to the group of beautiful girls sitting with the rich girl's mother.

Jacob shrugged. "A couple of them were a package deal with my father's new wife. The others are barely out of diapers. We're not close. I assume that's your brother." He nodded toward the security guard making his way toward the table.

"Steve," Jill said.

"How would you like to get out of here?" Jacob asked. "I don't mean to be forward but you seem uncomfortable, and I am uncomfortable. I'd like to get to know you better."

"Um..."

"You have something planned?" Jacob asked.

She nodded.

"I don't want to miss that."

CHAPTER THREE
WHAT HE'S MISSING...

"Back off Trevor," Jill's brother Steve growled.

Jill's head jerked to see Trevor storming toward her. Steve put his arm on Trevor's shoulder and pushed him away from Jill and Jacob. Turning to Jill, Steve said under his breath to her, "Get this over with."

"Jill, I need to speak with you," Trevor said.

Standing, Jill put her hand on Steve's arm, "It's all right."

"What do you want?"

"Why are you here?" Trevor's eyes were slits of rage and indignation.

"To celebrate your new life," Jill said. "I'm very happy for you."

"Bullshit," Trevor fury packed words spit at Jill. "You show up in your 'get lucky' boots to celebrate my new life?"

"What I wear is no concern of yours," Jill said. "Anyway, I'm just a one night stand."

"Ah Jill, what did you expect me to say?"

"I love her with every cell in my body, every fiber in my being, every thought in my head, and every action in my life." Jill imitated his voice. "That's what you used to tell everyone, including me."

"Jill, please try to understand. I still love..."

"Don't even start. You threw me away. You threw away our friends. We were all too low class for you. Yet..."

"I know that look. What are you up to?"

"All your low class ex-friends are here, Trev. Look around." Jill leaned into him. Her face was less than an inch from his face. "We came to wish you a nice new life as far away from us as possible."

She watched surprise, then fear flash through Trevor's eyes. Taking his glass of champagne, she drained the glass then gave it back to him.

"Thanks," she said.

She raised one eyebrow in challenge to Trevor. He opened his mouth then shifted to neutral. Jill turned to see what he was looking at and found Megan, wearing a server's uniform, holding a cordless microphone.

Jill beamed at her oldest sister. Only Megan could be completely loving and absolutely disapproving at the same time.

"Go on sis," Megan said.

Jill took the microphone.

"May I have your attention, please? I'd like to make a little toast to the happy couple."

The crowd moved to get a view of Jill and the rich girl came to hold Trevor's hand.

"But first, in order to launch Trevor into his new life, we wanted to share some photos with you."

The lights fell and a screen came down from the ballroom ceiling. The band began to play, 'The way we were.' As the crowd became silent and Trevor's rich girl started screaming, a photo flashed on the screen.

"I don't know what's here.... Oh you can't turn it off. When you trust a working person to set things up for you, you should check his loyalties first."

The rich girl stomped to the back of the ballroom to scream at the ballroom staff.

"Um... this is a photo of Trevor and me at our junior high school dance. Aren't we cute?"

A picture of Trevor and Jill dressed as Raggedy Ann and Andy filled the screen. The photo vibrated with joy and laughter. The image changed to a picture of two wrists with matching 'Soul Mates' tattoos in scripted blue letters.

"Those are our tattoos."

Jill turned over her arm to show the tattoo still inked on her wrist. Glancing at Trevor, he held up his wrist. His blank wrist combined with his nasty smile knocked the wind out of her. She gasped for breath. She gawked at him.

"Go on." Megan slipped her arm around Jill's waist.

Jill nodded.

The screen shifted to a legal document—their wedding license.

"This is our wedding license. We got married three years later. My parents died when I was ten so we had to talk my sister Megan into it."

"I was against it," Megan said.

Jill laughed at Megan's strong tone. Megan was always so smart about everything.

The image shifted to their wedding picture. She wore a short white rayon dress that cost twenty dollars at Sears. Trevor wore a borrowed tux three sizes too big. Sitting on his bended knee, she was laughing at something he'd said. They were kissing in the next photo.

"I was sixteen and he was seventeen. Here's our first apartment. Oh and that's a picture of our puppy, Scooter."

An image of a tiny mutt puppy flashed on the screen.

"He was a wedding present. Scooter got hit by a car a couple years ago."

While the screen flashed through three or four pictures of them playing with Scooter then showed a picture of them kissing in their high school graduation robes.

"We graduated from high school." Jill laughed. The picture switched their graduation party. "I'm pretty drunk here."

She was sitting facing Trevor, on his lap, wearing only small panties and her graduation hat. Trevor's face was buried in her neck. She heard laughter and cat calls. Looking up from the screen to the crowd, she realized they were doing something no one expected—these rich people were enjoying the show.

The picture changed to one of Jill standing sideways.

"Ok, you can't tell, but I'm pregnant here. Trev wanted a photo every week."

The screen flashed through nine months of her growing baby belly. Then there was a photo of Trevor kissing Jill while she held a one minute old Katy.

"That's Katy. Her name is Katherine, after my mom, but we call her Katy. Isn't she beautiful? She's almost four." Jill beamed.

The images flashed through countless pictures of Katy. Infant pictures changed to toddler pictures. Image after image, Jill watched her pretty baby grow up. They seemed so happy in the photos. The image shifted to Christmas.

"You can see the date on the picture. This was last Christmas. That's a picture of Trev and me at Keystone."

They were sitting on the ski slope, with their snow boards, wrapped in each other. 'I love Jill' was cut into the snow and Trevor was kissing her face. They looked so blissfully happy. Images flashed through a family Christmas pausing at a New Year's Eve party. Taken at midnight, Trevor and Jill were making out in the corner of the picture. The back of Jill's gold t-shirt read, 'Trevor's wish' while a large 'J,' the rest unseen at by the angle of the picture, was visible in the back of Trevor's matching t-shirt.

When the next image flashed across the screen, the crowd gasped.

"These are our divorce papers. As you can see, Trevor divorced me two days later and that means..."

"You're still married," a man's voice yelled from the back of the room. "Lawyer, sorry."

The crowd laughed.

"Until tomorrow," Jill said. She took a step toward Trevor who was shaking his head. "I wanted to give you a few things to help you in your new life."

The band began to play 'I will survive.'

"First, here's my wedding ring. While I see you managed to get her a diamond, my little thirty dollar ring was good for nine years. You should keep it."

She pulled the ring from her left hand and placed it in Trevor's hand.

"I think you should have these."

There was a whistle from the back of the room as Jill unzipped the beautiful boots. She gave the boots to the rich girl.

"He calls these his 'get lucky' boots. They're a little big for you but you can get them altered. Just put them on, honey, and you'll have a good time," Jill said. Megan touched Jill's arm then helped her step into the black pumps. "Thanks."

"I guess that's it," Jill said.

"No. It's not," Steve yelled from the back of the room.

"Oh," Jill nodded.

In her heart of hearts, Jill hoped Trevor would see their happy pictures and change his mind. She let out a breath. He wasn't going to change his mind.

Megan was right, as always.

Trevor only saw dollar signs.

Lowering her head to cover her last hope exploding in her heart, she unbuttoned her shirt. Reaching into her shirt, she retrieved a folded piece of paper. Candy gave her the long stem white rose.

"This is our wedding present for you, Trevor." Her eyes full of tears, Jill's voice caught on the words. "We terminated your parental rights. You're not Katy's daddy anymore."

"No, Jill, no," Trevor shook his head back and forth as his voice rose in desperation. "No, you can't do that."

"You haven't even seen her in six months!"

"I..."

"It's done," Jill said. "You signed the papers when Mike had you sign the financial papers."

"Then it's legal," the lawyer in the back of the room yelled.

"We're leaving, which means you high class people don't have low people to serve your dinner or your drinks or even play in your band. Pete said if you bring your invitation to the Kitchen on Colfax, he'll feed you dinner as a freedom present for me."

"Good luck," Jill said.

She gave Trevor the rose, then she couldn't resist the magnet like draw of him. She kissed his lips. He moved to draw her deeper, his lips pulling at hers, but she shifted away from him.

"I'm not yours to kiss anymore. No matter how much I love you…" her voice, barely above a whisper, caught and tears dropped. "You chose someone else. I had nine wonderful years with my soul mate. That's more than most people have in a life time. I have no right to complain."

She put her hand on his chest then she nodded.

"Good night."

As she embarked on a hip wagging trip across the floor, someone clapped. She looked over to see Jacob then his father clapping. The rich people began to cheer for Jill. She blushed and left the room.

"That's the girl, isn't it?" Jacob's Dad asked.

Jacob nodded.

"She is very much like your mother."

Jacob watched Jill through the glass wall as she rode the escalator down from the Seawell Ballroom.

"She's really just herself."

"You are a damned fool if you don't snatch up that woman," his father said under his breath. His weeping daughter came over to him.

"Now sugar," he said. "I told you not to gloat about stealing someone else's man."

"But Daddy…"

~~~~~~~~~

2 WEEKS LATER

"He's been here every night," Candy said to Jill. They met in motion behind the counter at Pete's Kitchen.

"So?" Jill replied. Leaning through the cook's window, she pointed at the check. "José, can you make sure those hash browns are a little crispy?"

"You should talk to him," Candy continued. She filled two coffee mugs and walked toward the floor.

"I told you, Candy. He's in love with some married girl." Jill called after her.

Candy shook her head. She was almost to the booth when she turned back to Jill, "Go talk to him."

Jill straightened her bright pink uniform with its little white apron and walked over toward Jacob. He was reading the newspaper at the counter. He looked up to watch her walk over to him.

"What's up?"

"I was wondering if you would marry me, but I'd take a date or a conversation or maybe another kiss." Jacob's face flushed with emotion. "How was that? I've been practicing."

"Very smooth," Jill replied. "What about the married girl?"

"What married girl?"

"The one you're in love with?"

"Oh her. She's divorced."

Jill sat down on the bar stool next to him.

"Why aren't you with her?" She knocked him with her shoulder. "You should go get her."

Jacob's eyes held Jill's. In one fluid movement, he kissed her lips. Surprised, Jill pulled back to look at him again.

"You okay Jill?" A beefy cook appeared across the counter. He scowled at Jacob.

"Yeah, Risto. Thanks. I'm okay."

Jill smiled at the cook. The cook leaned into Jacob and Jacob sat back on his stool.

When the cook turned away from them, Jill asked, "I'm the girl?"

"From the moment I laid eyes on you nine years ago." Jacob nodded.

Blushing bright red, Jill looked away from Jacob.

"I'm not very lucky at love. But I guess you know that," she said. "I promised myself, well and Megan, that I wouldn't ever even date again, let alone fall in love."

"Give me one chance. We don't even have to call it a date. In fact, it won't be a date. I can take you to a movie or..."

"I'd like to go to the zoo."

"What if I take you and Katy to the zoo tomorrow?"

Jill blushed.

"I don't know. I've read it's not good for babies to have other men around. But I can't really afford to take her so..."

"No romance, no hanky panky, no date. Just the zoo. Well, maybe some lunch and the zoo." Jacob held his hand out for her to shake.

"Lunch and the zoo sounds like a date, but okay." Jill shook his hand.

"When do you get off?"

"In an hour," Jill said.

"Can I take you home? I mean, in my truck... I know you walk to work. We could walk. I mean, it would be great if you would let me take you to my home but I don't want to be too forward... or move too fast or ..."

Jill laughed. Walking back to her station, she said, "Sure."

CHAPTER FOUR
THE NON-DATE LOOMS

"Four more hours."

Jacob tapped his alarm clock to make sure it was working. In four hours, seven minutes, and thirty seconds, he would pick up Jill and Katy for a trip to the zoo.

Sick of staring at the ceiling, Jacob got out of bed. Sarah, his three-year-old yellow Labrador retriever, lifted her head from the covers to watch him walk across the wood floors to the bathroom. Sarah's tail thumped a rhythm against the bed when he returned. He wandered across the open space to the refrigerator. Retrieving a bottle of cold water, he plopped down in a sagging arm chair. The pre-dawn light greeted him through the ancient leaded glass windows. Sarah wandered over to him.

"Ok, I'm nervous," Jacob said.

Sarah shook her entire body then barked one sharp bark.

"You're absolutely right," Jacob said.

Pushing himself from the armchair, he went to his closet to dress. A few miles pounding the pavement would help. He could burn at least an hour running in City Park.

Then what?

Jacob and Sarah jogged down the long flight of stairs from his third floor attic apartment to the front door. Sarah sat while Jacob fumbled with the door, then the security door. Like a gentleman, he held the door for Sarah. She romped to the slip of grass lining the flagstone sidewalk. Jacob locked the doors then stretched while Sarah finished her business.

Turning on his heart rate monitor, Jacob noticed he had wasted another fifteen minutes. He groaned at his own impatience. He waited nine years to even talk to Jill and today...

Unable to finish the thought, he whistled for Sarah. Passing through the iron gate, they set off down Race Street. They walked one short block. Turning right onto Sixteenth Avenue, they took off toward East High School. Jacob and Sarah fell into a slow, time burning jog to warm up. They made their way down the City Park Esplanade. Nodding to the grand lady of the Thatcher fountain, they ran into the park.

The exertion helped unravel his anxious mind. As his feet worked the pavement, his mind drifted to memories of Jill.

His mother, Celia, and her best friend, Delphie, had gone to Pete's

Kitchen every Friday night after their Herbs and Arts Spiritual group. They prayed for Celia's health from six to ten then celebrated with pancakes, eggs, and sausage. As a professional tarot reader, Delphie's cards said his mother would meet someone significant that night. Celia joked that she would meet a handsome man who would fill her last year on earth.

They met Jill.

Jill had just started working at Pete's Kitchen. She was young, bright and always smiling. His mother and Delphie watched her blossom. Jill used to tell Celia and Delphie that they were replacements for her mother. Like good surrogate mothers, they bought the puppy Scooter as a wedding present.

Every Saturday morning, Mom and Delphie regaled Jacob with Jill's latest adventure. From arguments with Trevor over having a baby to whether or not she should quit high school, Jacob had a ring side view to 'the infamous Jill's life.' That's what he called her, 'the infamous Jill.'

But Jacob could care less.

Freaked out by his family's implosion, he focused on playing high school sports, getting laid, and partying with his friends. Sure, he moved into his mother's three story money pit he called 'the Castle.' Yes, he knew cancer ate the very core of his mother. Of course, he went to visit his father's sec-witch-ary's day old infant.

These family matters were simply a break between sports, sex and friends. See the sec-witch-ary's baby, start as a safety for the East High Angels and trounce their arch-rivals Montbello High. Go with Mom for chemo, get laid. At eighteen-years-old, Jacob was handsome, popular, and completely self-absorbed.

Turning up Twenty-Third Avenue to run the steep incline of the Park Hill Golf Course, Jacob remembered the day he met the 'infamous Jill.'

The doctor told his mother she wouldn't see Easter. In response, his sister refused to return from UCLA for her "fucked up family." Of course, his parent's divorce was final so Dad was marrying his sec-witch-ary.

And Jacob tore his ACL playing weekend warrior Ultimate Frisbee. Surgery and rehab kept him off the track field that spring. Angry and bored, Jacob filled dumpster after dumpster with Castle junk. Pulling up moldy carpet, Jacob realized the carpet continued into an almost hidden room. Jacob yanked, pulled, and pushed his way into a gorgeous birch paneled office space.

Climbing roses and Virginia Creeper, covering the lead windows, gave the room a green cave like feel. Bright birch peaked through decades of dust on the floor and the bookshelves lining the walls. After a week of cleaning, and filling the shelves with cut flowers, he and Delphie moved his frail mother's hospital bed into the gorgeous room. To celebrate, they walked to Pete's Kitchen.

Jacob racked his brain. He didn't remember the walk to Pete's, the wait for a table or even what he ate. He only remembered Jill. Jill was so excited to see his mother and Delphie that she never looked at him. Her hair was short, her hips were round, and...

Was it love? That's what he called it now.

His mother never left the house again. After her death, he couldn't handle her favorite restaurant, Pete's Kitchen. He graduated from high school and left Denver forever. Or so he thought.

He picked the farthest college away from Denver, Bowdoin College in Maine. As he had during high school, he played sports during the school year and worked as a carpenter in the summers.

But he remembered the girl. That amazing girl.

He spent time with a lot of girls, but no woman held his attention for long. His last girlfriend told him he was haunted and should 'get help.' It wasn't until he moved back into the Castle, and started playing midnight hockey, that he saw Jill again. She was pregnant, exhausted, and more beautiful than he remembered.

And today he was going to spend the day with Jill and Katy.

Just spend the day. That's all.

Zoo and lunch. Easy.

Ah fuck.

~~~~~~~~

Jill liked to get up early. When Trevor lived here, he grumbled through the morning, and a pot of coffee, before leaving for school or work or studying or, as she knew now, the rich girl. The cool quiet morning was a gift of Trevor's betrayal. Even though she slept only a few hours, she woke early to steal an hour for herself.

Jill loved Sundays.

Megan and Tim kept Katy while Jill worked at Pete's. Sundays were a ritual of breakfast with Meg, church, then free time with Katy. Sometimes, they just ran errands. Other times, they spent the day at the park. Katy talked non-stop about every little thing happening around her. Yes, Sunday was absolutely Jill's favorite day of the week.

So why did she say she would go to the zoo with that guy?

Her mind went blank. It just happened.

He was cute. Turning on the shower, Jill grinned. He was very cute.

But, the Megan in her mind reminded, so were a lot of men. Stepping under the blast of water, Jill tried to imagine another man in her life. Nope. No men. She pressed her hand against her heart.

Still, she felt good when she was with Jacob. Safe. Warm. He held her hand when he walked her to the apartment last night. She was prepared for him to want a kiss or to come in. But he kissed her hand in a funny, shy way, right at the base of her thumb, then said 'good night.' He waited until she waved from her window then walked down the street. She watched him until he walked out of sight.

With Jacob, she didn't feel the flash intensity of Trevor. Hot or cold, Trevor was an in your face person who demanded everything he wanted. He wanted Jill morning, noon and night. As almost a conditioned response, her body leapt to attention when he turned his mind in her direction. For nine years, early Sunday mornings were spent rolling around in bed with Trevor.

Trevor was in bed with someone else this morning.

And Jill was alone.

Stepping from the shower, Jill was gripped with anxiety. What was she going to wear?

And why did she care?

~~~~~~~~~

After running stairs, doing a half hour of body weight exercises and throwing the ball for Sarah, Jacob was out of time wasting ideas. Plus he was getting hungry. The lure of the Cap'n drew Jacob and Sarah home. Turning from Sixteenth Avenue onto Race Street, Jacob noticed two things at once—Dephie's car, parked in front of the house, and Jill's brother Mike, sitting on the front steps waiting for him.

Jacob groaned.

Pushing open the metal gate, Sarah ran forward to say 'hello' to Mike. With a nod of his head, Mike followed Jacob up the stairs to his apartment.

"You know the front door doesn't work," Jacob said.

"Maybe you should install a bench for your waiting visitors," Mike said.

Jacob unlocked the door at the top of the stairs and Sarah bound into the apartment.

"Damn Jake, you stink," Mike said.

Jacob gave Mike a dark look. Mike had come straight from a night of driving drunks around Denver in the limo. He stank of beer, cigars, and boredom.

"Hey, I just got off work," Mike said.

"Breakfast?" Jacob asked.

"You know it," Mike said. Mike went to the cabinet to get Sarah a dog treat. While Mike and Sarah played 'find the treat,' Jake pulled out box after box of cereal from the cabinet. Mike grabbed the gallon of Royal Crest Milk from the refrigerator.

"You cleaned up a bit," Mike said. He gestured around the apartment. "Nervous about something?"

"Very funny." Jacob set two bowls on the table.

"It has been requested of me to ask you to be very nice to my sister," Mike said. "Where's the Crunch Berries? I've never known you to not have Crunch Berries."

"Get it yourself."

"I'm a guest! Sheez."

Jacob frowned at Mike then retrieved another box of cereal from the cabinet.

"How did you find out?" Jacob asked Mike.

"You told Jill that you play hockey. Megan asked me about you after your step-whore's party."

"And you said?"

"Jake's a good guy, plays hockey, eats lots of cereal." Mike shrugged as if there was nothing else to say about Jacob.

"So today?"

"Candy heard Jill say she'd go somewhere with you. She called Megan... Shit man, you'd know how this worked if you ever talked to your sister," Mike said. "What's it been two years?"

"Hey, we swap Christmas cards," Jacob said.

"Yeah," Mike said. "Like I said, you'd know how this thing worked if you ever dealt with your family."

"I deal with my father every single day," Jacob said.

"Yeah, at the company you own. Why did you tell Jill it was 'your father's company'?"

"Because it is my father's company."

"That you own," Mike said. "What are you doing today?"

"Zoo, lunch, that's all," Jacob repeated his mantra.

"Yeah right," Mike smirked. "Well, be nice. She's really had a tough time of it. I know you saw that slideshow. It makes everything look so hunky dory. But Trevor was a hard person to live with. Jilly's whole life was consumed by that guy. You know she worked two jobs so he could go to college. Then wham. He's off screwing your step-whore. And..."

Jacob held his hand in front of Mike's face. Mike stopped talking. He poured a second bowl of Crunch Berries to finish the box.

"You heard all of this before," Mike said.

"When it was happening." Jacob nodded his head. "I will do my best to be nice to your sister. Scout's honor."

"Pfft, you were never a scout," Mike said. "Shit college boy, you weren't even in the military. Hey can I shower here? I got to get to Mass."

"Help yourself," Jacob said.

"Damn, you are nervous," Mike yelled from the bathroom. "I could eat off the tile."

Jacob shook his head and returned to the sagging arm chair. The sun was up now, only a couple hours to go.

~~~~~~~~~

"When are you meeting him?" Jill's best friend Sandy whispered in Jill's ear. The music was starting for Mass.

Jill held up ten fingers.

Sandy fanned herself with her hands as if she was hot.

"That man is gorgeous," Sandy whispered. "And very rich. Did you see February's 5280? He's 'Bachelor of the Year.' Third time! They said it's rumored he owns that construction company. I'd do anything he wanted just to get a piece of that... change."

Jill hit Sandy's leg.

"Church?" Jill said between her teeth. She gave Sandy her 'shut up' stare.

Sandy laughed.

"You should have let me do your hair," Sandy said.

Jill gave Sandy a strong look then shook her head.

"Oh right, you don't care what you look like. It's not a date," Sandy whispered. "I bet you're wearing those sexy undies Tanesha got you."

Jill blushed.

"I knew it!" Sandy whispered. "Just do him and cash in for a while. Why not? Not everything is soul mate love. Plus, you've got to be horny. What's it been? Seven months. I can't go that long."

"Church?"

"Have you seen Jake's hands? Carpenter's hands. I'd let him hammer on me..."

And the priest began Mass.

~~~~~~~~~

"You're home early," Jacob said. He stepped aside to allow Delphie to enter his apartment from the Castle. "How's Sam?"

"Sam is very fun," Delphie said. She flushed in her flamboyant way. "Very passionate. Very Aries. They don't call him 'Big Sam' for nothing."

Jacob dropped his head and held up his hand. He really didn't want to know about Delphie's sex life.

"You should try it sometime," Delphie said.

Delphie moved into the Race Street Castle when his mother was ill and never moved out. When Jacob was in Maine, Delphie hung on as the Castle fell down around her. After four years of Jacob's Castle refurbish, she lived in a comfortable, safe apartment of her own on the second floor of the house.

"I'm not a virgin, Delphie," Jacob said.

"Could have fooled me," Delphie said. Looking in a mirror, she fluffed her bright bottle red hair. "Some Bachelor of the Year."

"I didn't ask for that award. I wouldn't even let them take my picture. How is it my fault that they stalked me? Fuck."

Delphie turned from the mirror. Her eyes assessed Jacob.

"Stop psychic-ing me. Just spit it out," Jacob said. "I have to be somewhere."

"Ah Jakey, can't a girl come visit her best-friend's son?"

"No," Jake said.

Like a five year old, Delphie twirled back and forth causing her flowing gauze skirt to flip from side to side. Jacob smiled at her.

"You're glad I made you go to your step-horror's engagement party," Delphie said.

"Yes, Delphie. I never would have gone if you hadn't made me go. Thank you. Now what?"

"Have a big day today?" Delphie asked.

"You know I do, so why ask?"

"What are you doing?"

"I'm taking Jill and Katy to the zoo. We're going to get lunch. That's all. No date. No hanky panky. Just lunch and zoo."

"Uh huh," Delphie said. "The cards say the day isn't exactly what you planned."

"What ever is?" Jacob said. He picked up his wallet, keys and phone. "You did not leave 'Big Sam' to tell me I'm not the master of the universe. What is it?"

"Jill is equally attracted to you and frightened of you. Be yourself—honest, true, kind. And you'll do fine. Remember soul mates are just people who arrive to teach you something. Jill is still learning the lesson Trevor came to teach her."

"Thanks Delphie, I'll be myself." He bent forward to kiss her cheek. "You're a gem."

Walking to the door of his apartment, Jacob saw the clock on the wall.

"Ah crap, I'm late."

Flying down the stairs, he heard Delphie yell, "Don't worry, she's late too."

When he reached the bottom of the stairs, he turned to wave 'good-bye' to Delphie.

"And Jakey? Katy's allergic to bees."

He was locking the door when he heard Delphie say, "She'll die if you don't get her to the hospital."

Shaking his head at Delphie's never ending drama, he ran to his Lexus SUV. After six hours of waiting, he was late.

~~~~~~~~~

"Rich people call it being 'stylishly late,' Jilly," Tim said from the driver's seat of the family van. "He'll think you're stylish."

They were stuck in traffic on Colfax Boulevard. Road construction left only one lane open in the four lane boulevard. And that lane was jammed with cars. Their direction waited while cars heading downtown used the lane.

"It's not polite. That's all," Jill said. "He's nice enough to take us to the Z-O-O. The least I can do is get there on time."

"Mike says he's a nice guy."

"He was Bachelor of the Year!" Jill gave the information that freaked her out the most. The information she had just learned from Sandy.

"Now Jill, did you see that article?" Megan asked. "My boss gets that magazine, 5280. The magazine couldn't get him to do an interview or sit for a picture. The picture with the article was a telephoto shot of him running. They call him the 'mysterious Bachelor of the Year.' A guy like that isn't going to care if you're a few minutes late."

"I thought 5280 singles were all gay," Tim said.

Megan smacked Tim on the arm. He laughed.

"Mommy, what's gay?" Katy asked.

"You don't know what GAY is?" Megan's oldest son, Ryan asked. "Are you a retard? Gay is where boys like boys. It's gross. They do it everywhere all the time."

"RYAN!" Megan yelled from the front seat. "In the first place, that is not a very nice thing to say. You wouldn't like it if someone said you were gross. And in the second place, we do not have prejudice in this family. Gay people love each other like I love Daddy and Daddy loves me."

"Yes, Mom," Ryan said. He widened his eyes at Katy and mouthed 'gross.'

"Mommy, what's gross?" Katy asked.

Jill looked at Katy. She couldn't help but laugh at her sincere question. Tim and Megan joined Jill's laughter as did Megan's three kids. The van started to move and within minutes they arrived at Jill's apartment.

Hopping from the back of the van, Jill rushed to the front of her building. No Jacob. Her stomach dropped.

Behind her, Jacob stepped from the driver's seat of his SUV. When she turned, she bumped right into him.

"Sorry I'm late," they said in unison.

Jacob smiled.

"Shall we?"

CHAPTER FIVE
THE NON-DATE

"I haven't been here in a long time," Jacob said.

He turned right from Twenty-Third Avenue into the Denver Zoo then took an immediate right into a parking lot.

"You can't park here," Jill said. "This parking is only for..."

Jacob waved a white security card in front of a post and the gate rose.

"Oh," Jill said.

Jill wasn't sure what to say. Only really rich patrons were able to park in this lot. She and Katy usually parked at least a mile away. But that was on Free Admission day when all of Denver came to the zoo. She'd never paid to get into the zoo. Of course, she'd never dated anyone who had a job.

Dated.

Is that what she was doing? She shook her head slightly. No, this was not a date. Friends? She barely knew Jacob. No, they weren't friends.

What was she doing?

He pulled into a spot that was stenciled in block letters: 'MARLOWE.' Trying for cool, she said, "Why are you parking here?"

"It has my name on it," Jacob said.

"But your last name is Lipson," Jill said.

"Actually, my name is Jacob Marlowe." Jacob laughed. Holding his hand out for her to shake, he added. "It's nice to meet you, Ms. McGuinsey."

"We're Ropers, now." Jill sighed. Squaring her shoulders, she imitated his tone, "Jillian Roper and my daughter, Katherine Roper."

They shook hands. Jacob winked at Jill and she laughed. He moved to get out of the Lexus SUV.

"But your Dad's name..."

"Is Lipson," Jacob settled back in the driver's seat. Turning to look at Jill, he said, "My mother was the last of the Colorado Marlowes. My parents gave me her surname. You know, I'm carrying on the family name and stuff like that."

Jill nodded.

"Ready?" Jacob asked.

Jill nodded. Stepping out of the SUV, she opened the back door for Katy. At the apartment, Katy took one look at Jacob and clammed up. She didn't squirm when Jill changed her clothing. Katy even waited patiently while Jill slipped into her jeans. In fact, Katy hadn't said a word in a Katy ice age -

fifteen minutes. Katy's silence added to Jill's general unease.

By the time Jill opened her door, Katy was out of her car seat. Katy held her arms out to Jill. Lifting her daughter into her arms, Jill felt a little less strange. For a moment, Katy and Jill hugged each other in silent bliss.

Jill jerked out of her revere. Jacob's waiting! Trevor always wanted to 'get going.' 'Hurry up, Jill. Why does it take you so long?' He'd always say.

When she rushed around the SUV, Jacob had unpacked Katy's stroller and held Jill's purse. He was already wearing her backpack. Jill flushed with gratitude.

Embarrassed at her response, she bent to put Katy into the stroller. Certain Jacob had moved off, she stood up quickly. She found him holding the handles to steady the cheap stroller. She smiled then took her purse from him.

"I should probably push," Jill said. "She gets very shy..."

"He can push," Katy said.

"You don't have to..."

"I'd love to," Jacob said.

Jacob and Katy set off across the parking lot leaving a stunned Jill behind. Certain they would leave her behind, she hurried to catch up with them. But Jacob stopped walking. He turned, smiled at her and reached for her hand.

"Do you mind?" he asked. "I don't want to lose you."

Smiling, she took his hand.

"So Katy, what do you like at the zoo?" Jacob asked.

To Jill's amazement, Katy actually answered. Katy was the quiet, obedient child around Trevor. Of course, he wouldn't have it any other way.

"Everything," Katy said. "I like animals. The zoo has special animals you don't find on the farm."

"The farm?" Jacob asked.

Jill cringed when Katy began singing 'Old MacDonald.' Trevor hated the sound of Katy's singing. She was about to hush Katy when Jacob joined in the song. Jill was so surprised, she stopped walking. Feeling the tug of Jacob's hand, Jill took a few quick steps to catch up.

Trying to gain some sense of normal, Jill said, "We have to go here for a ticket."

"I have a pass," Jacob said.

"Oh," Jill said.

Her cheeks went bright red. Overwhelmed with the 'I don't belong' feeling, she let go of his hand. She was out of place. She glanced back at the car. Why had she come?

Noticing Jill's distress, Jacob stopped walking. He touched her arm and

Jill looked up at him.

"My mother loved the zoo. She came here every day the last year of her life," Jacob said. "She left a donation when she died. That's why I have the parking spot and the pass. You know last Colorado Marlowe and all. This is my first time using it so I don't really know what I'm doing."

Jill nodded.

"Would you mind if we agree to something?" Jacob asked. "Can you just ask me about things rather than deciding there's something wrong with you? This is all very new to me. Talking and being clear is the only way I know to make it better... more comfortable... easier."

His empathy brought tears to Jill's eyes. Blinking back her emotion, she nodded.

"I'll try," Jill said.

"Great! I'll try to do the same," Jacob said. He stopped walking. "Where am I going?"

"This way!" Katy said at the same time Jill said, "Through the gate."

Jacob gave the volunteer his pass. The elderly woman searched Jacob's face then said, "I knew your mother. They don't make them any better than Celia Marlowe."

Reading the woman's name tag, Jacob said, "Thank you, Shirley. We all miss her."

Shirley, the volunteer, looked up to see Jill for the first time.

"You must be Jill," Shirley said. "It's nice to finally meet you."

Flabbergasted, Jill gawked at the woman. Shirley bent down to give Katy a zoo sticker.

"And who are you?"

"I'm Katy," the little girl said. "Who are you?"

"I'm Shirley," the volunteer smiled. Standing up, she said, "Is this little one yours?"

"Yes," Jacob said.

"Celia's grandbaby... she looks just like her." Noticing the forming lines, Shirley said, "I better get busy. It's nice to see you Jake. Enjoy your visit."

Jacob, Katy and Jill moved into the zoo.

"What was that?"

"My mother was loved by a lot of people," Jacob shrugged. "Don't take it too seriously."

"She knew my name! Why did you say...?"

"What was I going to say?" Jacob asked. "No, Shirley. I'm on a non-date with my step-horror's fiancé's ex-wife."

Jill's head jerked up to catch his eyes. Jacob laughed.

"Your step-horror? Mike called her your..."

"I was trying for polite," Jacob said. "Ladies present and all."

Looking at Jill, he could not contain his joy for being with her. He beamed. She smiled in return.

"Where to first?"

"Elephants!! Elephants!!" Katy bounced in the stroller.

"She likes to see the elephant's first," Jill said. "But we can go wherever you want to."

"Elephants it is," Jacob said. "Where's that?"

"This way! This way!" Katy said.

Jill laughed. Impulsively, she put her arm through his elbow. He smiled. They began their journey into the zoo.

They went about a hundred feet before Katy wanted to get out of the stroller. While Jacob looked away, Jill kneeled down to explain to Katy that she couldn't walk. Katy loved to run really fast and then walk slow. It was too hard for adults to keep up with her. And they didn't want to irritate there new friend, Jacob.

Jacob's head jerked to Jill when she said his name. He made a puzzled face. When Jill looked up, he said, "Can I talk to you for a minute?"

"Sure. Katy, stay here."

"Yes Mommy."

Jill's stomach dropped. Even though she and Katy had been on their best behavior, Jacob was mad. Stepping away from the stroller, she racked her brain. What had she done?

"I wanted to say that I don't mind keeping up with Katy. You don't have to keep her in the stroller for me."

"But she'll get tired then we'll have to carry her."

"Of course. That's what kids do. Do you mind keeping up with Katy?"

Jill looked up at Jacob and gulped. She wasn't quite sure how to respond. She bit her lip and shook her head.

"Do you mind carrying Katy? Because I don't mind carrying her."

Jill shook her head. "You're not mad?"

"Absolutely not. What would I be mad about?" Jacob shook his head slightly. "I have the special delight of going to the zoo with a kid. I'd be pretty stupid to be mad at a kid for being... a kid."

Still biting her lip, Jill shrugged. Jacob smiled.

"Let's free the hostage," he said.

Jill unhooked Katy from the stroller.

"Why don't you go to the elephants while I take this back to the car?"

"Are you sure?"

"Yeah, I can be there and back in a few minutes," Jacob said. "I'll meet you there."

Before Jill could respond, Jacob took the stroller and jogged through the zoo. The further away Jacob ran, the better Jill felt. Taking Katy's hand, they skipped to the elephants. Katy's delighted chatter at the elephant mommy and the elephant baby filled the air, and Jill's heart. Katy's wonder helped Jill feel more grounded.

When Jacob returned, carrying a green balloon for Katy, Jill was happy to see him. They bonked heads trying to tie the balloon on Katy's wrist. Jill laughed and he blushed. Before they could say, 'I'm sorry,' Katy was off to see another animal.

After quick stop at Monkey Island, Katy pointed her finger and ran to watch the penguins eat lunch. Katy's mind, and conversation, bounced from topic to topic. She was fascinated with Bear Mountain but the Apes scared her a little bit. She stood against the Plexiglas barrier while an ape stood to watch her. Backing away from the Plexiglas and the ape, Katy cried for the ape behind the glass. While Jill comforted her soft hearted daughter, Jacob bought tickets for the train. The laughing ride on the train cured all Ape related problems.

Stepping off the train, Katy said, "I have to go potty, Mommy."

And Jill froze.

Katy took forever in the bathroom. She did everything BUT go to potty. Every public restroom was at least a fifteen minute procedure. When Jill and Katy were alone, Jill marveled at the songs, conversation and general observations Katy made in the restroom.

But when Trevor was with them?

He was furious. 'Why doesn't she just go?' or 'What kind of a mother are you to let her take so long?' She tried to explain that there were always other mother's camped out waiting for their three or four year olds. But Trevor insisted she was manipulating Jill to purposely disrupt his life.

More than once, he left them. Jill and Katy had to take the bus home from the Zoo or the Rockies game. When they got home, Jill would lock Katy in her room so Katy wouldn't have to witness Trevor scream at Jill.

"What happened?" Jacob touched Jill's arm.

"Katy has to use the restroom," Jill said. "I'm really, really sorry. She takes forever and..."

"I wondered where it came from," Jacob said.

"What?" Jill was so surprised by his statement that she jerked out of her Trevor related panic.

"Well, as a guy, you wait forever for women in the bathroom. Waiting for Valerie? My sister? I'd practically evolve into a new species before she came out again." Jacob smiled. "I didn't realize four year olds curled their hair. Does Katy have a propane curling iron too?"

Jill couldn't help but laugh. She shook her head. "A new species?"

"You'll see. You'll have the opportunity to wait for Val and you'll know what I mean." Jacob laughed. "How about this? I'll sit right here and you guys can go in."

"Will you be here...?"

"There is no chance, not one, of me ending this non-date," Jacob smiled. "I'm having a great time!"

"Me too," Jill said.

"I might get some food. Do you want anything?"

"French Fries! French Fries!" Katy said.

"Anything else?" Jacob asked.

"We can share a hamburger or chicken strips," Jill said. "There's juice and water in the backpack."

She pointed to her backpack he insisted on wearing.

"I wondered what felt cool on my back!" Jacob said. "I'll meet you here."

With one last look to Jacob, Jill and Katy went into the restroom. And Katy took forever. Using this time as alone time with her mother, Katy reviewed all the animals she had seen and what she wanted to see. She asked questions about Jacob. Miraculously, Katy even went potty. After a quick hand washing, they were out the door.

Jill scanned the area for Jacob.

He wasn't there.

Jill had to bite her lip to keep from crying. The one moment she let her guard down to have a good time, look what happened? He left.

Feeling Katy tug her hand, she looked down to see Katy pointing. Jacob sat at a table talking to two octogenarian zoo volunteers. Jill hadn't seen him behind the volunteers. She felt a wave of relief.

"Here she is!" The elderly man said. He kneeled down to Katy level, "How are you, Katy? I'm Edward and this is my wife, Mary."

Katy shook his extended hand.

"I bet you're hungry," Edward said standing. "We don't want to keep you. We wanted to meet Celia's granddaughter and say 'Hello' to Jake. We've seen Delphie, but we haven't seen Jake since Celia died."

In that moment, Jill realized she knew Celia. Like a scene from a movie, Jill remembered meeting Jacob at Pete's Kitchen all those years ago. Every detail, from how frail his mother was to the illegal jolt of attraction she felt for Jacob, flashed across her brain. Shaking her head to clear the memory, Jill wandered to the table.

Katy was already eating her French Fries when Jill sat down at the table. She watched Jacob and Katy discuss the advantages of ketchup. Jacob had set up lunch including the fruit juice and water from Jill's backpack. He bought a couple hamburgers, chicken strips, and lots of fries. For dessert? Denver Zoo crunch cereal, of course.

And they ate everything.

One last bite and Katy was off!

Jill wiped Katy's hands while they walked. They found more penguins at Bird World. Katy bounced along the metal guard rail past the hoofed animal. When a buffalo caught Katy's eye, she stopped stalk still. While Katy and the buffalo shared a silent communication, Jill and Jacob stood behind her.

"I realize I knew your mother," Jill said.

Jacob nodded.

"She was very kind to me in a difficult transition in my life," Jill said. "Sometimes, when I get down, I talk to her... in my head, you know? I always feel better when I talk to your mom. I think of her as my guardian angel. I called her Celly... Celly Marlowe... not Celia. I guess I thought your mom was a Lipson."

The buffalo looked away and Katy ran into the cul-de-sac where the white wolf pack lived. The animals greeted Katy with a wild howl which she imitated. Jill and Jacob returned to their places behind Katy.

Jacob smiled, "Most people know her as Celia Marlowe. My dad was always just 'the husband' to her magnificence. I felt lucky to have known her."

"Me too," Jill said. "She had this friend... crazy red hair..."

"Delphie?"

"Delphinium, like the flower. She gave me a reading before I married Trevor. She told me Trevor would betray me three times before I was finally done with him. I thought the whole thing was hilarious." Jill sighed. "I told Trevor and... Well, he wouldn't let me go back. After Celly died, then again when I was pregnant with Katy, Delphie offered a free reading but I..."

"Delphie can be a bit much," Jacob said. "She lives with me... I mean in my house... I mean..."

"I know what you mean," Jill said.

Jacob smiled.

"I hate to think of it. You know? Trevor's only betrayed me twice," Jill said. "I hate to think of what the third time will be."

"Then don't," Jacob said. "Just be here with me."

On impulse, he slipped his arm around her. When Jill leaned into him, their eyes caught with a jolt of electricity. She lifted her chin and his mouth made an easy journey toward her luscious lips. Their lips were almost touching when they heard:

"Stupid bee. You won't hurt me again. I'll squish you and..."

"KATY! NO!" Jacob and Jill screamed at the same moment.

CHAPTER SIX
Disaster in the Form of a Honey Bee

They were too late. As Katy's fingers closed to squash the honey bee, the bee stung her. Clamping her hand closed, Katy screamed in terror and pain.

"Oh my God." Jill dropped to hold her daughter. "She's hyper-allergic to bees."

"Show me your hand. Katy, show me your hand. Katy, show me your hand," Jacob screamed.

He knelt next to the shrieking girl and pried her tight fist open. Using his zoo pass, he flicked the stinger from her hand.

"We have to get to the hospital," Jacob said. "JILL!"

Jill looked up at him. Her worst nightmare unfolding, Jill went completely blank. Horror overwhelmed her. Katy was going to die!

Jacob wrestled Katy from her arms.

"Hold my hand." He commanded Jill.

He grabbed Jill's hand. While Katy howled in his arms, Jacob hauled Jill through the zoo. The balloon, tied to Katy's wrist, trailed behind them like a green beacon. Running past Edward, the volunteer, he yelled for Edward to call Children's hospital at St. Joseph's. Katy was heading toward anaphylactic shock. Several people dialed their cell phones at once. The crowd stepped aside and Jacob raced through the zoo.

In his arms, Jacob felt Katy get ever warmer. Somewhere near the front gate, she stopped crying. Her throat closing, his tiny burden began to gasp for air. Her skin burned under his hands. He picked up the pace while dragging Jill behind. From the edge of the parking lot, he unlocked the Lexus. Flying to the front passenger seat, he laid Katy on his lap.

With great effort, Katy pulled in breath. Ripping an inhaler from a plastic Walgreen's bag, he shot Primatene Mist into Katy's mouth and counted down one minute. He was about to spray the inhaler again when Katy coughed and took a clear breath.

"Oh thank God," he said.

Moving quickly, he strapped Katy into her car seat then buckled Jill in the passenger seat.

The message that 'Celia's granddaughter was in trouble' had gone out over the zoo airwaves. Elderly volunteers appeared from nowhere to help. The volunteers blocked the road so Jacob had a clear shot.

Jacob, Jill, and a wheezing Katy sped out of the parking lot. The tires squealed as they turned left onto Twenty-Third Avenue. For once in his Denver life, Jacob hit every green light and missed any road construction.

The emergency staff waited at the curb. Yelling orders, the doctor began treating Katy in her car seat. As if in a trance, Jill stood watching the emergency team. Jacob came around the car to wrap himself around her. Nestled in his tight embrace, Jill began to sob. He covered her face when the nurses carried Katy from the car and onto a stretcher. A nurse cut the forgotten balloon from Katy's wrist. With Jill in his arms, Jacob watched the green balloon disappear into the bright sky.

"Mr. Marlowe?" An official looking woman stood next to him. She held a clipboard jammed with forms.

"I need to move the car," he said. He set a credit card on her clipboard. "Can I fill those out when I get back?"

"Sure," she said. Pointing to the man standing next to Jacob, "We have a valet."

Still shielding Jill in his arms, Jacob gave the man his keys.

"We've had a horrible shock. Is there a place we can...?" Jacob asked.

"Of course," the woman smiled. "I'll take you to a quiet place where you can talk. But I do need..."

"Sure," Jacob said. "You'll let them know we are back here."

"Of course."

They followed the woman through the hospital to a small empty waiting room. Jacob settled Jill on his lap. While he held her, stroking her hair and back, Jill cried her heart out. When her tears evened and her breath was deep, he got her some water.

"I'm going to call Mike," Jacob said. "I have a friend who works Emergency at Denver Health. I'm going to call him as well. He might be able to help. Is it all right to get my friend's help?"

Jill nodded her head. Watching Jacob on the phone, she felt almost drunk from the release of emotions. She was so used to being in control, so used to having to be in control, that she felt ungrounded. When Jacob slipped his arm around her, she tucked herself into him. Surrounded by his warmth and scent, she was safe.

She only let go of Jacob when Megan peeled her from his embrace.

Mike arrived not long after Megan. Her two oldest siblings were all set to take over when Jacob's doctor friend, John Drayson, came into the room. Tall with dark curly hair, he shook Jacob's hand then spoke with Mike. Mike introduced him to Jill as the husband of an old Army friend.

"It's very unusual for a child to have this kind of reaction," Dr. Drayson said. His accent was foreign, British she thought. His cobalt blue eyes were present, clear and kind.

"I was stung when I was pregnant," Jill said. "I... I'm allergic to bees... I didn't have insurance... I mean for the baby... what the state gives you... but not for an allergic reaction. I got really sick."

"What about Katherine? Has she ever been stung?" Dr. Drayson asked.

"About a year ago," Jill said. "We were at the Botanic Gardens. Trevor wanted to take a family break. He was... studying for finals. She likes to run out ahead and just ran into the bee. Trevor wouldn't let me take her to the Emergency room because he... he didn't want the disruption or... the expense, I guess. I was horrified that she would die... but Trevor said it was my fault for not watching her. I'm not a very good mother. I took her to Walgreen's. It's across the street from Pete's and I know some of the pharmacists... from working at Pete's.... It was the only thing I could think of... The pharmacist was very kind. He told me to give her Benedryl. He made a place for us by the pharmacy so he could make sure she was all right. It took a while, but the Benadryl eventually worked. He told me she might die the next time she was stung."

"Her reaction makes more sense. Without treatment, any allergic reaction can get stronger with each event," Dr. Drayson said. "This is the Trevor from the engagement party?"

Jill's head jerked up to look at the doctor.

"My wife and I were there as Jacob's guests. You put on quite a show. My best-friend was the lawyer who kept shouting from the back. You've traded up, my dear." Dr. Drayson nodded his head toward Jacob. "Is there anything else you can tell me?"

Jill shook her head. Biting her lip, she whispered, "Trevor said... I... Is Katy going to die?"

Dr. Drayson smiled, "She's very sick. The allergic reaction went through her body. They're working to keep her body from getting too hot... kind of like a bad fever. She's responding well and seems very healthy. They gave her steroids to fight the allergic reaction. It will be a while before we know for sure. For now, they're cautious but very hopeful."

Jill nodded her head. "Is she in pain?"

"The doctor put her to sleep in her car seat. She won't remember any of this," Dr. Drayson said. "She's well loved and strong, the kind of strong that comes from great mothering. You got her here quickly. These doctors are the very best. She has every chance."

"John?" A doctor stuck his head in the waiting room. "I heard you were here. Do you mind...?"

"One minute," John said to the doctor. Returning to Jill, he said, "If it's all right with you, I'll remain as your liaison. At this point, there isn't anything for you to do. You can stay here with your family. I'll let you know when I know anything."

Jill nodded. "Thanks."

"It's my pleasure. Jacob has helped us with a number of quandaries. I'm delighted to have the opportunity to return a favor," Dr. Drayson said. He and the other doctor walked from the room.

At the same moment, Jill's sister Candy came into the room. Candy hugged Jill. The two sisters joined Mike and Megan near the back of the waiting room.

Jacob stood near the door watching the siblings all talk at once. Overwhelmed by the sound of everyone talking, he was grateful when a hospital staff clerk came to the door. He tried to flag Jill, but she was absorbed in her family. Slipping out of the waiting room, Jacob followed the clerk to a cubical where he began filling out Katy's admission forms.

Yes, he would be responsible. No, Katy didn't have insurance. Of course, he understood that the bill might be thousands of dollars. The woman sneered at him when he said he would pay cash. Of course, feel free to run my credit.

The clerk ran his social security number, then it was 'Thank you, Mr. Marlowe. Credit card is fine. Is there anything else I can do for you?' He was just about to leave when she asked him to autograph her copy of 5280. He shook his head as if he didn't understand what she asked and left the cubicle.

Standing near the door of the waiting room, Jacob watched Jill and her family interact. Their voices would get loud, as if they were arguing, then someone would laugh. Once one sibling laughed the rest of them followed.

Intimidated, Jacob convinced himself that he should probably just go home.

Jill could call him if she wanted to see him again. He was passing through the outer door when Steve, Jill's middle brother came walking in.

"Hey," Steve said. "Running away?"

Trying to come up with a lie, Jacob stalled for time with a smile.

"Megan and Mike are at it, huh?" Steve said. "God, they drive me crazy. I thought they would be over their bossy brigade by now. Not yet?"

Jacob shook his head.

"Yeah, well. That guy's looking for you."

Jacob turned to see Dr. John Drayson flagging him.

"How's Katy?" Jacob asked.

"She's improving. Are you leaving?"

"Nah," Steve said. "We're going to get a beer."

"Being involved with a woman from a huge Catholic family can be a nightmare." Dr. Drayson's intelligent eyes laughed at Jacob. "Listen, they need to keep Katy overnight. They wanted me to ask because you are paying cash. She'll also need follow up treatment. A lot of follow up treatment. Are you all right with that?"

"Of course," Jacob said. "Whatever she needs."

"Good," Dr. Drayson said. "I take Irish Breakfast tea with a spot of steamed milk. And a sweet."

"Sweet?"

"Anything chocolate works. This hospital's food is particularly bad. I know because I've picked up call at every hospital around Denver. Have to pay my historic restoration contractor."

"Your contractor has large hospital bills and appreciates your diligence in payment."

Dr. Drayson laughed, "You might want to get dinner."

Jacob and Steve watched Dr. Drayson walk into the hospital. Turning to Steve, Jacob said, "Beer?"

"Pasquini's is close. You paying?"

"Sure," Jacob said.

"Then let's take the Brits suggestion and have dinner," Steve said. "They won't miss us. By the time we get back, they should have settled down a little bit."

"We'll get them dinner too?" Jacob asked.

"Shit, you're paying," Steve said.

Jacob laughed.

~~~~~~~~~

Jill noticed Jacob leave with the administrative woman. She kept one eye on the door hoping to see him come back. But he hadn't come back. After an hour passed, she knew he had left her.

"I'm going to use the restroom," Jill said.

"I'll go with you, Jilly," Candy said.

"I think I need to be alone," Jill said. "Thanks."

"You sure?" Candy's worried face said more than she would ever speak.

Jill nodded. Jill found a single toilet restroom and locked herself inside. Sitting on the toilet, she reviewed the day. She can't remember when she'd had a better time–at the zoo or anywhere. She bit her lip wishing she had kissed Jacob earlier. She wanted to… thought about it… but it was… what did he call it? Right. A non-date.

Then all of this.

She would leave too. God.

Pulling up her underwear, she noticed she was wearing the pretty slip of lace Tanesha gave her for the engagement party. Sandy was right. She hoped Jacob would take the beautiful panties off her. Not after all of this…

Jill was brushing her hair when she realized that she hadn't thought about paying for Katy's care. Her usual focus on the bottom line slipped in her distress of Katy. Leaning forward to wipe the mascara smudges from under her eyes, Jill furrowed her eyebrows.

Did Jacob give that woman a credit card? Why would he do that? Katy wasn't his child and he certainly didn't owe Jill anything. She nodded to herself in the mirror. Time to face the music.

Squaring her shoulders, Jill washed her hands and went to find that administrative woman. Jill clutched her chest when she heard that Jacob had settled everything and taken full responsibility for Katy. The woman looked Jill up and down. With a raised eyebrow to speak her opinion, the woman asked Jill exactly what was her financial arrangement with Mr. Marlowe. Flushing at the woman's implication that she was a prostitute, Jill backed into Dr. Drayson.

"Katy would like to see you," he said.

CHAPTER SEVEN
WHO ARE THESE PEOPLE?

They were half-way through a pitcher of Fat Tire before Jacob realized Steve wasn't just killing time. Steve wanted to check out his sister's new potential boyfriend: Jacob. After chatting with their waiter, Dustin Kidder, about Katy, Steve ordered a couple of Pasquini's calzones and another pitcher of beer. And Jacob waited for Steve to get around to what he wanted to say.

Dustin brought the calzone's and beer before Steve's demeanor shifted. Steve was ready to talk. Jacob shifted back in his seat to give Steve space to unfold his story, the story of his parents' death.

The entire family was on vacation in Costa Rica when his parents and Jill went out for groceries. At nine years old, Jill went everywhere with her mother. As usual, they left Megan and Mike in charge.

But there wasn't anything to take charge of.

The family had a cottage right on the beach of a small private cove. Steve and Candy were in the ocean when their parents left. Mike made a complicated sand castle complex and Megan read a romance novel in the sun. The afternoon slipped away.

No one noticed that their parents hadn't returned until it was getting dark.

Terrified, the siblings went to the police. Nothing. They called the consulate. Nothing. When news came, it was bad. The Costa Rican national police arrived near dawn. Their parent's car was hit by a tractor trailer. The truck driver was swatting at a mosquito and swerved into their lane. Their parents' rental car was destroyed. His parents were dead and Jill was missing.

Desperate for help, they called the father of a school friend, Senator Patrick Hargreaves. After the Senator's intervention, the police reluctantly agreed to show Mike the wreckage and identify the bodies. To this day, Mike refused talk about what he saw.

Jill was just gone. Kidnapped? Stolen? No one seemed to know.

Senator Hargreaves told them to return to Denver. He would continue to put pressure on the consulate to find Jill. Grief stricken, they returned to their empty house in Denver.

Mike and Megan were in charge of the family. Their parent's life insurance paid off the house, but not much more. Megan had just graduated from high school. She turned down her full scholarship to Regis University and went to work. Mike quit high school, took his GED, enlisted in the Army and sent every paycheck home. Steve and Candy continued at Machebeuf on a family tragedy scholarship.

"All the luxuries of a Catholic education," Steve smirked.

"What about Jill?" Jacob asked.

"We were just getting our feet under us when Senator Hargreaves called," Steve said. "Some friar found Jill among the congregation of a church in Costa Rica."

"What?"

"Yeah, he called it 'angelic intervention,'" Steve said. "This guy remembered meeting the whole family at an ordination in Denver. Through Catholic Charities, he was able to get Jill home in two days."

"Wow," Jacob said. He set cash in the bill folder and handed it to Dustin. He said to Dustin, "I don't need change."

"I'll bring the rest of your food when it's ready," Dustin said.

"Thanks," Jacob replied. Looking over to Steve, he asked, "Where was she?"

"Honestly? We don't know," Steve said. "She was healthy... seemed fine. The friar said that a farmer found her in his field. The farmer and his wife had other kids so they just cared for her."

"Was she all right?" Jacob asked. "Did they hurt her?"

"No, she was healthy. She has a scar on her leg and the doctor says her leg was broken and set. She wasn't malnourished. Except for the leg thing, she wasn't hurt... in any way," Steve said. "She was kind of blank. She still does that when she gets really freaked out."

"She went blank today," Jacob said.

"Freaky, isn't it?" Steve smiled at Jacob's nod. "She was blank for a while, then wham, she was Jill again. She didn't remember Mom and Dad were dead, where she had been all that time, nothing.

"I'll tell you this," Steve continued. "Mike's looked for this farmer and can't find him. He's looked for the friar and can't find him either." Steve shook his head. "It's like they never existed."

"Now that IS freaky," Jacob said.

"I guess I'm telling you all of this so you can understand. We are very protective of Jill. She's like a special gift from our dead parents. They were great parents... really great."

"She's very special."

"Trevor couldn't stand us. He used to harass Jill to pick between us and him. He told Mike that he abandoned Jill and Katy because of us! Prick."

Jacob shrugged his eyebrows at the obvious.

"We couldn't stop her from being with Trevor but... We're always here for Jill."

"I wouldn't expect less," Jacob said.

"Good, then why were you running away?"

Dustin brought three plastic bags filled with calzones, salads, and breadsticks to the table.

"Here's the tea and the Raspberry Decadence," Dustin said. He set a separate brown bag down. "Dude, you'll let me know about Katy?"

Steve and Dustin did a complicated little hand shake that ended in a hand bump. "Yeah, I'll let you know."

Dustin grinned at Jacob.

"Thanks," Jacob said.

"No problem, man. Any friend of Steve's and such," Dustin said.

The men began walking back to the hospital with the food.

"Running away?" Steve asked.

"I got overwhelmed. My sister and I are... not close. She does her thing in Hollywood and I do mine here. I guess your parents' death pulled your family closer while my mother's death drove me and Val apart."

"It's a lot," Steve said. "If you stay with Jill, are we going...?"

"I don't have any problem with Jill having a family. I left my life and business in Maine to help my father. I know what it means to have family," Jacob said. "I... This was our first date... It's not even a date. We called it a 'non-date.' Just the zoo and lunch."

"My sister's a pricey date." Steve laughed.

"I'd rather buy Christian Loboutin's," Jacob said.

Steve laughed. "Lots of guys try to get with Jill. If she's willing to go on a non-date with you, she must be pretty interested."

"Or desperate to get to the zoo," Jacob said.

"I think she likes you," Steve said.

Approaching the hospital, Jacob saw Jill talking to Dr. John Drayson outside the hospital. When she saw Jacob, she beamed. Jacob grinned in response. Even with his hands full of food, he managed to hug her 'hello.'

"Katy's going to be all right," Jill said into his chest.

"I'm so glad," Jacob said. He kissed her cheek.

"Me too," Jill said.

"We brought dinner," Steve said. "Your tea and Chocolate-Raspberry Decadence, sir."

"Thanks" Dr. Drayson laughed.

"Would you like to eat?" Jacob asked.

Jill nodded.

Stepping back from Jacob, Jill was about to kiss him when Steve said,

"Come on, Jilly. No make outs on the sidewalk."

Jill laughed. She caressed Jacob's cheek then followed the men inside for dinner.

~~~~~~~~~

Valerie Lipson opened the door of her Malibu condominium, their Malibu condo, and walked into the hall. Standing at the door, she gazed across the apartment to the pounding surf. She would miss this view.

Her eyes shifted to her engagement ring tucked into its Harry Winston box on the floor. People magazine said Ronald Winston, Harry's son, personally selected the yellow diamond. Wes paid a cool three and a half million dollars for perfection in a size seven. Valerie tugged her note from under the ring box and set it in front. Wes would see the note first.

One last check. Yep, she had everything.

Valerie pulled the door to the condo closed and locked the bolt. Holding the keys in her hand, she closed her eyes. If she had keys, she could always come back.

In one swift motion, she shoved the keys through the mail slot.

Standing, she picked up her suitcase and walked to the elevator. A trip home to Denver to reset her life. A fresh start. That's exactly what she needed. Her BMW M3 convertible roared to life in response to the thought.

Flicking on her blinker, she felt real regret. She wished she could be what Wes needed. With a sigh, she merged into Pacific Coast Highway traffic.

How long was she engaged this time?

Longer than the last two... Valerie counted the months on her fingers. Five months. Valerie shook her head. Three engagements, hundreds of men, and the red headed witch was still right.

Wes's face flushed red when he asked: "Please marry me, Val. All I want to do is take care of you for the rest of my life."

And the only thought in Valerie's head was, "See Delphie, you were wrong! I can love someone other than Michael Roper."

She squealed when he gave her the ring. They made Viagra love for hours. When Wes fell asleep, Valerie cried into her pillow.

She would make this work. She was going to make this work. She had to make this work. She was going to love Wes.

The day her engagement to Hollywood producer Wesford Kapanski was announced, the blogosphere vibrated with nasty comments and vicious opinions. Perez Hilton posted a photo of Val and Wes a huge white X over them. Every night, Entertainment Tonight did the 'Val Count' for the number of days they were engaged. Vegas set the line at fifty to one that Val would marry Wes.

Valerie worked to love this man.

But no amount of love making, ocean views or expensive gifts removed her ever-present thoughts of Mike. Caffeine helped. Alcohol was better. But nothing ever really washed that man from her mind. This morning, she realized that becoming the seventh Mrs. Wesford Kapanski wasn't going to cure her.

"You will only have one love, Val," Delphie said to a sobbing Val. Mike left for basic training ten minutes before. "You will cause yourself great hardship if you can't allow yourself to love him, marry him, and make him your world. He is your true love. Children born of love, like your parents,' are only satisfied with true love. There's no more powerful force in this world."

True love?

God. No one believed in true love any more. After six years of starring on a popular soap opera, Valerie knew everything there was to know about love. Men cheat. Men lie. And women suffer.

Not that she didn't learn that from her father.

Delphie was wrong about her parents. She had to be wrong about Mike.

"Where you going, hon?" The clerk at Frontier Airlines ticket counter asked.

"Denver. The soonest available," Valerie said.

"You're Valerie Lipson," the clerk said.

Valerie smiled her movie star smile. "Do you watch *Our Loves, Our Lives?*"

Surprised by the question, the clerk looked up from her typing. She shook her head. "My husband works for your father. Lipson construction. You look like your brother, Jacob."

Valerie's smile dimmed. Of course, Frontier Airlines was based in Denver, home of Lipson construction.

"I bumped you to first class on me," the clerk said. "Your father's been really great to us. He gave my husband a month off when our babies were born. He even cosigned on a loan so we could get into our house. My husband's never been happier at a job. I... I just wanted to say, 'Thanks.'"

Valerie smiled at the woman. Everyone loved her scumbag father. This woman couldn't help it if she was fooled by the bastard. Valerie paid for her ticket and thanked the woman. She wasn't going to go diva on a poor stupid airline clerk.

Looking at her ticket, Valerie realized she had a few hours before her flight. Walking toward security, Valerie waved to the bank of paparazzi photographers.

"Val! Val!" They screamed. "Over here Val."

"Val! TMZ! Where you goin'?" the videographer for TMZ.com asked.

Valerie waved then started up the escalator.

"Where you going, Val?"

"I'm going home, boys," she said. Then without even realizing what she was saying she murmured, "I'm going home to my husband."

Like any great actress, Valerie didn't respond to her own words. She smiled and waved again as if she never said a thing.

While her stilettos pounded the concrete passage way, her mind returned to Mike.

"I can't just work for your father!" the 17 year-old Mike screamed. "I take a job with your father and I'll never be my own person. You need a real man. Day by day, you'll lose respect for me. I can't live with that."

"Please don't go," the 15 year-old Valerie begged. "I'll work for my father! I can take care of your family. Let me take care of your family. Please don't leave me."

"Oh Val," Mike said. "Oh honey."

He wrapped her in his arms and they cried together. When morning came, he left for basic training. That was the morning Delphie pronounced her fate, her curse.

Valerie ordered a cosmopolitan at the LAX bar. Finding a spot near the back, she opened a magazine. She slipped in her iPOD ear buds so no one would bother her or her memories.

She was "Mike's girl" to everyone in Denver. UCLA had given her a fresh slate. She started with UCLA boys, then graduated to producers and movie stars. One after another, she tried to find love again.

Mike would arrive at her dorm room in his dress uniform. He never cared who was there. He just wanted Val. More than once, he found her in bed with some random guy, and still he didn't care. He'd shrug and say, 'What can I expect? I'm the one who left.' But her promiscuity hurt him. He flaunted his own liaisons in return.

They went back and forth hurting each other until the summer between her junior and senior year, the summer everything went bad.

Her precious mother was diagnosed with terminal cancer. And her mother's true love? He fucked his secretary and was stupid enough to get the whore pregnant. Her childhood home was sold before she had time to retrieve her things. Mom and Delphie moved into that tenement on Race Street. Jake, her funny, kind, lovable, partner-in-crime little brother, managed to transform himself into a complete jock asshole.

And Mike was stationed at Fort Irwin in Barstow.

For six months of sheer bliss, she had Mike every weekend. Her parents' divorce settlement included a fourth of the construction company. Jake bought her portion the very next day. With her new found millions, she and

Mike bought a tiny house in Monterey. They were married on the beach by a minister. Jake and Mom received a picture of Mr. and Mrs. Roper kissing on the beach.

Valerie was in heaven. She didn't make Mike her world. He was her world—her morning, noon and night. She graduated a term early to be with him, near him. While her childhood family burned to the ground, Valerie and Mike rose like the phoenix from its ashes.

"Valerie Lipson?" A short, thin Hispanic man stood next to Val's table. "Raphael Acosa from US magazine. I'm wondering what you meant when you said you were going home to see your… We couldn't quite catch the last word. TMZ is saying that you are going home to your husband. Ma'am, everyone knows you are marrying Wes. Are you and Wes already married? Are you married to someone other than Wes? US magazine would love to have an exclusive interview…"

Valerie stood so quickly that the man was forced to take a step back. Smiling her movie star smile, she said, "My brother lives in Denver. I have a family business meeting tomorrow. Gosh, I'm not sure what TMZ heard." She shrugged. "If you'll excuse me. I need to freshen up before the flight."

"We're sitting together on your flight, Val," the reporter said. "We at US magazine wanted to show you our commitment to telling your true story."

"Thanks. I'll see you on the plane," Valerie said.

She made a bee line for the restroom. Locking herself in a stall, she called her publicist. It was time to tell the truth.

~~~~~~~~~

"Ok, well this has been fun," Mike said. "I've got to get to work. Jill, you know how to get a hold of me right?"

Jill hugged her older brother, "Thanks Mikey."

"Candy? You'll remember to do that thing we talked about?" Mike asked.

"I watch 'Val Count' every night. We are up to one hundred and forty-nine engaged days." Candy smiled to reassure her brother.

"Great. And you," Mike pointed at Jacob, "I'd like a word."

Jill shot a surprised look at Mike, then to Jacob. Jacob just smiled. Leaning to kiss her cheek, he said, "I'll be right back."

Jacob followed Mike through the hospital to the front door.

"Jill said you're paying for everything," Mike said. "And that the money lady asked Jill if she was trading sex for the hospital bill."

Jacob took a step back. He shook his head slightly, "What?"

"I want to know how you're going to expect repayment."

"I… I never thought about it." Jacob flushed bright red. "I…"

"Good, that's what I told Jill," Mike said. "You haven't heard from Val have you?"

Jacob shook his head.

"She's been engaged a long time this time... You think..."

"Honestly?" Jacob asked

Mike nodded.

"No," Jacob said. "Val's still Val inside."

"I hope you're right," Mike said.

With a nod of his head, Mike walked toward the parking lot.

~~~~~~~~~

"What's Val count?" Jill asked Candy.

"Mike is obsessed with this soap opera actress," Candy said. "She's engaged for like the third time. Entertainment Tonight is doing an engagement watch. I watch it every night then call him with what they say."

"Who's the girl?" Megan asked.

"Valerie Lipson."

Megan jumped up from her seat and walked to the water cooler where Steve was standing. They shared a long look.

"I'll tell you if even half of what they say about her is true, she's a real bitch," Candy said. "I mean, I don't get it. Mike's great looking, a wonderful person, amazing artist, but he doesn't want to be set up, won't go out with girls or boys for that matter. He's obsessed with this... prima donna actress."

Megan closed her eyes. Turning around, she looked from Candy to Jill. It was time they knew the truth.

"Meg, what's wrong?" Jill asked.

"Mike's married to Valerie Lipson."

CHAPTER EIGHT
THE PAST, PRESENT AND FUTURE

"But Valerie Lipson is Jacob's sister," Jill said. "How...?"

"Val and Jake aren't Catholic. Remember that huge fight Dad and Mike had? That was over Valerie," Megan said. "Dad forbid Mike to go out with Val because she wasn't Catholic. Mike disappeared for a week. Mom was hysterical. She made Dad go after Mike."

Candy and Jill nodded.

"They met skiing when Mike was fourteen or something," Steve said. "Remember how much Mike used to ski in the winter? Camp in the summer?"

"Every moment he wasn't working or in school," Candy said.

"That was so he could be with Val. They dated from the time they met. Mom and Dad didn't know," Steve said. "When they got married, Mike figured we would be against it because Dad was against it. So he didn't tell us."

"We only found out when..." Megan's face flushed red and her eyes filled with tears.

"When what?" Candy said. "We aren't children anymore, Meg. You don't have to protect us."

"Mike died; or, they thought he was dead."

"WHAT?" Candy and Jill said in unison.

"I... I really shouldn't tell you this," Megan said.

"Yes, you should," Steve said. "If you don't, I will. It's time to stop the secrets, Meg."

"Around the time Jake's mom died...." Megan began her story.

~~~~~~~~~

"I wonder if you might help me," Valerie said.

When the Frontier Airlines clerk moved from the ticket counter to the boarding pass counter, Valerie stood in her line. She signed autographs and talked to fans in order to keep the US magazine reporter at bay.

"Absolutely. What can I do?" the woman said.

"There's a reporter from US magazine and..."

"Oh don't worry, hon. I took care of him. He wanted to sit next to you but I put him in the back of the plane. I radioed the gals on the plane. They will let you off then hold him for a while. You should be able to make a quick get away."

Val's face registered real relief, "Thanks."

"You're father's a great man. I'm happy to do what I can." She passed Valerie her boarding pass back over the counter. "Just watch me. I'll let you know when it's safe to board."

Valerie blushed and nodded. "Thanks."

Continuing to buffer herself from the reporter, Valerie signed autographs and chatted with fans. She watched the line of passengers board the plane. Confident he had corralled Valerie on the flight, the reporter boarded the plane. When the agent nodded, Valerie made her excuses then moved down the ramp to the plane. The flight attendants settled Valerie in the front seat with a glass of champagne.

She slipped in her iPOD ear buds and returned to her memories of the best time of her life. As always, those memories of love and laughter collided with the reality of that awful spring.

Valerie and Mike were naked, wrapped around each other, when the dreadful news came. Mike was going back to the Middle East and her mother wouldn't live to see Easter. Jake begged her to come home, but she wasn't going to give up her last month with Mike.

She wasn't sure how it happened. She was on the pill, after all. She only knew when. She was pregnant when he left.

Unbidden, Valerie's mind ticked through the markers of that horrible spring:

February 27th:
Valerie gets pregnant and Mike leaves for the Middle East.
February and March:
They talked every night. He sent her crazy pictures. In response, she sent him pictures of herself naked. She didn't tell him about the baby. Her mother had a bunch of miscarriages. Valerie wanted to make sure she was really, really pregnant. She was going to tell him April 15th as a tax joke.
April 5th:
Mike went on a week-long mission. No problem, he'd call when he was done. She was brave for him in their last phone call but cried herself to sleep that night.
April 15th, 8 AM:
Opened the door to two somber Army men. Mike's team was ambushed. Mike was presumed dead.
April 15th, 8:25 AM:
Sedated by the doctor.
April 15th, 7 PM:

Awakened by telephone:

"Mike?"

"No. It's Jake. Come now, Mom's dying."

<u>April 16th, 1 AM:</u>

Walked in on father sobbing at mother's bedside.

"I can't do it," he sobbed.

"You have to," Mom said. "Do what we planned. Take care of your new family. Jake and Valerie need you… more now because I won't be here."

"You're my whole life," her father said.

"Then do it for me. Stick with our plan."

"Ah, Celia. I can't live without you."

<u>April 16th, 7 AM:</u>

Celia Marlowe Lipson drew her last breath with her children and best-friend by her side.

<u>April 20th, 8 AM:</u>

Valerie and Jake reviewed their mother's memorial plans with the mortician. Shaking the mortician's hand good-bye, she felt a burning, ripping, thousands of times worse than a cramp. Jake took her to the hospital. Her last connection to Mike was dead.

<u>April 24th, 8 AM:</u>

More than ten thousand people celebrate the life of Celia Marlowe Lipson.

<u>April 28th:</u>

Paperwork waited at Monterey. Mike was officially dead.

<u>April 29th:</u>

Valerie moved the band from her wedding set to her right hand where it remained today. Hoping the Pacific would cleanse her misfortune, she threw the diamond solitaire into the ocean.

<u>April 30th:</u>

Jake helped Valerie pack the Monterey house.

<u>May 5th:</u>

Valerie settled into her new Hollywood Hills home, called her agent, and got an audition.

"Ms. Lipson." The flight attendant touched Val's arm. She gave Valerie a Kleenex to wipe her dripping eyes. "We're taxiing right now. I thought you might want to get your possessions together so you can make a quick exit. Do you need a ride home?"

"I arranged for a car," Valerie said.

"I called ahead. There are a lot of photographers waiting for you. We're going to sneak you out the back. What company is meeting you?"

"Prestige," Valerie said.

"I'll call them. They can send a second car," the flight attendant said.

"Michael Roper usually drives me. Would you mind asking for him?"

"Sure," the flight attendant said.

"Thanks," Valerie said.

~~~~~~~~~

"You have about an hour before visiting hours are over. They woke up Katy so you could spend some time with her. They'll put her to sleep again before you go," Dr. Drayson said. "I'd encourage you to enjoy your time with her then go home and get some rest. Katy will need you to be one hundred percent tomorrow."

Jill nodded. She had already called in sick to work tomorrow. She knew Katy would need her. She dreaded having to desert her at the hospital. Following Dr. Drayson back through the ICU, she worked to keep the horror from her face. Her baby was swollen, her skin was bright red, and she was hooked to a bunch of machines. When Katy opened her eyes, she was Jill's girl.

"Mommy," Katy said.

Jill's eyes filled at the sound of her daughter's croaking voice. Katy hadn't been able to speak the last time she was awake.

"Katy-baby." Jill bent to kiss her daughter.

The nurse lowered the guard rail so Jill could sit on Katy's bed.

"Mommy, I'm sorry. I made you cry." Katy's red swollen finger caught a tear from Jill's eye. "I didn't mean to get sick."

"Oh baby," Jill said. "I'm just happy to see you."

"Are you going to ask Jacob to be my Daddy?"

Jill burst out a laugh at her daughter's question.

"I think he would be a good Daddy," Katy said.

"We'll see, Katy-baby. We'll see."

~~~~~~~~~

"Ma'am," the driver said.

He held open the door to the small limousine and Valerie stepped into the back. The flight attendant escorted Valerie to an employee's garage where the limousine was waiting.

"Michael usually drives me," Valerie said.

"I apologize, Ma'am. Mr. Roper was previously engaged. We attempted to shift his assignment but his client specifically requested him six months ago."

Valerie watched the man come around the limousine then step into the driver's seat.

"Wedding?" Valerie asked.

"Bachelor party." The driver started the car. "Better him than me. Where am I taking you?"

"Race and Colfax," Valerie said.

"So, Val. Are you going to marry Wes?" The driver looked at Valerie through the rear view mirror.

Valerie smiled her movie star smile.

"What's this about a husband?" the driver asked as the window to the passenger compartment closed. Valerie clicked off the microphone.

Slipping on her sunglasses, she tried to figure out how to see Mike and not seem desperate.

Desperate.

For two years, four months and fifteen days she was desperate. Desperately lonely. Desperately sad. Desperate to move on. Desperately lost.

Then Michael Roper returned to her life. She was leaving the Ivy in West Hollywood on the arm of a handsome, and secretly gay, actor when she saw Mike. Fifty pounds lighter and broken, Mike Roper stood on the sidewalk waiting for her. If the actor hadn't been holding her up, she would have collapsed to the pavement. Somehow, they managed to miss the watchful eye of the ever present paparazzi. They escaped to her home in the Hollywood Hills.

They didn't leave the house for a month. They argued until they made love. They made love until they were exhausted. They ate whatever could be delivered, bathed together and barely dressed. The incredible draw toward each other remained impossibly strong.

But the obstacles were much greater.

Losing Mike, her baby, and her mother in the course of two weeks was too much for Valerie. She had become bitter and pessimistic. She would never trust him, or anyone, again. While her words lashed at him, her hardened heart froze him out.

Mike's unspoken experience left him shattered. Moment to moment, his moods were unpredictable. One moment, he would sob. The next moment, he was punching walls and screaming at the top of his lungs. Then, worst of all, her best-friend and lover would appear from inside the wreckage of this man. Valerie ached for her Mike.

A month after Michael Roper returned to her life, he disappeared again. He left a note saying he had to 'get right' before he could be with her. By the time he reappeared, she was a star on one of the most popular soaps and engaged to the gay actor.

As the limousine pulled up in front of the Castle, Valerie wondered what to do about Mike.

~~~~~~~~

"Where to?" Jacob asked.

They were sitting in his Lexus SUV outside the hospital. With her sisters' help, Jacob and Steve were able to get Jill into the car. Jill didn't want to 'abandon' Katy at the hospital. Sitting in the passenger seat, Jill looked longingly at the hospital.

"I should stay here," Jill said. "Katy needs me here."

"I will bring you back before Katy is even awake to need you," Jacob said. "I promise."

"I don't want to go home," Jill said. "I can't... I can't look at her things."

"Ok," Jacob said. "Would you like to come to my house?"

Jill bristled then nodded. She knew what was expected of her. Jacob started the car and moved toward Seventeenth Avenue.

"How did you know?" Jill asked.

"What do you mean?" Jacob asked.

"The emergency room doctor told me that if you hadn't given Katy the Primatene Mist, she would have died. Katy's only alive because of you. How did you know she would need it?"

"Delphie said Katy was allergic to bees. She said Katy would die if I didn't get her to the hospital," Jacob said. "I went to Walgreen's on the way to your house. That's why I was late."

"Oh," Jill said.

"The pharmacist must be the same guy who helped you before. He remembered Katy and told me what to do. One shot every minute until she breaths clearly. I only needed one."

"And you believed Delphie? Delphie, the crazy tarot card reader? I thought you said she was a joke?"

"She's very dramatic," Jacob said. "I mean her spirit guide's name is 'Naomi.'"

"Naomi?"

"Like from the bible," Jacob said.

"So she's Ruth?"

"Something like that," Jacob said. "You can see what I mean. Drama. Anyway, I've never known Delphie to be wrong. I mean, sometimes she mixes up the signs or misinterprets things. Like she told Mom that Mom would meet someone significant. They decided Mom was going to meet a new man. But they met you. Even so... I've never known Delphie to be... just wrong."

"So Trevor will betray me again," Jill said.

"He already has," Jacob said.

Jacob pulled the car into the driveway of the Castle. He pressed a button and the iron gate opened to allow him access to the open backyard. When the iron gate opened, Sarah and another dog came barking and running toward the car.

"Scooter," Jill said under her breath. "Why do you have Scooter?"

"Trevor took Scooter to the Dumb Friend's League. He told them he found Scooter on the street," Jacob said. "Delphie knew he would be jealous of Scooter. She wasn't sure what Trevor would do. So Mom had an identification chip put in Scooter with Delphie's address and phone number. The Dumb Friend's League ran the chip and called Delphie. That was right before I came back to Denver."

"Trevor said Scooter was dead. That stupid bastard. I can't believe... Oh God, Scooter..."

Jill jumped from the SUV to greet her old friend. Standing near the back of the truck, Jacob watched Scooter give Jill kisses on her mouth in delighted reunion. When Sarah nudged his leg, he rubbed her ears then threw the ball she had dropped in front of him.

Looking up, Jacob saw Valerie come down the back steps and into the garden. When Valerie smiled at Jacob, he knew she was finally 'just Val' again. He ran across the lawn to hug her.

In the dimming light of the summer night, Delphie stood on the back porch of Celia's Castle. Watching the reunion of Jill and Scooter, and Jacob and Valerie, Delphie said, "Just like we thought Naomi. They're finally all together. Now, the fun begins."

CHAPTER NINE
WHAT DID YOU SAY?

"Jill! Is Katy Ok?" Sandy yelled into her cell phone.

"Katy's okay. They're keeping her overnight," Jill said. "Where are you?"

"Funky Buddha. You wanna join us? I'm here with Tanesha and Heather. We are hoping to find some fun."

"No..."

"Jilly, what's wrong?" Sandy asked. "Wait, hang on. I'm going to go the sidewalk so I can hear you."

Jill paced Jacob's apartment. After playing with the dogs, Jacob brought white wine and cheese to the deck. They drank wine, ate fancy cheese and those little crackers she had only seen on TV. Jacob's sister, Val, and Delphie kept her laughing with funny stories about each other. She was all but asleep when he suggested she come upstairs to take a shower. He took her up to this gorgeous apartment, set out a towel and a bathrobe for her, then disappeared into the house.

Jill knew what was expected of her. After all, why would he have brought her to his house? She showered with his lavish soap and shampoo then wrapped herself in his plush bathrobe.

Looking at his comfortable queen sized bed, she panicked. She couldn't go through with it. She couldn't sleep with some guy just because she thought he was cute... or he paid for the hospital... or she liked his house... or she loved his mother... or... vexed with herself, Jill called her best-friend Sandy.

"Ok, sorry, I couldn't hear you," Sandy said. "What's wrong?"

"Jacob took me back to his apartment."

"You mean after he paid for the hospital, he took you back to his place? What's it like?"

"It's gorgeous. I mean the furniture needs replacing, maybe some colors on the wall and there's a lot of electronic equipment. Typical guys' place, you know. But it's all wood floors, cut-glass windows, and... The house is amazing. He calls it the 'Castle.' You'll just die when you see it."

"So what's the problem?"

"I don't think I can..."

Jill heard Heather ask for an update and Sandy explained what was wrong with Jill.

"Listen. There is only one reason a man brings you back to his place,"

Sandy said. "Is there a bedside table?"

"Um… yeah," Jill said.

"Open the drawer," Sandy said.

"Ok," Jill said. She slid open the antique table drawer.

"Condoms?" Sandy said.

Jill dug through the drawer. A reading light. Kleenex. Earplugs. A pair of glasses. A dog treat. A bag of throat lozenges. She gasped when she saw them. Jacob had condoms in this drawer!

"That man is ready to play," Sandy said. "Good for you."

"I don't think I can do it. I mean, I know the accounting lady said I was going to have to but I can't just SLEEP with someone."

"Honey, I don't think he brought you to his apartment so you could sleep."

"I know… What do I do?"

"She wants to know what to do," Sandy said to Tanesha and Heather.

Jill heard her friends laugh. Tanesha grabbed the phone from Sandy.

"Jilly, it's Tanesha. I think you should enjoy that gorgeous man. You might just figure out why people actually like sex."

"But Tanesha, I barely know this guy."

"You know him enough for him to pay off your hospital bill. With the emergency room, what's that gonna be? 20k? 30k?"

"I don't know," Jill mumbled.

"Honey, have some fun. You deserve it. That's all I wanted to say," Tanesha said. "She's all yours."

"I couldn't have said it better," Sandy said.

Jill heard Heather in the background, "Tell her we want every detail!"

"Yeah, make sure we get all the details. You know what I would do if I was in your situation."

"I know. But how do I…?"

"Just take off your clothes. He'll take care of the rest."

"Okay." Jill heard a door close downstairs. "I think he's coming."

"Have fun! We love you!" Her friends yelled into the phone then hung up.

Jill slipped off the soft terry robe and stood in the middle of the room.

~~~~~~~~~

Figuring Jill needed some time to herself, Jacob checked on Val, talked to Delphie, and answered some calls. Jill was almost asleep on the deck, so he assumed she would have crawled into bed by now. Tip toeing up the last few steps, he nudged the door open. Sarah bound into the apartment.

And there was Jill. Naked. Standing in the middle of the room. In one glance, his eyes took in her round hips, taut belly and perky breasts. His entire being rose to attention.

"Whoa," he said. He spun around to face the door. "What's going on, Jill?"

"The hospital lady said you told her I'd have to work off the hospital bill," she said. "I figured…"

Jacob collapsed into himself.

"I'm sorry. I don't know what I said to that woman," Jacob said. "She was just a nasty clerk."

"You mean you DON'T want to…"

Jacob turned to Jill. Forcing his eyes to stay on her face, he walked across the room. While his eyes caressed her face, he collected her hands with his hands.

"Nothing would make me happier than to make love to you. Not. One. Thing. But only when we want to… when you want to… when it's right. Not as payment of some stupid debt."

"Why did you bring me here?"

"I don't know," Jacob said. "You didn't want to be at home without Katy. At my house, Scooter's here to cheer you up. And I have cereal."

Jill started crying. She didn't resist when he pulled her into his arms.

"God, Jill. You're not a whore or a prostitute or whatever else. Don't short-change yourself. You're wonderful."

"What did you mean then?" Jill said into his shoulder.

"I don't think I said that. After that horrible woman found out who I was, she was hitting on me. She even wanted me to sign her 5280. She probably said that to you so you'd be mad at me."

"I'm not mad at you," Jill said.

"Good." Jacob pulled back to look into Jill's eyes. "What will ease your mind about the hospital bill?"

"Nothing," Jill said. "I hate being poor. I promise you. I will pay off the bill even if it takes forever."

"If that makes you feel better, all right." Jacob held his hand out to her and they shook on her promise.

He walked to his closet and picked out a clean white t-shirt for Jill to sleep in. She pulled the t-shirt over her head then wandered across the floor to find her panties.

"You have so much that money can't buy." In order to keep from jumping Jill, Jacob started talking. "You have family who that will drop everything to support each other. You have Katy. You have love and laughter in your life every single day. You have…"

He stopped talking when she bent over to pull on the beautiful panties. Taken back by her full hips and muscular legs, all thought escaped his head.

As she turned back toward him, Jacob adjusted his face, and himself. Noticing his motion, she gave him a wry smile.

"Money makes the world work," Jill said.

"Not really," Jacob said. "Come on. I promised no hanky panky on our non-date. You need to rest. Tomorrow is going to be another long day. Let's just rest for a while. I can take the couch..."

"I don't mind if we share a bed," Jill said.

Jacob nodded. "Bathroom?"

Jill shook her head. He took her hand then held the covers for her. He went into his closet to change into another white t-shirt and slipped into the bed next Jill. When he held his arm out to her, she snuggled against him.

"I guess I made a fool of myself," Jill said.

"Welcome to the club." Jacob chuckled.

"How did you get so much money if you don't care about it at all?"

"Oh Jill, that's a long complicated answer and you're exhausted. Let's save some excitement for our second non-date."

Jill stretched up to kiss him.

Snuggled together, their lips began a gentle exploration of each other's mouth and tongue. When Jacob moved to kiss her face, he found her cheeks wet with tears. Pulling back to look at her, he saw that she was crying.

"What is it?" he whispered.

"I just feel really sad," Jill said. "I'm sorry. I'm so sorry."

Jacob pulled her into his arms. Tucked against her chest, Jill began to sob. He stroked her back and head until her emotional storm abated.

"Your shirt is drenched," she said.

"Easy remedy," Jacob said.

He gave her a tissue for her nose then pulled off his shirt. She tucked herself against him and fell sound asleep.

"I love you, Jill," he whispered.

She stirred with his words, opened then shut her eyes. He smiled. Closing his eyes, he fell into a blissful sleep.

~~~~~~~~~

Jacob woke to the sound of his Blackberry buzzing. Someone sent him a text. Jacob shifted his shoulder and Jill rolled over. The clock read 3:07 in glowing red numbers. The site managers start up at five, so it couldn't be work. He lay back against the bed.

The blackberry continued its persistent buzz.

Someone needed his attention.

Slipping from the bed, Jacob crept across his apartment. He dug around in his laptop case until he found his vibrating phone. Looking at the face, he saw the same text repeated three times.

"Where the fuck is my sister?

Mike.

"She's asleep," Jacob texted back.

"Stupid fucker," Mike texted.

Hoping to not wake Jill, Jacob slipped out of the apartment. He had just reached the bottom of the stairs when Mike pounded on the door. Jacob opened the door.

Mike hit him like a ton of bricks. Jacob stepped aside, redirecting Mike's energy, and Mike fell forward.

"I cannot believe you would take advantage of my sister when she is vulnerable."

Mike took a swing at Jacob, which Jacob easily avoided.

"You done?" Jacob asked.

"No."

Mike shifted to throw Jacob over his hip, but Jacob defended his position. The men stood in the small landing looking at each other.

"You want me to be with your sister. You've said that over and over again," Jacob said. "Plus nothing happened."

"Then why don't you have any clothes on?" Mike was mad but calming down.

"She cried on my t-shirt. I took it off because it was soaked," Jacob said. "Besides, who are you? The morality police?"

"As far as my baby sister is concerned, asshole."

"I've never come after you about my sister. And she was fourteen years old!"

"Fifteen. But I was only seventeen," Mike grinned. "I love Val. You know that."

"I love Jill. You know that. So what's the problem?"

Mike looked at his boots for a moment, then shrugged. "Breakfast?"

"Sure," Jacob said.

Jacob pointed to the door that connected the attic stairwell to the house. Mike nodded.

"Val's here," Jacob said as Mike passed through the door. Mike stopped walking.

"What? Why?"

"She said she didn't want me to have all the fun. Tomorrow's the step-whore's prenuptial meeting." Jacob put his hand on Mike's back. "Cereal?"

Mike nodded. They went through the darkened house to the original kitchen. Even though Jacob had installed small kitchens in the apartments, everyone used the main kitchen. Jacob pulled cereal boxes from the cabinet then retrieved the Royal Crest milk from the refrigerator. Mike ate a bowl of Captain Crunch before saying anything else.

"Trevor came to the hospital," Mike said. "He made a huge-ass fuss. I guess he saw something on the news and put two and two together. He rushed into Katy's room saying this proved that Jill was an unfit mother. I guess he was all but foaming at the mouth. That crazy fucker tried to take Katy from the hospital. He said he was going to kill Jill for putting his daughter in harm's way."

Mike poured another bowl of cereal. His hand and the milk hung in the air.

"Katy took one look at her father and started screaming in horror. I..." Mike shook his head and poured milk on his cereal. "Did Val mention me? I mean, do you think I should call her?"

"You and Val have a complicated relationship. If you want to call her, I know she'd like to see you."

"Then why didn't she tell me she was coming?"

"A very good question to ask Valerie. If it helps, she didn't call, email or text me either." Jacob shrugged.

"I drove this bachelor party tonight. Stupid fuckers. They picked up hookers for blow jobs all around. While his wasted friends cheered him on, the groom screwed some girl in the alley behind Vinyl," Mike said. "All I could think was why does this jerk deserve to be married?"

"You and Val will work it out eventually," Jacob said.

"God, I hope so," Mike said.

"You were telling me about Trevor?"

"How did you know he would show?"

"I just figured it would happen. Who was there?"

Jacob had asked his midnight hockey team to keep an eye on Katy in case Trevor showed up. Mike set up a schedule so someone was there at all times.

"Colin."

Mike smirked.

"What?" Jacob asked.

"Colin beat the crap out of Trevor when Trevor was in high school."

Jacob raised his eyebrows, "What?"

"Colin's little sister is about four years older than Trevor and Jill. Trevor started really hassling Erin. I mean, Colin's what six-four, six-five? Erin's not five feet. She's tiny... smaller than Jill even. Colin was home on leave before he went into Special Forces. He went to pick up Erin at school and saw Trevor pawing at Erin. Colin isn't known for his restraint, especially when it comes to his sisters."

"So Trevor's there ranting and raving about how he's going to take Katy, minus the hospital bill of course. Colin took one look at Trevor and laughed. You know all those Hargreaves are fucking nuts. I guess, he tossed Trevor onto the sidewalk." Mike laughed. "Trevor was so freaked he scrambled away."

"He told Colin that he was going to find Jill," Mike said. "I had just dropped the assholes off at the bride-to-be's house when Colin called. I found Trevor trying to get into Jill's apartment."

"What did you do?"

"I called the cops. But then I couldn't find Jill and… I guess I went a little nuts." Pointing his spoon at Jacob, Mike said, "You should be glad I'm not Colin."

"So noted. I have a black belt in Brazilian jujitsu."

"Well, big whoop-de-fucking-do. They teach everybody in the military. Colin's like an expert in every martial art." Mike shrugged, "Sorry man."

"It's not a problem," Jacob said.

"Why'd you bring her here?" Mike asked.

"She didn't want to go home. She said it would be too hard to be around Katy's things. She was freaked enough about money so I didn't want to check us into the Adam's Mark. Plus Scooter and Sarah are here."

"She saw Scooter?" Mike asked.

"The dogs were really what she needed." Jacob nodded. "She played with them for a while then took a shower. She's exhausted. What a horrible day."

Jacob looked up from his cereal when Mike didn't respond. Mike's face was completely blank. Jacob turned to see what Mike was looking at.

Valerie.

Val's dark hair hung in waves over the spaghetti straps of her silk shorty. She beckoned Mike with her hand. Like a man in a trance, Mike stood from the table and walked to Valerie. Jacob was just closing the door when Valerie giggled then squealed.

Guess Valerie and Mike are 'on' again.

After cleaning up their cereal, Jacob went back upstairs to his apartment. Jill stirred when he came in but fell right back to sleep. Sarah had taken his side of the bed. Rather than fight the dog, he went to the table to work. He needed to clear his day so he could be available for Jill.

One last glance at Jill and he set to work.

CHAPTER TEN
ONE STEP FORWARD

Mike slipped Val's long hair over her shoulder so he could caress her back. He was sitting behind her in the big bathtub tucked against a glass block window to the Castle's backyard garden. Her elbows wrapped around his knees. The light from the setting moon danced against the wavy glass.

"Are you going to ask me for a divorce?" Mike asked.

Valerie turned to look at him. Her motion in the warm water caused her breast to float into Mike's hand. He smiled. Unable to risk looking at her face, his eyes focused on the beautiful nipple rising to his touch.

"No," Valerie said. "I was going to ask you if you'd like to make a go of being married."

Mike's head jerked up in surprise.

"I've tried to love without you. I'm incapable of loving anyone other than you, Michael Roper. And too terrified to let myself just love you."

Mike nodded.

"Say something," Valerie whispered.

"I'm afraid if I say anything you'll change your mind," Mike said.

She turned and leaned back against him.

"What about this Wes guy?" Mike asked.

"I had this dream... I... I saw Mom. She was knitting this beautiful golden blanket. When I got closer, I saw that every strand of the blanket was one of the people she loved—me, you, Jakey, Jill, Delphie, even Dad. The sun surrounded her in the hazy warm light. She smiled at me and... When I woke up... I guess it was yesterday... I realized that I only want to be with you. I think about you all the time, every day, almost every minute of every day. I..."

"I think about you all the time too," Mike said. "Is this guy gay?"

Valerie laughed. "You mean, am I back because my fiancé is gay? No. I'm back because I want to be with you."

"I heard that..."

"What?"

"That you have a movie coming out on Friday. You said told TMZ you were going home to your husband to generate press for the movie," Mike said. "Candy watches Entertainment Tonight for me when I'm working. I... It's the only way I get to hear about you every day."

"I don't know why I said that. It just came out," Valerie whispered. She shook her head, "I… I'm sorry. I've really hurt you. I… I don't have any excuse…"

"I'm sorry for everything. I never should have left you. I regret it every single day," Mike said. "I can't imagine what it was like for you. You lost your family then me… To lose your mom…"

"It was the baby that really did me in."

"What baby?"

"Before I tell you, I want you to be clear: I left Wes. I left the ring, the beach condo, and everything. I don't want to be with him. Tomorrow, Wes is going to say he loved me enough to encourage me to sort out my life. My publicist talked him into it as a way for him to save face. He can be vicious if he's humiliated."

"But that's not true?"

"No, that's not true. I left him a note saying I was leaving. I don't know why I said that at the airport. It's like my soul spoke the truth–I wanted to come home to my husband," Valerie said. "I was just one of Wes's women, one in a long line of trophy brides."

"Why would you want that?" Mike asked. His voice held hurt and confusion.

"It's safe. I don't have to risk…"

"Losing again," Mike finished her sentence. He settled her back against him and kissed her head.

"I want to be here with you. This is my choice and my choice alone. It's been a long time since I've made my own choice… It feels good… right."

"What about the meeting tomorrow?" Mike asked. "Jake said you have a…"

"The meeting got me off my ass yesterday. I've wanted to come a million times, a billion times. I've wanted to beg you like I did when we were kids. I just never had the courage."

"And now?"

"I want to see if we can make it work. I mean… If you …"

"There's nothing in this world I want more than to be your husband every single day," Mike said. "But Val, what baby? How…?"

He didn't know how to ask the question. He knew she wasn't pregnant with his child.

Valerie turned again to look at him. He looked away when her eyes filled with tears.

"We were pregnant–you and me. I didn't tell you because I wanted to be sure. Remember you asked me if my breasts were bigger or if I'd gained weight?"

Mike nodded. "Your body changed. I could see it in the photos."

"Couple days after Mom died, I lost the baby."

"Oh Val," Mike said. He held his arms out to her. She nestled her head on his shoulder. "Oh God..."

For the first time since that awful month in Hollywood, Mike cried. Lying together in the bath, he cried for himself and her. He cried for their baby. Then in jerky unplanned sentences, he told her about the days and nights he was dead to the world.

When the bath water cooled, they migrated to soft blankets in front of the fireplace. With his head on her lap, he told her about the one thing that got him through—the unbreakable love in his heart for Valerie, for her.

When the sun peaked over the horizon, Mike slipped Val's original wedding ring from her right hand. His eyes held the question which she answered with a nod. He slipped the ring where it belonged, on her left ring finger.

And they began again.

~~~~~~~~~

Jill woke when the early morning light hit her eyes. Stretching in Jacob's comfortable bed, she smiled. The sheets smelled like Jacob. She turned toward the warm body next to her to find Sarah. Sarah licked her face and Jill laughed. Hearing the odd sound that woke her, she sat up to see what was going on.

She wandered across the open loft toward the sound. Passing the sagging couch, she saw Jacob sitting at his round dining table. Wearing only his white boxer briefs, he spoke quietly into a Bluetooth device connected to a cell phone. He was also texting someone on his Blackberry. The sound that woke her was his fingers blazing across his Blackberry keys.

Unsure of what to do, she stopped walking. Her eyes darted from his muscular legs, flat belly and round muscular shoulders. Her hand moved instinctive to hold the rising heat in her belly while her eyes settled on the dark line of hair that ran like an arrow from his belly button. In that moment, Jill noticed something she hadn't allowed herself to see.

Jacob was a hunk!

Embarrassed, she turned to go back to bed when Jacob smiled and winked at her. She smiled at his greeting. She waved her hands to indicate she didn't want to interrupt. But Jacob walked to her. Without breaking the conversation, he kissed her lips and hugged her.

"Good morning," he murmured.

She sighed. She melted into his embrace

"Ok, you know where to find me if you need me," Jacob said. "Right. I'll be there."

Jill moved to step away from him but he held her in place.

"Thanks," Jacob said. He pulled the ear piece from his ear and tossed it on the table. Returning his attention to Jill, he said, "How are you feeling?

"Really good," she said. "You're a balm for any insomnia."

"I'm glad. Katy is doing very well. They'll release her to our care this morning. Rest, quiet, stuff like that. I was able to cancel most of my day, but I have to attend a meeting at eight-thirty. I shouldn't be too long, but I have to go," he said. "I thought Mike could take you to the hospital. That way, you can be there when Katy wakes up. I'll come and get you when I'm done. Will that work?"

"I know you have a company to run," she said.

"Help my father run," he said. He kissed her nose. "The company runs itself. I mostly run interference for my father. That's what the meeting this morning is about—one of my father's messes."

Jill smiled. "I've never been with anyone who had a job, so I don't really..."

Jacob laughed.

"How about some cereal?" Jacob asked.

"I understand it's the house specialty," she said. "Crunch Berries?"

"Mike finished them yesterday. I was going to get more at Walgreen's but I talked to the pharmacist for too long. I can go right now."

Jill shook her head. Wandering to the table, she saw Jacob's Blackberry vibrate. She flushed with guilt. She shouldn't distract this important man.

"You have a phone call," she said.

"Also I have an assistant. If anyone really needs me, they text," he said. Jacob pulled the boxes from the cabinet. "Would you like me to get some Crunch Berries or can you choose something from my vast selection?"

Jill's pierced brow relaxed. She laughed. "I love cereal."

"See! I knew you were a girl with taste."

"What are you working on?" Jill asked. "Oh, I probably shouldn't ask."

"No, it's okay. We have a group which estimates jobs. They estimate what we'll spend down to the gallon of gasoline, what company resources will be required and how much we'll make from each project. It's a hard job, really hard. We have some talented people who keep us in business."

Jacob sat down in his chair. He turned the laptop for Jill to see.

"They send me these projections and I look them over. I run the numbers, double check their work, look at the work schedule, stuff like that. If it seems reasonable, I send the entire thing to my father to see if he wants to do the project. Pretty boring. I get a bunch of these every Monday morning."

"Can I see?"

"If you sit on my lap," Jacob said.

Jill plopped down on his lap.

"Mmm." His hands stroked her legs.

"I'm pretty good at budgets and numbers, so this is interesting to me. I never knew how companies did this kind of thing."

Jacob kissed the back of her neck while Jill pretended to study the spreadsheet.

"You have beautiful skin," he said.

Jill turned her head to look at him. "Jacob."

"Hmm?"

"You have a busy morning," she said.

"Mmmm," he said.

She leaned away from him to catch his eyes.

"Yes, busy morning," Jacob said.

Jill stood from his lap. "I don't want to get in the way of your..."

Their eyes caught with a jolt.

Jacob lifted Jill off her feet. Jill wrapped her legs around his hips. Their lips caught and he carried her to bed. There was no hesitation, no sadness this morning. Jill was hot, relaxed and ready for him. He pulled off her t-shirt and panties at the same time she dragged down his boxer briefs. They joined with fast rising heat. Jacob kept a slow easy rhythm but Jill pulled for him. They rose in fast union. In one blinding flash, Jill stopped moving.

"Oh," Jill said.

Jacob pulled back to check if she was all right. He smiled. She began to release in waves of pleasure. Patient, but insistent, he continued the pace until she began to rise again. Caught in her rising heat, he gave in to his passion. Together, they slipped over the cliff. They held each other tight through the rise and fall of blissful sensation.

"Stay right there."

He kissed her lips, her nose, then rose to attend to the condom. When he returned, she held her arms out to him. He dropped into her arms.

"How are you?" he said.

"Really, really good. Thanks. You?"

"I feel amazing. You don't feel funny or sad or embarrassed..." He stopped talking when Jill laughed.

"Oddly no," she said. "If you do that again, I'm your slave."

He laughed. "I hate leaving you, but I need to take Sarah out for a bit before I get ready to go. Would you like to come with us?"

"I think I'd like some time to myself," Jill said. "Is that all right?"

"Of course. I washed your clothes from yesterday but they aren't quite dry. I have sweats that might fit you."

"Sweats are great."

Getting up from the bed, he began to dress in running gear. He gave Jill a pair of sweats. She rolled down the top to make them work. In the t-shirt and sweats, she had a charming sexiness that almost dragged them back to bed. She smiled at the look he gave her.

He scooped her up in a hug. His lips found her mouth. With effort, he broke from the kiss.

"This is so not how I wanted to do this," he whispered.

"Regrets?"

"Only that I have to keep moving," he said.

Jill stepped back from him to help him gain some control. He smiled his thanks.

"Delphie would love to see you. When you're ready for company, just open the door to the house. I'll be back soon."

He brushed her lips with his mouth. He picked up Sarah's leash and Sarah waited at the door to the stairs. Opening the door to the stairs, he turned to look at her one last time.

"I love you, Jill. I always have."

He closed the door before she could respond. Jill went to the windows to watch Jacob and Sarah but the iron fence perimeter of the Castle front yard was surrounded by paparazzi photographers. She saw Jacob whistle for Sarah then head around the back. Unsure of what to do, and not wanting her picture taken, she plopped down in the sagging armchair.

Yesterday, her mind was consumed by her Trevor-screwed-up life. Today, she was... She smiled. Happy.

In a burst of emotion, her fear and guilt returned.

What would Trevor think?

She heard Trevor screaming voice telling her that she was a worthless whore. Jill pressed her hands against her ears. But the voice in her head continued its rampage. She was almost in tears when she heard a knock on the door to the apartment. Without thinking, Jill walked across the apartment to open the door.

"Don't let that man steal your happiness, sweetie," Delphie said.

Jill dropped into her arms.

CHAPTER ELEVEN
THE BUSINESS OF LIFE

"Are we ready?" Jacob asked. "We can get past the paparazzi through the tunnels."

Standing by a locked door in the main Castle kitchen, he looked from Valerie to Mike. After years of preparation, he had no idea if they could get away from the photographers that stalked his sister. Today would be the first time they tried the tunnels.

Jill slipped her arm around him. He smiled at her.

Today was a first for a lot of things.

"Mike and I have cleaned the tunnels but they are old coal tunnels. There's only so much we could do," Jacob said. He pointed to the long overcoats with hoods on hooks by a locked bead board door. "As long as Delphie isn't going out, there's one for each of us."

"I'll stay here Jake," Delphie said. "I don't like those tunnels. Too many sad spirits down there."

"I'm so sorry." Valerie hugged Delphie. "This is all my fault. If I hadn't let the driver take me home the paparazzi would have never found us."

"Honey, I'd rather be stuck here because you and Mike are back together than be stuck here because it's snowing or the doors won't open or Jake blew something up or I'm sick or..."

"Thanks," Valerie said. "I've missed you."

"We've all missed you, Val," Delphie said. "It's nice to have you home."

"We need to go!?!"

Jacob's impatience and worry echoed through his voice. Delphie made her usual cutesy face at Jake's frustration.

"Is he always like this?" Valerie mock whispered to Delphie.

"YES. I'M ALWAYS LIKE THIS!" Jacob said in a terse voice

Mike looked from Delphie's smile to Jacob and burst out laughing. Everyone laughed. Even Jacob gave in to a smile. Jacob passed out the overcoats.

"If Val's staying, we'll have to get some more of these coats."

"Just one?" Jill asked.

"Well, Katy too." Jacob beamed at her.

"Sheez, now who's wasting time? Explain the locks," Mike commanded.

"There are two locks," Jacob pointed to a modern dead bolt and a refurbished antique lock. "You can unlock this deadbolt with a key from both sides of the door. This old lock can only be opened from the inside."

"Which is why I have to stay," Delphie said.

"We usually leave the old lock open when we go out through the tunnels, but with all this attention." Jacob pointed toward the growing crowd and paparazzi outside the Castle's metal fence. "I don't feel comfortable leaving it unlocked. There are two locks at the workshop. Those are regular key bolts. There's also a security system in the tunnels that's connected to both doors. You can turn off the system from inside the Castle or inside the workshop. It goes back on when either the door is closed at the other end or thirty minutes passes."

Jacob opened the door. Pointing to key padded lock box, he said, "This box has the key to the deadbolt in it. It will open to each of our birthdays. Our birthdays are the security code as well."

"Except mine," Jill said.

"Right, but you know Mike's right?"

Jill nodded.

"We'll add yours," Jacob said. Jill kissed his lips.

"I thought we were late?" Mike asked.

"Nervous?" Valerie asked.

"No, I'm torn between bashing his teeth in and puking."

Mike pulled Jacob away from Jill and Jacob laughed. He flicked a switch and a dim thread of lights appeared in the darkness.

"There's a switch at each end," Mike said. "There are also flashlights and head lamps if you need them. Just toss them in the baskets at each end. Since we're so late, we should probably skip the headlamps and hold hands."

"There's a series of stairs—eight stairs and three landings—here and twelve stairs on the other end."

Jacob pulled an overcoat over his Armani suit then flipped up the hood. He held his hand out for Jill. Hand in hand, they entered the ancient tunnel. Created in the 1800s, the tunnels were used to move heating coal from the train tracks throughout Denver.

"How far is it?" Jill whispered after they had been walking a while.

"It's half mile," Mike said. "You don't have to whisper."

"I just feel... like I should whisper," Jill said.

"Me too," Valerie whispered in response. "Maybe we feel all the sad souls Delphie was talking about."

"It's a dark place," Jacob said. "We're almost there. You can see the stairwell up ahead."

They climbed the stairwell. Jacob pointed to another lock box with a key pad. He punched in his birth date and opened the box. He used the key to open both locks. Holding the door for Jill, Valerie and Mike, Jacob set the key back on it's hook and re-engaged the security system.

He walked through the door to an open warehouse space. One end of the warehouse was a wood shop. Tidy stacks of wood, windows, woodworking tools and work tables filled half of the space. Opposite from where they stood, there were four aging cars—a Jeep Wrangler, an old Bronco, a 1960s Mustang and an ancient silver Mercedes lined up in front of the garage doors. The cars were clean and clearly well maintained. Jacob added his overcoat to the line of hooks near the door.

"This box has keys to the door as well as key to the cars. I thought Mike would take his Bronco." Jacob threw the keys to Mike. "Val? Are you okay with the Jeep?"

"Why are all of our old cars here?" Valerie asked. "That's Mom's old Mercedes and that..." She pointed to the Mustang. "That's mine!"

"I thought no one would expect the famous Valerie Lipson to drive an old clunker. Delphie drives Mom's Mercedes. I can't bring myself to..."

"Thanks Jake." Val's eyes brimmed with tears. "You really thought of everything."

Jacob smiled. He pressed the garage opener and they peered out at Detroit Street. The residential street was silent. No helicopters. No photographers. Just a few high school kids walking along the back of East High School.

"Yes!" Mike said. "I knew we could do this!"

Valerie laughed then pulled him to her. They kissed and whispered back and forth by the Jeep.

"We'll catch up with you at the hospital," Jacob said to Jill. "But don't wait for us. We're not exactly sure how long we'll be. If you can take Katy home, you should do that. I'll find you when we're done."

Jill hugged Jacob. She whispered in his ear, "Thanks. I..."

"God damn it. Can we go?" Mike asked. He opened the driver's side of his Bronco.

Jill blushed and stepped away. Jacob walked her to the passenger side, waited for Jill to hop in, and then closed car door.

"I remember this car," Jill said to Mike.

Mike laughed and revved the Bronco's engine.

"Ready?" Jacob asked Valerie turning on the Jeep.

"I feel a little... nervous, I guess," Valerie said.

"About?" Jacob asked.

Backing out, he waited until the garage doors to close before pulling out onto Detroit Street. He drove a half block, then turned right on Colfax.

"Just being here, I guess," Valerie said. "You must think I'm an idiot, but it's very scary for me to make these changes and take these steps."

Stopping at the light, Jacob looked at Valerie.

"I think you're very brave." Jacob smiled. "You're also not alone Val. I'm here. Delphie's a trip but she loves us."

"And Dad," Valerie said. "Will he be there this morning?"

"Just for a bit," Jacob said. "Are you ready for...?"

Valerie stared down Race Street when they passed. The paparazzi surrounded the Castle and news helicopters buzzed overhead. The Denver Police were containing a growing crowd of fans around their home. Valerie felt like she was watching a feeding frenzy. Everyone wanted a piece of her.

"Hey," Jacob said. He touched her thigh to get her attention. "Max is waiting for us in the parking garage at his office. He'll escort us to his office. Our step-sister and her Trevy-toy are already there working on the prenuptial agreement."

Valerie nodded, "I always call her the step-whore."

"You do? I thought Mike made that up," Jacob said.

"He got that from me," Valerie said.

"After the 'Valerie worked pornography' thing?"

"After she told 5280 you 'caught AIDS at the bath houses,'" Valerie said.

"Ah yes, how could I forget my slutty gay life?"

"You must tell Jill about being gay, little brother. Not telling her is really cruel."

Valerie looked at Jake and they cracked up laughing. They were laughing so hard that Jacob almost missed his turn onto Lincoln Street. Jacob turned into the parking garage and drove deep into the bowels of the Cash Register building. They were met by their friend, and lawyer, Max Hargreaves.

~~~~~~~~~

"We have to do something before we go to the hospital," Mike said.

"Mike, I want to get my baby! I've been trying to get to Katy all morning!"

"Do you want to get to Katy or keep her safe?"

"What do you mean safe? Katy's not safe?"

Stopping at a traffic light at Eighteenth Street, he turned to Jill.

"Trevor came to the hospital last night."

"What? What do you mean?"

Dread settled over Jill like a bad thunderstorm.

"He came some time around midnight. He was there for a while before he found Katy. He told everyone at the hospital he was going to take Katy from her hospital bed. He tried to get the doctor to say this proved you were a bad mother."

Jill bit her lip to keep from crying. Mike shook his head at her then continued driving toward downtown Denver.

"Jill, you cannot possibly believe him."

Jill's eyes filled with tears.

"I... I'm not a very good mother. I try. I really try. I love her so much. But she gets sick or hurt... That doctor? Dr. Drayson? He gave me an Epi-Pen for myself and one for Katy when she gains some weight. I... I didn't even know they existed. And they're like a hundred dollars... a piece! And..."

Mike face flushed.

"That's just bullshit, Jill. My God!"

Mike hit his hand against the steering wheel. Jill began crying into her hands.

"Ah Jilly," Mike said. "I'm sorry."

"I can barely afford to feed her... Trevor should have full custody. At least he can take care of her..."

"Stop it," Mike said. "Just stop it. Katy freaked out when Trevor came into her room. They had to sedate her. The hospital social worker called Social Services. They came out to investigate."

"They're going to take her? My Katy? She's in custody of Social Services?"

"No. Jill, stop it. You're freaking out for no reason," Mike said. "You need to hear what happened. Stop the hysterics and listen."

Jill bit her lip and nodded. She took a deep breath to calm her horror then nodded. "Okay. I'm okay. What happened with Social Services?"

"They filed a report against Trevor. The hospital social worker said she'd never seen a person so angry and out of control around his hospitalized kid. She felt he was an imminent threat to Katy... and to you. He said he was going to kill you."

Jill nodded.

"He went to your apartment to find you. I called the cops and he was cited but let go. Jill." Mike put his hand on her shoulder. "Look at me."

Jill looked up at her brother.

"I left a message for Diane Radman last night. Remember your lawyer? She's already been to the hospital. She's going to meet us at the courthouse. Diane was able to get a couple people to testify this morning. She thinks you'll finally get that restraining order."

"You don't think it's better for Katy to be with Trevor? At least he's rich now."

"No." Mike laughed. "I don't think that. No one thinks that. Look Diane's right there waiting for you. I'll drop you and park."

Mike pulled up the curb where a fit woman with curly red hair stood. Wiping her eyes, Jill got out of the Bronco. Diane gave Jill a hug, then began preparing her for court.

"We have to be in the courtroom with all the documents, and witnesses at 7:30 a.m. to get on the 8:00 a.m. docket," Diane said. "If we miss the 8:00 a.m., we'll try to get on the 3:00 p.m. docket."

Standing in line for security, Jill took a breath to steel herself for another restraining order hearing. Every day—from the moment Trevor asked for a divorce to today—had been like a terrifying roller coaster. She couldn't remember a more difficult and horrifying seven months.

And...

Remembering this morning's warm, loving conversation with Delphie, Jill smiled.

"I think we'll get it this time," Diane said. "Just tell the truth about what he's really like. Enough people have seen him now that he's going to have a tough time getting out of it."

Jill nodded and followed Diane into the courtroom. Sitting in the crowded court, her mind lingered on the 'best not to waste time' morning shower with Jacob just a half hour ago. By the time Mike sat next to her, she felt herself again.

Life was terrifying and getting so much better.

~~~~~~~~~

"Dad," Valerie said as quiet exhalation.

"Hi baby," Her father replied.

They stood in front of each other for the first time in almost ten years. Similar in coloring and feature, their eyes scanned each other's faces in hesitant longing and mistrust.

"I..." They both started.

Her father smiled at Valerie then nodded. He touched her arm.

"It's nice to see you, Val." Turning to Jacob, their father said, "I've done my part. I'll be with your mother."

"See you later, Dad," Jacob said.

Jacob and Valerie watched their father walked toward the suite's exit. At the door, he turned to raise his hand to them then walked out.

"What does he mean be with Mom?"

"He reads Mom the paper every day. Remember he used to do that when we were kids. After the job sites are up and running, he spends the morning at the cemetery."

"Guilty conscience," Valerie sneered.

"Or something," Jacob said. "You know Val, not everything is as it seems."

"Thank you, Buddha." Valerie followed him into a conference room.

"What? What are YOU doing here?" their step-sister asked in horror.

Hopping to her feet, she pulled at the seated Trevor. Trevor stood slowly as Jacob and Valerie sat down across from the couple. They sat in silence for a moment.

"My Daddy will be so mad when he finds out you are here to ruin my life AGAIN," the vicious blonde screeched at them. "And the week of my wedding."

"Actually, your Daddy is still in prison," Valerie said in an even tone.

Their step-sister launched herself across the table at Valerie. Jacob blocked Valerie from the attack while Trevor held their step-sister back.

"Now kitten, you can't to get too upset," Trevor said. "Remember what the doctor said. Getting upset is bad for the baby."

As the couple made dreamy eyes at each other, Jacob and Valerie leaned back in their chairs. Jacob looked at Max, who nodded. Jacob raised an eyebrow.

"I hate to break up the love here. But we have a lot of ground to cover," Max Hargreaves said. "Will you please return to your seats?"

"I will do what I like around my... employees," the step-sister said with a dismissive flip of her hand.

"Actually, I am employed by Jacob and Valerie," Max said. "Please sit down."

The couple plopped down holding hands. When their step-sister noticed Jacob again, she squinted her eyes. Her lip curled with disgust.

"We'll see how you act when I run the company," she spit at him.

"Ah, that's exactly why we wanted to be here today," Valerie said.

Max gave Valerie a stern look. She shrugged her apology.

"Before we start," Max said, "I will remind you that you signed a confidentiality agreement. You are restricted from mentioning any detail from this meeting, including who is present at this meeting. Is that clear?"

The step-sister and Trevor nodded their heads. Max laid a document in front of the couple.

"You'll see from these documents that Lipson Construction is owned in it's entirety by Jacob and Valerie Marlowe-Lipson," Max said. "You'll note the date of purchase."

Max pointed to a date on the paper.

"Four and a half years ago, Jacob and Valerie Marlowe-Lipson purchased the remaining shares of Lipson construction from their father for ten million dollars."

"But..." Their step-sister's oft pouting lip began to vibrate.

"Please let me continue," Max said. "At that time a seven year plan was set into motion converting Lipson Construction from private owner to an employee owned company. The initial transfer of ownership began at the beginning of this year and should finish within the next three years."

After a moment of stunned silence, their step-sister flipped her hair.

"I'll just inherit from Daddy," she said.

Valerie wanted to slap her smug little face. This wicked woman had nearly destroyed Valerie's life by selling Valerie's personal information, hacked from her father's accounts, to the press. From photos to lies, the press paid thousands of dollars for Valerie's tidbits. Every time Valerie moved or changed her phone number, this little witch sold Valerie's private life to the highest bidder. When Jake put a stop to her antics, she came after him. Of course, Jake could care less.

Valerie was about to scream at the step-whore when Jacob reached for her hand. They had agreed to let the lawyers discuss the details then follow up with options. Valerie held Jacob's hand with both of her hands. She could do this.

"At the time of the Lipson Construction purchase, six trusts were set up." Max retrieved the corporation sale documents and presented another document. "Each of your mother's children received a one million dollar trust payable on their twenty-fifth birthday. In the event that Mr. Lipson does not remain married to your mother, she will receive a two million dollar trust. You will also notice that only Mr. Lipson's children will inherit wealth or possessions from Mr. Lipson. You'll notice your mother's signature here... and here."

"But... but... that's just them," the step-sister said pointing to Valerie and Jacob. "What about my little sisters?"

"That's an interesting point of discussion for another time..."

CHAPTER TWELVE
CHICKENS COME HOME?

Walking from the bright day into the dark hospital lobby, Jill was unsure of where to go. Jacob said Katy had been moved to a private room. Stepping toward the reception area, Jill opened her mouth to ask for Katy when she heard:

"MOMMY!"

Trailing an attending nurse, Katy ran down a hallway toward Jill. In a rush of emotion, Jill lifted her precious daughter into her arms. For one moment, for a lifetime, sensation and sound slipped away in a cloud of joy.

The world stopped as a mother held her small child.

~~~~~~~~~

"What does this mean in reference to our..." Trevor corrected himself. "I mean honey bunny's financial support? It was her understanding that her father was going to support her."

Valerie took a breath to remind the little malicious 'honey bunny' that her father was in prison, but Jacob placed the toe of his boot over her shoe. Valerie nodded. I can do this.

"The trust attorneys will discuss the nature of the trust. I am the Marlowe-Lipson's contract attorney," Max Hargreaves said. "The final contractual issue is that the trusts are payable at the age of twenty-five. I believe you are..."

"Twenty-one," the step-sister said with a flip of her hair.

"According to this contract, you are not able draw from your trust for four more years. You will note here that your mother is the one who specified the age. I believe she thought the trust would give you financial support after you graduated from college." Max pointed to a handwritten addition made by the step-sister's mother. "I don't think anyone could have foreseen..."

Max looked from the step-sister to Trevor then stopped talking.

"I'll just talk to Mommy. She'll change this in an instant," the tiny blonde said.

"These contracts cannot be modified without voiding the entire agreement. I'm fairly certain the parties involved, including your mother, will not renegotiate."

"We'll see about that," their step-sister smirked at Max.

There was a tap at the door and Jill's lawyer, Diane Radman, stuck her head in the conference room.

"Excuse me for a minute," Max said.

Max and Diane whispered back and forth near the door. Max nodded, then shook her hand and she left the room.

"Why is she here?" Trevor asked.

"Who is that, Trevy?" the step-sister asked.

"That's Jill's attorney," Trevor said.

"This is an outrage. What bullshit is that trailer trash pulling now?" The step-sister jumped to her feet. "That bitch can't take care of her own child! My God, her negligence put our child in the hospital. And now she wants to horn in on MY business."

Valerie put the pointed toe of her Jimmy Choo's into Jacob's calf to keep him from exploding. He grimaced his thanks to her.

"Now smoochums," Trevor said. He stood to wrap his arms around the tiny woman. "You have to be patient. We'll have custody soon enough."

Max set a piece of paper on the table.

"This is an ex-parte restraining order. Signed by the judge a half hour ago after the testimony of a Homeland Security Agent, a hospital social worker, as well as a neighbor from your old apartment building. This order says that Trevor may not cause physical pain or injury or the threat of pain or injury to Jillian or Katherine Roper. Further, Trevor is not allowed any contact with Jillian or Katherine Roper. You may wish to hire an attorney to explain the ramifications of this agreement. There will be a permanent order hearing in fourteen days."

"What?" Trevor's face flushed bright red with fury.

Unable to rip their eyes away, Valerie and Jacob watched Trevor flash into full blown rage. As his voice raised and his entire body went red, Max touched their shoulders. The contract portion of the meeting was over. They stood to follow Max out of the room. Trevor would need to calm down before he learned about honey bunny's trust.

~~~~~~~~~

"I waited for you for about forty hours, Mommy," Katy said.

Katy walked between Jill and Mike toward her room. The nurse said Katy was well enough to go home, but they needed the doctor to release her.

"Forty hours?"

"Maybe fifty. A long time and I'm really little. That's most of my life! I woke up and missed you. Then that nice lady? The one I was walking with? She said I was really, really, really sick but I don't remember being even a little sick. Was I really sick, Uncle Mike?"

Mike held Katy's other hand as they walked toward her hospital room.

"You were very sick, baby," Mike said. "We were really scared for you."

"Mommy? Do you like that guy who took us to the zoo? Do you think he would take us to the zoo again?"

"I don't know, Katy-baby. Probably."

"I really liked him. I thought he was nice and cute too. Plus he likes ketchup on his French Fries like I do and he got me a green balloon. I love green AND I love balloons. A green balloon is the best balloon. Mommy, what happened to my balloon?"

"I don't know, sweetie," Jill said.

She hoped Katy wouldn't be upset by the loss of her balloon. Sometimes, Katy could intensely focus on a single object. She would cry uncontrollably until she had that specific thing. But today, Katy shrugged.

"I bet that guy... Mommy, what was his name?"

"Jacob," Jill said.

"I bet Jacob can find me another balloon. Don't you think Jacob can find me one, Uncle Mike?"

"I'm sure he can, Katy," Mike said.

"He's going to be my Daddy."

Shocked, Jill's head jerked to look at her daughter.

"And THEN he's going to make me a little sister!"

Jill burst out laughing.

~~~~~~~~~

"A million dollars? I get a million dollars?"

The step-sister squealed with delight. She clutched Trevor and they kissed. Valerie snatched Jacob's hand in an effort to remain silent.

"Yes and no," the trust attorney said. "You get the annuity on one million dollars."

"What does that mean?" Trevor asked. After his rampage, Trevor was eerily reserved and calm.

"You receive the interest generated from the trust's investments. The trust is currently making around four percent."

"What does that mean in dollars?" the step-sister said.

"You will receive forty thousand dollars," the attorney said.

"A month?" Trevor asked.

"A year."

"WHAT?" The step sister launched to her feet. "I can't live on forty thousand dollar a year!"

Valerie had to take a few deep cleansing breaths to keep from beating the crap out of the step-sister. The paltry forty thousand came from her parent's blood, sweat and tears. Jacob put his arm around her to reassure her. Valerie looked at him and nodded.

"Why don't I get the million dollars?"

"The principle of the trust cannot be touched. In the event of your death, the trust will become property of the primary owners."

"Who is that?" Trevor asked.

"Jacob and Valerie Marlowe-Lipson."

"What do butt-boy and sluttina have to do with MY money?" the step-sister screeched.

"Jacob and Valerie Marlowe-Lipson are the only people who can negotiate any of the details of the trust."

"What does that mean?" Trevor asked.

"The trust is set to begin annuity when your fiancé is twenty-five. It is our understanding you wish to begin payments now. Jacob and Valerie are the only ones who can change that date."

"Oh," the step-sister said. She plopped back into her chair. "Can they change the amount?"

"No," the attorney said. "The only thing that will change your annuity is a significant change in the stock market."

"Oh," the step sister said. "What about my wedding?"

"Jacob Marlowe-Lipson promised his father at the time of sale of Lipson Construction that he would pay for your mother's children's weddings," Max Hargreaves said. "He has already paid for your engagement party and will make the final payments on your wedding after Sunday."

The step-sister was slow to process the information. Nodding, she looked from Valerie to Jacob as if to assess what to do next. When Valerie looked at Trevor, she felt a chill run up her spine. He was working something else out.

The step-sister's face shifted to a big, charming smile.

"Ah come on. Val? Jake? You have lots of money. This little trust is just sitting there. Everyone knows how generous the Lipson's are. Why not show your sister a little generosity and give me my money now?"

~~~~~~~~~

"Lots of water. Rest," Jill said to the doctor.

She held Katy in her arms while Mike carried Katy's car seat and her medications. After her initial burst of conversation and activity, Katy was worn out. Katy pressed her face against Jill's neck.

"Meds every four hours," the doctor said.

"Yes," Jill said. "I... Thanks."

"She's a great little girl," the doctor said. "We're going to miss having her around. Were you able to schedule the follow ups?"

"I... I have the list of people. I'll call when Katy's settled."

"Perfect," the doctor said. "Bye Katy."

Katy lifted her head from Jill's shoulder and waved to the doctor. They walked out of the hospital toward Mike's Bronco.

"Mommy?"

"Yes, Katy-baby," Jill said.

"I think I'm sick," Katy said.

"I know, Katy-baby," Jill said. "We'll get you home and you'll feel better."

"Oh... home... how nice," Katy murmured.

Katy was sound asleep when Jill settled her into her car seat. Katy slept through the drive to the apartment, the trip upstairs and her return to her own bed. Jill left her door open so she could hear Katy if she needed anything.

"I'll leave the car," Mike said. "That way if you need to go to the doctor or get something, you can just get it."

"Are you sure?" Jill asked. "I don't want to take your wheels."

"I'm sure," Mike said. "Trevor took your car?"

Jill nodded.

"You can keep this one," Mike said. "If I need it, I'll come get it. The Castle's only a couple blocks from here. You're all right here?"

Jill nodded.

"Val and I want to have the family over for dinner tonight... you know, to talk about being married and all. Do you think that will be too much?"

"No, I think it will be nice to get together around something happy. Is Meg planning a pot luck?"

"Of course."

"Great, I'll bring some pot."

Jill made their usual joke and Mike laughed.

"Love you, Jilly." Mike hugged his sister.

"Love you, Mikey."

Jill walked Mike to the door. Leaning against the door, she almost collapsed to the floor in sheer relief. She and her baby girl were finally safe and sound at home.

~~~~~~~~~

Valerie and Jacob stood at the elevator outside the attorney's office. Exhausted from the emotional meeting, they leaned against each other in silent support. Expecting Max, they turned to look when the office door opened.

"May I speak to you for a moment?" Trevor asked. "No, just Jacob."

Valerie watched Jacob walk to the door of the attorney's office. She couldn't see Trevor's face to read his lips or hear what he said, but when Jacob stumbled back from Trevor, she caught Trevor's eyes. Pure evil shone clear and cold in that man's eyes. Trevor nodded in satisfaction. Jacob shook his head as if he didn't understand what Trevor said. Trevor put his hand on Jacob's shoulder.

"Jacob Marlowe, the elevator is here," Valerie bellowed in her bossy older sister voice.

Jacob jerked at the sound. When he turned, she saw that he was blanch white.

"Get. Your. Ass. On. This. Elevator. NOW," Valerie said.

Jacob walked toward her as if he was in a trance. Trevor looked like the cat who ate the canary.

"NOW," Valerie commanded.

Jacob jerked out of his trance and trotted to the elevator. When the doors closed, he all but collapsed to the floor. Valerie bent to him.

"What is it?"

"He said... he could smell Jill on me... But I showered, Val. How? He said... He's going to tell Jill I set this whole thing up so I could fuck her... I... I orchestrated everything... even Scooter... and the pregnancy... and the tattoo removal and... Val, even Scooter. And... and... she'll believe him because... they're soul mates... I... Jill loves him...I..."

Valerie's lip curled. Half carrying, half dragging her little brother to the car, she stuck him in the passenger's seat. She wrenched the keys from his hand and started the Jeep. Jacob mumbled something. The tips of his fingers came together then opened over and over again. Valerie leaned her head to his mouth.

"She's all I ever wanted and, poof, she's gone. She's all I ever wanted and, poof, she's gone. She's all I ever wanted and, poof, she's gone."

"STOP IT!" Valerie commanded.

Jacob jerked present.

"I'm here now. No one is going to shit on my little brother and get away with it. We will go, right now, and talk to Jill."

Jacob moved his head up and down as if he understood but he was too horrified to understand what she was saying. Valerie drove the Jeep through the parking garage. Stopped at the sidewalk, she saw what she expected–paparazzi. Max told them the step-sister called Star Magazine to calm Trevor's restraining order rage.

"There she is! Val! Over here! Val!"

The photographers jogged toward the Jeep. Valerie smiled her movie star smile and waved as she drove off.   Turning left on Colfax Avenue, Valerie laughed.

"Guess that's the end of the step-sister's trust! Break the confidentiality agreement? Lose the trust! I KNEW it!"

Valerie expected Jacob to laugh with her but he was off in his own world. Continuing up Colfax Avenue past the Colorado State Capitol building, she shook her head.

Ain't love grand?

CHAPTER THIRTEEN
ONE STEP BACK...

Jill was sitting on her balcony when she saw Jacob and Valerie park in front of her building. At the sight of the Jeep, her heart started a little happy dance. Stopping by the mirror, she brushed her hair and put on some lip gloss. She paced back and forth with nervous excitement until there was a knock at the door.

Opening the door, she saw Valerie and Jacob bickering back and forth.

"Hi!" Jill said.

When Jacob turned he looked lost and sad. He opened his mouth, then closed it. She hugged him and brushed her lips with his but he was completely unresponsive. He mumbled something.

"What?" Jill asked.

"I'm sorry. I'm so sorry."

"What's going on?" Jill asked. She shook her head at him then remembered Valerie. "Please come in."

"Wow, this is really nice," Valerie said. She stepped into the apartment and looked around. The furnishings were inexpensive but well cared for. The walls of the apartment were painted in bright colors. And the tattered ancient carpet was covered with bright throw rugs. "Did you do all of this?"

Jill blushed and shifted a piece of hair behind her ear.

"I like to make things homey," Jill said. "Can I get you some coffee? Water?"

Valerie grabbed Jacob's arm and pulled him into the apartment.

"Water would be great," Valerie said.

Jacob opened his mouth again then shook his head. Leaving Jacob near the door, Valerie followed Jill into the efficient galley kitchen. Jill opened an ancient refrigerator and pulled out a Brita water filter. She put a few ice cubes in three glasses and poured the water.

"What's wrong with him?" Jill whispered.

"He's had a terrible run in with your ex," Valerie said.

"Trevor?" Jill made a dark face. "What happened?"

"I was hoping he would tell you but he's too freaked out."

"Does this happen?" Jill asked.

"Sometimes. He needs to go fix something. In fact," Valerie went out into the other room, "Jake, go fix something. Here's the key to the Jeep. Come back here in two hours. Shower first."

Jacob looked at his sister and nodded. He looked at Jill and almost burst into tears.

"See you in a couple hours," Jill said. She smiled and waved.

Jacob nodded and walked out of the apartment.

"Where is he going?" Jill asked.

"To one of his projects. He'll break down a wall or fix a floor or hammer on something for a while. You'll see. He'll be back to himself."

"But Lipson Construction does underground utility and roads."

Valerie laughed, "You really don't know anything do you."

"We haven't had a lot of time to get to know each other."

"Is there a place we can talk?"

"Sure," Jill said.

Valerie followed Jill out onto a small balcony with blooming flower boxes and even a tomato plant. Due to near constant paparazzi attention, Valerie hadn't sat on a balcony in years. She delighted at the shady outdoor spot.

"What do you want to know first?" Valerie asked.

~~~~~~~~~

Jacob pulled up to a hundred and fifty year old boarded up house. The Denver Square was a two story red brick box with a wide open porch. The most prominent feature on the house was a couple of bright yellow "CONDEMNED" posters tacked to the front boards. He parked the Jeep in the shade of a hundred foot maple.

Jacob went to the back of the Jeep where he kept a pair of work jeans and a t-shirt. He laid his suit jacket and tie inside the Jeep. In quick practiced motions, Jacob changed from his suit to his work clothing. He left the suit in a tidy wrinkle free pile. Running a construction company, and working construction on the side, Jacob sometimes changed on the street a couple times a day.

He walked up wide flagstone sidewalk, past the barren front yard and dry rot porch to unlock the front door. For all of the house's exterior woe, the interior was spotless. Gleaming hardwood shone from every surface. The ceiling of the entry depicted cherubs reaching down from heaven. Jacob wandered on a paper path through the living room past a stone fireplace to the open kitchen.

He wanted to make sure the kitchen was installed over the weekend. Everything was in except for the countertop. He read the note saying that the granite shipment was delayed and would be installed on Wednesday. He stuffed the note in his pocket as a reminder to call the installers when he got back to the car. The thought of the car brought back him back to Jill.

"Ah crap."

Jacob's voice echoed through the empty house. He let out his first real breath since Trevor said he could smell Jill on Jacob.

"What does that mean anyway?" Jacob asked the empty house.

Valerie was right. He needed to focus on what he was good at—restoring neglected beauties.

"Like you," Jacob said to the house.

The new owners were doing a walk through in a week. They hoped to move in by the end of the month so they would be settled by the time their twins arrived. Jacob smiled. Yes, restoring old houses was something he did very well.

Noting the delicate trail of gold inlay on the stair railing, he walked up to the second floor. He hated to do it, but the owners wanted to replace the cut glass windows on the second floor. They compromised when Jacob told them he could replace the glass but keep the original window frames and sills. He planned to take the windows out on Sunday. But yesterday he had a non-date with Jill.

Jill.

Jacob felt his entire body constrict. Can't think about her yet.

After popping out a South facing window pane, he went to the three double hung windows at the front of the house. The window's wood trim and sill had been stripped, varnished and wrapped in paper so he could remove the windows. Popping off the inch molding that held the window in place, he heard a noise behind him.

"I'm surprised you're here," Mike said.

"The gold inlay looks amazing. Did you finish the entry?"

Mike nodded.

"It's gorgeous. I bet their twins will look just like the cherubs."

Mike shrugged. "Want some help?"

"Yeah."

~~~~~~~~~

"So that's what he means when he says 'my father's company.'" Jill nodded. "I thought he was just… faking or something."

"No, Jake loves to restore old things. Fix messes, that's what Mom used to say. Give him a mess to fix and he's happy."

"No wonder he's interested in me," Jill said.

Valerie laughed.

"What happened with Trevor?" Jill asked.

"Your ex is going to tell you Jake put him up to the whole thing so Jake could… um… sleep with you."

Jill curled her lip with disgust. "Trevor is such a weirdo. Everything is someone else's fault. Trevor never makes a choice and is never, ever wrong."

"I know plenty of men like that," Valerie said. "But Jill, you have to know a few things so you can be prepared."

Jill nodded.

"First, Jake had no idea you were our step-sister's fiancé's anything. In his boy mind, you lived on a whole other planet than them. He knew our step-sister was serious about someone through our father. Jake promised Dad he would pay for the girls' weddings. So Dad let him know she thought she might get married soon."

"Huh," Jill said. "Jake paid for the engagement party."

"Jake paid for the engagement party."

"I wondered because no one expected to get paid… for their work, you know? Because of me. But everyone got checks. That was Jake."

"That was Jake. He wasn't going to go to the engagement party but Delphie talked him into going. He brought some friends along to keep him company. He figured he would hang out with his friends, write a check and go home."

"Dr. Drayson said he was at the party. He helped us at the hospital."

"John's married to Alex Hargreaves. Max is Alex's identical twin. Max is our lawyer."

"Twins? Really?" Jill said. "Wait. I know them. They come into Pete's. I call them 'my lucky twins.' Brown hair, big eyes, tall but very thin?"

"That's them. They're kind of hard to miss."

"Are you friends with them? They're like the Catholic elite here in Denver. Their brother Colin testified this morning at the restraining order hearing and their Dad helped find me. Anyway, I like them but I'm a little intimidated by them." Jill blushed and looked down, "But then…"

"What?"

"I was terrified to meet you! I watch *Our Loves, Our Lives* whenever I can. Candy, my sister, tapes it for me. She watches it for Mike. We'd do anything for Mike. Then we got hooked. Candy's a pastry chef because of Mike. OH!"

Jill put her hand over her open mouth. Valerie smiled.

"Putting things together?"

Jill nodded, "You paid for Candy's school after Mike died."

"I promised Mike I would always take care of his family. I tried to get you to go to college, but Meg said Trevor took your first semester tuition."

Jill nodded.

"We have to talk about Jake," Valerie said.

"Ok," Jill said.

"Jake didn't know you were divorced until he came to the apartment right after the New Year. The owner was going to tear the building down and sell the lot. Jake came by to see if he wanted to refurbish the building."

"This place?" Jill looked surprised. "There's nothing here a wrecking ball wouldn't fix."

"Exactly. But Jake gets called because he pays top dollar and saves owners a lot of hassle. Anyway, he had finished touring the building when you came home from the market. You were bawling in your car. The elderly lady lives on the first floor saw Jake gawking at you."

"Mrs. Robinson," Jill said. "She's a menace but has a big heart."

"She told Jake your husband divorced you the day before leaving you penniless with a baby. That's how he found out. But he didn't know that your husband was marrying our step-sister."

"Ok, why do you keep saying that?"

"Because Trevor is going to say Jake knew about it all along."

"Oh, I see. He was just waiting to pounce at the engagement party. For a pouncer, he was very... sweet."

"Jake's very sweet. Anyway, Jake carried your groceries up to your apartment that day. You don't remember?"

"Those days are a complete blur. I remember some guy but when I went to thank him he was gone." Jill's face flushed with the memory of those painful days. "Trevor came that day for his stuff... He took the car. Oh. You're saying Trevor saw Jacob."

"He must have," Valerie said.

"Oh," Jill said.

"Jake bought the building so you wouldn't have to move. He thought losing your home would send you over the edge."

"Jacob's the new owner? Really?" Jill chuckled. "He fixed my dishwasher. We've lived here five years and the dishwasher has never worked. Huh. Mrs. Robinson told everyone I was the reason we didn't have to move but I thought she was just a crazy old nuisance."

"She was right," Valerie said.

"But Valerie, what happened this morning?"

~~~~~~~~~

"He says to me that he'll tell Jill I set everything up so I could fuck her and dump her. Another bitch on my list. Because that's how guys like me operate."

Mike tugged his side of the window. The window slid across the paper wrapped sill. They set the window onto the floor. Jacob went to work on the next window.

"I thought you were gay."

"Oh, that too. I gave her AIDS."

"I told you he was awful," Mike said. "Did he go off when he got the restraining order?"

"I've never seen anyone get like that. Ever. We left the room." Jacob set his tool down to wipe the dust from the wood. "How did the hearing go?"

"Did you know Colin works for Homeland Security now?"

"I thought he still worked at the bakery," Jacob said.

"Colin gets up there and describes in detail exactly what Trevor said and did. The judge signed the order right there." Mike laughed. "Trevor's going to have a hard time going against a Homeland fucking Security Senior Agent."

"There's some good news. I can't imagine having to deal with Trevor... ever... let alone every day."

Jacob shook his head and returned to popping the trim from around the window.

"So what got to you?" Mike asked.

"Valerie called?"

"No," Mike said. "I came to put another coat of varnish in the railing and found you here. I thought you'd be with Jill and Katy. You guys seemed pretty hot this morning."

"I have to take these windows out," Jacob said.

He yanked off the last piece of trim. Mike stepped forward to help pull the window from the sill. Mike set his end down and pointed to a rotten area of the frame.

"I have a piece that will match," Jacob said.

"What did Trevy say that got to you?" Mike asked again.

"He told me he was going to tell Jill that I was responsible for all of this. Even Scooter! I took Scooter from them to make him look bad. She would believe him because she belongs to him. She will always love him and only him. He said... He said their souls are joined. Trevor owns her soul. But it wasn't what he said as much as... "

"The confidence he had when he said it? Yeah, that's how those guys were in Afghanistan. I mean, logically I knew they were lying. Val would never forget me or give up. I knew someone someday would come for me. But they were so sure, so confident in what they were saying... I... I believed them."

"Right."

They pulled the last window in silence.

"What are you going to do?" Mike asked when they set the last window down.

"Kill myself?"

Mike laughed. "Come on, lover boy. I brought a work truck. Let's load up these windows. You're taking them to the workshop?"

"To the window shop. They need to measure the frames to make the double panes," Jacob said.

"Ok, let's call the girls and tell them we'll bring lunch," Mike said.

Jacob nodded. "Valerie said to take a shower."

"Oh well, you wouldn't want to wash off the stench of Jill would you?"

Jacob laughed.

~~~~~~~~~

"But why would Trevor say all of that?" Jill asked. "I... We're divorced. He hasn't wanted to have anything to do with me or Katy since the day he left."

"He found out his rich wife is only worth about forty grand a year," Valerie said. "Now she's lost her trust because she violated the confidentiality agreement. But Jacob won't follow through on that."

"Why? Because she's pregnant?"

"How did you know?" Valerie said. "I was afraid to tell you."

"Oh, I know the man." Jill waved her hand in the air as if having a baby was like swatting a fly. "We were in high school and he wanted a baby. I'm the only reason we don't have fifty. Children are things, possessions, toys, not living growing beings. Speaking of which, I need to give Katy her medicine. I'll be right back."

Valerie nodded her head.

"I mean, you can come and meet Katy. I'm sure she wants to meet you. She's just still very sick."

Following Jill into the apartment, Valerie marveled at the way Jill had made everything feel like home. She watched Jill wake Katy then negotiate the medicine. Half asleep, Katy took the meds then let Jill kiss her before falling back to sleep.

"I think she's happy to be home," Jill whispered.

"There's no place like it," Valerie said.

Jill smiled. They refilled their water glasses and returned to the balcony.

"I'll tell you this, Valerie. I've never told a soul. I knew he was with someone else. I refused to believe it but I knew it. And when he gave me the divorce papers? We were in bed, of course."

"You mean he asked you for a divorce after you...?"

"Yeah," Jill said. "When he gave me the papers, the first feeling I felt was relief. Sheer relief. Stupidly, I signed them right there. My lawyer will never let me forget that stupid act. But Trevor? He was stunned. I took a shower. When I got out, he was gone. I'll tell you. I cleaned this place of every single item he owned—everything. I would have chucked it but I knew he's throw a fit. He filed the papers then came here! He expected to spend the night here!"

Jill laughed.

"What happened?"

"The manager threw him out. I... You know, Delphie said this morning that I know the truth when I hear it. And she's right. I might not always know a lie, but I always know the truth. I know you're telling me the truth, Val. Can I call you, Val?"

Valerie nodded.

"Trevor said, that day after New Year's and after he fucked me, he said, 'You and Katy are better off without me' and I knew it was true."

Valerie smiled. No wonder her mother loved Jill.

"When do you think Jacob's coming back?"

CHAPTER FOURTEEN
DREAD IS A FIVE LETTER WORD

"I know can you believe that crap? It's that Valerie Lipson. I mean, who cares?" Sandy said as Jill opened the door to the apartment. "Hi honey. How's our Katy?"

"Asleep," Jill said. Hoping to silence her friend, Jill held her arms out for a hug. Sandy hugged her.

"Oh I know! She's a total D-lister," Heather said. "Hey Jill, did you see the paparazzi around that mansion? The radio says it's that soap slut Valerie Lipson. You know, 'Denver's own star.'"

"What's she doing?" Tanesha asked. "Taking her clothes off again?"

The friends laughed.

"Hi you guys," Jill said. "Why don't you come in and meet my brother's wife?"

Stepping out of the doorway, she raised her eyebrows in a 'shut up.' Her friends were so caught up in their world that they missed her signal.

"You know what Perez says..." Heather started. Her mouth fell open when she saw Valerie standing in the living room. "What? What?"

Heather stopped walking so suddenly that Sandy and Tanesha bumped into her.

"You're right. I'm a total D-lister." Valerie shrugged. "I don't have any idea why anyone would give a shit what I do."

The women gawked at Valerie.

"I'm Val," Valerie said.

"Here's my question," Tanesha said. "Why would you work porn? I mean your Daddy's rich. Was it like a phase or some rebellion?"

"I never worked porn," Valerie said. "Listen, you came to see Jill and Katy I can just..."

"No," Jill said. "I'm not going to kick Valerie out because you guys are being rude. Knock it off."

"Well I want to know," Tanesha said. She put her hands on her hip as if she wouldn't give it up until her question was answered. "I mean, every girl has a chance to do porn. I have. Jill has. And we need the money. Why did you?"

"I never worked in the adult entertainment industry." Val's hands bounced her size 'A' cup breasts. "Don't really have the parts now do I."

"I saw those pictures," Sandy said. "You're bigger in the pictures."

"I was pregnant in the pictures," Valerie said. She shook her head slightly. "My husband was deployed to the Middle East. I took those pictures for him. The pictures were forcibly removed from him. They were sold to the press by my step-sister."

"Trevor's whore?" Heather asked.

Valerie nodded.

"She sucks." Sandy had a sheepish expression on her face. "Why does Perez hate you so much?"

"He has a crush on a friend of mine... You know, my first ex-fiancé? Sean?" Valerie shrugged. "He thinks I'm keeping him from his true love."

"Oh," Heather said. "Sorry. We didn't mean to..."

"It's all right." Valerie shook her head. "If people believe this stuff, I need to get used to explaining my life. It's just complicated, you know?"

The women nodded their heads in unison.

"Well, that Wes?" Tanesha said. "You know, I never liked that man. I always though he was... slimy. And too old. I bet he has to take those blue pills."

"TANESHA!" Jill's horrified voice echoed in the small apartment.

"Uh huh," Sandy and Heather said in unison. "We thought that too."

Valerie laughed at the truth reflected to her in these stranger's faces.

"I especially don't like him now," Heather said. "I mean you seem so nice. And he's just... bleck."

"Why?"

"He is not saying nice things about you," Tanesha said.

Val's took a quick in breath. "How bad?"

"Bad," Tanesha said.

Sandy and Heather's heads bobbed up and down.

Valerie closed her eyes. She crossed her arms so her hands held her in a tight hug. The world seemed to wobble on its axis. She felt like she might throw up or faint.

Feeling movement in the room, she opened her eyes. Mike. Mike wrapped her in his arms. Holding him to her, she knew she was right where she was supposed to be, exactly where she belonged.

Home.

~~~~~~~~~

Jill tiptoed across her living room. When Mike and Jacob arrived with food, Katy was ready to entertain. Even lagging a little, she kept the adults laughing with her endless stories of her hospital adventure.

After everyone left, Jacob insisted on caring for Katy to give Jill time to deal with her life. Jacob and Katy played with Barbie's for a while. He taught Katy how to play tic-tac-toe. When Katy's eyes drooped, they watched her favorite cartoons on videotape.

Jill peeked in a couple times to see how they were doing. Katy and Jacob went from playing on the couch to laying on the floor. Jacob made a bed for Katy out of the couch cushions. The last time Jill checked, they were sound asleep.

"Oh sorry," Jacob said. He woke when she touched him. "I haven't slept much in the last couple days."

"I don't know why." Jill smiled.

His chuckle woke Katy. Katy opened her eyes to watch them whisper back and forth.

"My boss called. He can't find something he needs. Would you mind watching Katy for an hour or so? I should be right back."

"I'm happy to hang out with Katy. Is that all right with you, Katy?"

Katy nodded her head up and down.

"Would you mind if Katy and I went to the Castle?" Jacob asked. "I'm sure Mike and Val could use some help getting ready for dinner."

"I want to go to his house, Mommy," Katy said.

"Ok Katy-baby, let's get you dressed for dinner. I'm going to get your stay the night stuff together so you can sleep if you need to."

Katy nodded.

"When does she take her medication again?"

"In an hour," Jill said. "Do you mind just hanging here while I take care of this?"

"Not at all."

Jill gave Katy a quick bath then dressed her in her hand me down 'fancy dress.' Katy was beginning to sag again by the time Jill finished packing Katy's pony bags. She carried Katy into the living room but stopped, stunned at the door. Jacob had cleaned up the toys and couch cushions. He even replaced the rug where it belonged. She shook her head as if she couldn't believe what she saw.

"Mommy, I think I need to sleep," Katy said.

"Should we stay here?" Jacob asked.

"No, she sleeps like a rock. If you don't mind keeping her with you, she'll sleep almost anywhere."

Jacob took Katy's worn leather saddle bags. He arched his eyes in question to Jill. She smiled and nodded toward the door. He opened the door so she could carry Katy from the apartment.

Walking down the hall, she said, "The bags are another long story. For now, you should know that these are Katy's pony bags. I'm sure she'll tell you all about them when she's feeling better."

He followed Jill out of the apartment. Jill set Katy in her car seat and was surprised when Jacob took the passenger's seat.

"You can drop us off at the workshop," he said. "We can take the tunnel into the Castle."

"I usually take the bus."

"You may as well take the car. Do you have money for parking?"

Jill looked in her purse. She had a dollar in quarters and a prescription for Katy. She would use the dollar for the meter but the prescription... As if he read her mind, Jacob set a hundred dollar bill in her purse.

"For the meds," he said.

She blushed. "I..."

"Don't worry. I'll put it on your tab." He winked.

"Thanks. I didn't know..."

"How to get the prescription filled? I figured as much," he said. Jacob took her cell phone and dialed his number. "Now you have my number. Just call me when you're done and I'll meet you at the workshop."

She nodded and drove to his Detroit St. workshop. Jill waved at Jacob and Katy when she pulled out. Driving down Detroit street, she watched them waving in the rearview mirror.

Her baby girl in the arms of her...

Boyfriend?

Ah shit.

~~~~~~~~~

"What's next?" Mike asked.

They were sitting in the Jeep. They had spent the last hour in Store of Lingerie in North Cherry Creek. The owner, Cindy Johnson, escorted them into a private fitting room where Valerie teased Mike with lingerie. Mostly, she looked at underwear and bras for her new Denver life. Jacob planned for everything, except decent underwear.

"Want to do something really fun?" Valerie asked.

"More fun than watching you try on lingerie for an hour? No, darling, there's nothing better than that."

In a swift motion, Valerie slipped her knee over Mike's lap. Sitting facing him, she kissed with long pulling motions. As fast as she was there, she moved back to the passenger seat. Mike was so dazed it took him a few moments to speak.

"Yes dear," Mike said.

"So you want to do something fun?"

"Whatever you say."

Valerie laughed. His arms moved around her to kiss her. She turned her head away. He laughed and kissed her cheek.

"What did you have in mind?" Mike asked.

"Safety deposit box."

"Your wish is my command."

~~~~~~~~~

"But… but…" Jill couldn't breathe.

"Get the fuck out of my office!" The rolls of fat under her bosses chin vibrated with his scream.

"I have sick time. I have vacation time. I…"

"I don't give a shit what you have or don't have. If you don't get the fuck out of my office, I will have you arrested!"

"My daughter…"

"You are such a whining little bitch," he said. Imitating her voice, he whined, "My daughter."

"Listen, you have no right…"

Jill started then jumped back when he let out a rage filled scream: "AGHHHH! I don't give a fuck about your daughter or you."

He jumped from his seat so fast that Jill cowered as if he was going to hit her. He pushed his bulk pat her to the door.

"Please, sir," Jill whimpered. "I'm very sorry you couldn't find the email. You're absolutely right. It's entirely my fault."

"Damn right it's your fault."

"I really need this job." Jill couldn't keep herself from begging.

"That's not my problem anymore."

He wrenched the door open and pointed.

"Please Mr. Ashforth."

"Get the fuck out of my office and my company. If I even THINK you're near the building, I will call the cops."

He grabbed Jill by the elbow and dragged her through the office. While horrified employees watched, he threw her out the door. Jill landed in a heap on the sidewalk. He threw her purse at her. Her purse opened in mid-air spilling its contents all over the sidewalk.

Her nylons ruined, Jill scrambled to pick up her purse when a woman ran across the street to see if she could help. Together, they picked up her belongings. When Jill looked back at her office, she gasped, bit her fist, and then went blank.

Unsure of what to do, the woman found Jill's phone on the sidewalk. The stranger pressed send to dial the last number Jill dialed. Maybe someone knew this poor woman.

"Hello? I'm sorry. I am in… uh… Denver. I saw this woman thrown out of an office. I think she was assaulted but I can't tell. She's very upset."

"Where is she?" Jacob asked.

"Brighton Boulevard and E. 36th St.," the woman said.

"I hate to ask you this, but will you stay with her. I certainly will compensate you for your time. She gets overwhelmed and…"

"You don't have to compensate me. I'll stay with her. I have time," the woman said. "Just come and help your friend. I've never seen anything so awful."

"I will be there as fast as I can get there," Jacob said.

Clicking off his cell phone, he looked at Delphie. They were standing in the middle of his apartment while Katy slept on his bed.

"You were right," Delphie said.

"Just tell me. She'll be all right?" Jacob asked.

He slipped his arms into the jacket his black Bioni 'power' suit. Delphie straightened his tie.

"She will be fine," Delphie said. "I'll stay here with Katherine. Just…"

"I know. Be myself," Jacob said. "Can I kill him?"

Delphie smiled. "You know what to do."

"You'll talk to Dad?" Jacob asked.

"I already have," Delphie said.

"Thanks," Jacob said.

"Jake?" Delphie hugged him. "I love you."

"Love you, Ruth."

He was halfway down the long stairs from his apartment when Delphie called his name. He turned and she threw him a box of Kleenex. Catching the tissue box, he stopped short for Valerie. Valerie came out of the house and waited for him on the landing. She nodded.

When Valerie walked across the grass, the crowd and photographers began screaming her name. Jacob ran toward the garage. Using his remote, he started the Aston Martin DBS while the garage door opened. Valerie moved toward the opposite edge of the property. The photographers and crowd followed Valerie and the driveway cleared of people. Jacob drove the silver two-seat sports car to the fence. With the Denver Police holding the stragglers back, Jacob hit the street.

Gratefully, Monday afternoon traffic was almost non-existent. He took Colfax to Park Avenue West. Even with a few red lights, he managed to make good time. Turning on Broadway, he made the easy transition to Denver's oldest warehouse district on Brighton Boulevard.

Nearing 36th, he noticed a Denver Police Cruiser and a policeman talking to Jill. She was sitting in the middle of the sidewalk. Jumping from the car, he jogged to her. He dropped to his knees to scoop her up.

Jill felt his safety first. Then she could smell him. Jacob. In a snap, she returned to the present. Seeing Jacob, she hugged him to her. He helped her to her feet then tucked her into his shoulder. Jill buried her face into his neck.

Jacob spoke with the police officer and took the business card of the woman who stayed with Jill. Wanting to get her somewhere safe before the inevitable storm of emotion, he led Jill to the Aston Marin. He was halfway around the car when Jill started to sob. Slipping into the driver's seat, he leaned over to pull Jill onto his lap. While the Aston Martin pumped out soft music and air conditioning, Jill cried her eyes out.

CHAPTER FIFTEEN
JUST LOTS OF BLOOD

"Homeland Security is saying we need to get the photographers off Race Street," the Denver Police Chief said. "That entire neighborhood is on top of the coal tunnels. No one can get in so I don't see why this is suddenly a problem."

"What did you come up with?" the Denver Mayor asked the City Attorney.

"A constitutional amendment. Freedom of the Press."

"God damn it! This isn't news. Its harassment... stalking at best! We're talking about Celia Marlowe's daughter and her husband. You remember Val? She waited tables at the Wynkoop."

"I know Val. She interned with us in high school," the editor of the Rocky Mountain New replied. "What did the other mayors say?"

"They feel powerless against the hoard of press. I'll tell you this, though. At least one mayor said it's good for business."

"Of course. That's what the Los Angeles Police Chief said. He said every time they get rid of the paparazzi, the business owners complain."

"Anyone complaining?" the Mayor asked.

"Dean, Pete's son, called a couple times. He's had their vehicles towed from his lot. He would be very happy if they left and never came back," The Police Chief paced the office. "The LA chief said the best we could hope for was that Miss Lipson would leave town."

"I'm not going to kick my dear friend's child out of town," the Mayor said. "God damn it. Valerie grew up here. She's one of us. That's not to mention what her parents have done for the city of Denver! Why don't we let Homeland clear them out?"

"That's like telling the world: 'NATIONAL SECURITY THREAT RIGHT HERE!' They come in with Black Hawks and soldiers. No fucking around," the Police Chief said. "With the Democratic convention in a month, we don't want Homeland involved."

"There is one thing we could do... When is the City Council meeting on this issue?"

"Tomorrow morning," the Mayor said.

"Let's call immigration. That'll fuck with them for a while," the City Attorney said.

"Curfew's at 11 p.m.," the Police Chief volunteered.

"Do it," the Mayor said.

~~~~~~~~

"He... he fired me," Jill said. "He just called me in to f-f-fire m-m-me. He said I... I..."

Her words were lost in her sobs. Jacob stroked her hair until she was breathing again.

"I thought you worked for Mabel," Jacob said.

"He... he... t-t-tricked her out of t-t-the company. T-they have a c-court date this w-w-week. I was just holding on until... until... Oh God Jacob, I lost my job!"

Jill buried her head in his shoulder. He returned to stroking her hair.

"She got the company in the divorce but he... he..." She wept into his shoulder.

"You work for Ashforth Pipe Supply?" Jacob asked.

"Your Mom got me the job right out of high school," Jill said. "N-n-now I... I... I'll never be able to pay you back... Katy will starve... I'll lose her for sure. Oh my God, where's Katy?"

Her tears evaporated the moment she realized she didn't know where her daughter was.

"She's with Delphie. Don't worry. Delphie's really good with kids. Val and I spent a lot of time with her when our parents were working."

Jill nodded.

"I left Katy's meds in the refrigerator at the office," Jill said. "I can't go back in there."

"Let me. Did you get the stuff from your desk?"

Jill shook her head.

"He's s-so awful. He used to j-j-just work the w-w-warehouse. The last three months have been h-h-hell. I just... He lost an email. He deleted it from his personal email box and then couldn't find it. He does that all the time. If I tell him, he deleted it? He gets furious. So I found the email then he fired me. He... he threw me out."

Jill lifted her shirt to show the developing bruise on her elbow where her boss grabbed her. Jacob kissed her elbow. She threw her arms around his neck in a tight embrace.

"I'm so sorry," Jacob whispered. He shifted and she released him to look at his face.

"I should probably get off your lap," Jill said. "What about the Bronco?"

"I'll call someone to get it. We have a job a couple blocks from here. They can pick it up and I'll get it tomorrow."

"You saved me again. Second time in two days," Jill said.

Jacob shrugged, "Fixing messes is my specialty."

"Like me?"

Jacob crushed her mouth with his mouth. He tasted her soft lips and delicate tongue. Jill felt a rush of passion overcome her senses. Pulling back, he took a breath.

"I better stop or this might get a little... public." He nodded to the police cruiser. "Are you all right here?"

"Yeah, thanks."

"Jill? Don't say you're a mess. You're the very best thing that has ever happened to me. Things are messy. That's true. But life is like that sometimes. We'll sort all of this out. Promise."

Jill nodded and slipped off his lap. Jacob gave her the box of Kleenex. She kissed his cheek and he slid from the car. Jill leaned her head back against the leather seat. Smiling to herself, she closed her eyes.

How did she get so lucky?

~~~~~~~~~

Katy opened her eyes. Sitting up, she looked around Jacob's apartment. Delphie was sitting near the bed knitting.

"Hello Katherine," Delphie said.

"I know you," Katy said.

"Yes, you do," Delphie said.

"But I don't know your name," Katy replied. Her small brow furrowed in concentration. "Did I meet you before?"

"A long, long time ago," Delphie said.

"Are you a friend of my Jacob?"

"I am a friend of your Jacob. I'm Delphinium. People call me Delphie."

Delphie set her knitting down and came to the bed to shake Katy's hand. After shaking hands, Delphie sat next to Katy on the bed.

"I thought your name might start with an 'r,'" Katy said.

"Yes," Delphie said. "Your Mommy is having a little bit of trouble. Your Jacob went to help her. So we have to carry on without her for a while."

"Ok," Katy said. "I'm glad Mommy has someone to help her now."

"Me too," Delphie said. "Would you like to go meet your Aunt Valerie?"

Katy nodded. "Will you help me go potty?"

"Of course."

Delphie helped Katy off the bed and they walked hand in hand toward the bathroom.

"I like you, Delphie."

"I like you, Katherine."

~~~~~~~~~

"Of course, Mr. Marlowe," the receptionist said. "I can escort you back."

"That's all right. I know the way," Jacob said. "Thanks for your help."

Walking through the office, Jacob could feel the tension crackle around him. The women office workers stood in clusters whispering to each other. As he approached the owner's office, a dirty dishwater haired woman darted in front of him.

"Mr. Marlowe! I didn't realize you were here," she said in a deep Wisconsin accent. Nervous, she pulled at her light pink sweater set.

"Hi Darla," Jacob said. "Mabel's not here."

Darla startled then shook her head.

"I need to speak with him. Is he in?"

"You have to forgive us. We've had a challenging day," Darla smiled.

Smiling, Jacob let the silence drag.

"Really, sir. Today's not a very good day to..."

Just then the owner's office door opened.

"Jacob! How the hell are you?"

"Great. Do you have a moment?" Jacob asked.

"I was just leaving for a meeting but I always have time for my best customer."

"This will only take a second," Jacob said.

"Please, come in," the owner said. "Darla, you stupid cow. I'm paying you. Can you work?"

Darla jumped and raced back to her desk.

Jacob followed the owner into his office. Ashforth indicated a chair in front of the desk but Jacob continued to stand. A glance around the tiny office told Jacob that Ashforth was moving out. Ashforth shut the lid of a toolbox stuffed full of large pipe wrenches with a flip of his foot.

"I'm here to tell you that Lipson Construction will no longer need your services."

Jacob turned to leave but the owner said, "It's because of that stupid incompetent bitch. You should pay ME for keeping her lazy ass here for so long."

Jacob spun in place and moved toward the owner. Catching himself, he stopped walking. He backed to the door.

"You don't want to make this personal," Jacob said.

"Why should I listen to a little twerp like you?" the owner sneered. "Did you ask your Daddy first?"

"I am Lipson Construction, you stupid fuck. DO NOT MAKE THIS PERSONAL OR YOU WILL UNLEASH A SHIT STORM YOU ARE NOT PREPARED FOR."

Jacob stalked to the door. He felt the owner follow him but he refused to turn around. In his mind, he longed for the owner to touch him so he could let loose his rage and indignation at this pathetic excuse of a man.

But the owner never laid a finger on him.

"You make sure your last invoice is on my desk by the end of the week," Jacob said. "You will hear from my lawyers."

Yanking the door open, Jacob saw the office employees clustered around the door. He pulled a stack of cards from his pocket and gave them to the women.

"Give me a call when you need a job," Jacob said. "Now, can someone show me the kitchen?"

"I'll take you," Darla said.

"Thanks. I hate to ask, but would someone mind boxing up Jill's desk. She didn't get a chance to do it."

"Mr. Marlowe, I was doing that when you came in. I was going to drop it by her place tonight." Another woman shrugged. "She sits next to me."

"Thanks," Jacob smiled, nodded to the women, then followed Darla to the kitchen.

"Did you just terminate your contract?" Darla asked. She bent into the refrigerator to retrieve Katy's medication.

"Yes," he said. "We were unaware of the ownership change."

"That was intentional. We wanted to keep every customer for when Mabel comes back. I'm sorry." Darla gave a weak smile. "Guess I should get my resume together."

"That's probably a good idea," he said. "Keep me in the loop, Darla. We can always use good people at Lipson."

"I heard you had another business. Molly does your books?"

Jacob nodded. "Send me your resume."

He shook Darla's hand and took the medication from her. Walking through the office, he picked up a box of Jill's possessions from the other women. He waved to the 'girls' and went out into the bright day.

Seeing Jill in the car, he smiled. Some messes were easy to clean up.

~~~~~~~~~

"What's happened?" Mike asked Delphie.

"As far as I can tell? Nothing," Delphie said. "Maybe Jake was wrong."

"He's never been wrong before," Valerie said. "He's better than Mom was. Between the two of you..."

Valerie jumped from her arm chair to pace the Castle living room. Mike held his arms out in case she wanted a hug but she shook her head. She was too anxious for comfort. For the billionth time, she wished she had even a twinge of her mother or brother's skill.

"Go over again what he told you," Valerie said.

"He said Jill was going to get fired and the owner was going to attack him."

"What about the blood?" Mike asked.

"He saw a lot of blood. Lots of blood," Delphie said. "That's what he said."

"What do you see?" Valerie and Jacob's father walked into the room from the kitchen.

"Lots of blood," Delphie said. "Just lots of blood."

~~~~~~~~~

Jill remembered what happened like this:

She was spacing out, listening to jazz and enjoying the cool air on her skin. If she thought of anything, it was that she had never been in such a nice car. With the air conditioning on and the music playing, she couldn't hear the street noises. She felt enclosed in a cozy bubble. She even slipped off her shoes and her torn nylons. Holding the Kleenex box in one hand, her fingers played with the torn nylons in the other hand.

Out of the corner of her eye, she noticed Jacob come out of the office. He winked at her. He held up Katy's medication and a box as if to say, 'That was easy.' Their eyes caught and he smiled.

Mostly, she remembered his beautiful smile. His teeth were so white against his sun kissed skin. Yes, his smile was something she would always remember.

A second later, his face flashed in horror then went slack. He fell forward toward the cement. As he fell, his right shoulder seemed to disintegrate. Blood sprayed from his neck. Jacob's fall to the ground revealed Ashforth behind him. Ashforth jerked the head of a twenty-pound straight pipe wrench from Jacob's shoulder.

Jill screamed, "NO!"

Fumbling with the locks, she somehow managed to get the door open. Jacob's body bounced on the sidewalk until he landed on his left side. Blood began to mist into the warm day. With both arms, Ashforth swung the pipe wrench over his head to bash in Jacob's head.

"NO!" Channeling Megan, Jill screamed in her bossiest voice. "DON'T YOU DARE."

Hearing Jill, Ashforth lowered the pipe wrench to step over Jacob's body. He spit on Jacob before moving his rotund body across the sidewalk toward Jill. Jill ran forward toward Jacob. They met in the middle of the sidewalk.

Ashforth hefted the pipe wrench over his head.

"LOWER THE WEAPON."

Ashford swung at Jill. Jill avoided the arching pipe wrench as if she was playing champion dodge ball.

"THIS IS THE DENVER POLICE. LOWER YOUR WEAPON."

Time shifted into slow motion.

Ashforth's pipe wrench bashed into the open passenger door catching on the roof of the Aston Martin. The window shattered in tiny pieces. Amidst the mist of Jacob's blood, the tiny pieces of glass floated through the air to the sidewalk.

As Ashforth lifted the pipe wrench over his head for another swing, the police officers stopped running and lifted their handguns. Ducking the pipe wrench, she continued toward Jacob. The glass tore at her feet. She felt, more than saw, bullets pass over her.

Ripping apart the cardboard Kleenex box, she slid on her knees next to him. She jammed a wad of tissue into the river of Jacob's blood coming from where his collarbone had been. The spray of blood stopped. Using her torn nylons, she tied the tissue in a neat pressure dressing. Yanking off her cotton work shirt, she pressed the fabric into his oozing, destroyed shoulder. Hoping to slow his bleeding, she pressed her weight into his shoulder.

Jacob opened his eyes.

"I love you, Jill."

He jerked and went slack.

Time returned to a normal pace.

She felt Ashforth lumber toward her then fall to the sidewalk.

One Denver Police officer ran past her to her ex-boss. Another police officer, a Hispanic woman, came to Jill.

"I have a weak pulse," the policewoman screamed into the microphone at her shoulder, "We need ambulance NOW."

~~~~~~~~

"He's still alive?" Valerie whispered.

"For now," Delphie said.

CHAPTER SIXTEEN
I WANTED SO MUCH LIFE

"Mom," Jacob whispered.

He felt his mother near. Gradually, her face came into view. Not her cancer ravaged face, but the face she wore when he was a very small boy. Like a thirsty man, Jacob drank in her image.

"Mommy."

"My baby boy," Celia said.

"I'm dead?"

"Not quite." He felt her hand touch his face. "I love you."

"I love you, Mom."

"I am so proud of the man you've become. You're kind and loving to everyone who knows you. Honorable. You are a wonderful person."

"Mommy."

Jacob stretched out his hand to touch her face.

In an instant, they were walking along a familiar shore. The day was bright and warm. There was a slight wind from the West that blew wisps of clouds through a bright blue sky. Their footprints in the tan colored sand were washed away by a slow white capped tide. They were alone on the shore. This youthful version of his mother slipped her arm into his elbow. They walked in silence for a while.

"I've missed you," Jacob said.

"I've missed you. I've been around. It's you who refuses..."

"To call you Naomi?" Jacob laughed. "Don't you think that's a bit... much?"

"The truth is always a bit much," Celia said.

"Are you... all right?"

"I was in pain for such very, very long time. It's nice to not be in pain. But I long for Ruth and you children. I miss Sam like a hole in my soul."

"He's lost without you."

"You've been a tremendous relief for him. I don't think he realized how much he needed you."

"It's hard for me to imagine Dad needing anyone... except you."

"Poor Sam. I really messed up his life... and yours."

"With the new wife, Tiffanie?" Jacob asked.

"Yes. I thought that ...

"With loving support and resources, they'd blossom," they said together.

Celica stopped walking to gawk at her son.

"You used to say that any time someone was… hurtful."

"I was wrong."

"Yes, but that's part of your beauty. Your belief in people." Jacob smiled. "Are you all right with Dad and Delphie?"

"Ruth?"

"Dad and Ruth."

"Of course," she said. "My best friend and my soul's love."

"They miss you and love you so much…"

Celia stopped walking and hugged her son.

"You don't have to explain it. I'm not jealous. We belong to each other—Ruth, Sam and I. And with you and Jillian, Jillian and Michael, Michael and Valerie."

Jacob kissed his mother's cheek. "You're very sweet."

She smiled. They walked for along the unending shore in silence. A river of palpable love flowed back and forth between them.

"I wanted so much life… Love… laughter… babies… I wanted to grow old… with Jill… Twenty-six years isn't a very long time to live. After years of thinking… hoping, I only… one chance… very fast… with Jill. I wanted to live… I liked living."

"Yes," Celia said. "Why haven't you stepped into your wisdom?"

"Why didn't you?"

"I never pretended I didn't know things. Never. I never told people… What is it that you say?"

"I just figured it would happen," Jacob said. "What am I supposed to do? I'm not going to read Tarot cards."

"You know tarot cards can be quite a mess. You might enjoy fixing that kind of mess."

They laughed.

"I did like sorting out messes," Jacob said.

"Then it's time to sort out the mess you're in."

Jacob gasped.

He felt tremendous ripping pain on his entire right side. A blinding white light filled his eyes. He would have thought he was 'following the light' except his ears filled with the sound of yelling people and screeching machines.

"He's back," the nurse said.

"Welcome back, Jacob."

Dr. John Drayson's lack of wings and British accent confirmed Jacob's non-descent to heaven. His gloved right hand, coated in Jacob's blood, held a scalpel. He leaned into the light so Jacob could see his mask covered face.

His cobalt blue eyes seemed huge through his magnifying glasses.

"We're hoping to keep you with us for a while. Nurse?"

Amidst the blazing light in his eyes and the agony in his right shoulder, Jacob felt the sharp stab of what felt like a four-inch diameter needle. A whoosh of pain relieving medication moved into his system.

"You need to hang around, Jacob," Dr. Drayson laughed. "Alex has her heart set on the leaded glass tulips transom windows you showed her. I was hoping you could get them in by our anniversary. What do you think?"

Jacob tried to laugh but the machines screamed.

Everything went dark.

~~~~~~~~~

Jacob opened his eyes. The room was dark and he was laying in a hospital bed. Looking to see who was holding his hand, he felt a stabbing pain in his right shoulder.

The monitors blared.

Everything went dark.

~~~~~~~~~

Hearing voices, Jacob tried to open his eyes. The effort was too much for him.

"We've been able to clean up a lot. He still has quite a bit of internal bleeding. If we continue to work, we will only do him a disservice." Dr. Drayson's staccato words broke through the darkness. "The trauma team removed a portion of his upper lung, ribs... His collar bone is crushed. His scapula shattered. His right shoulder girdle is all but destroyed. There's a break in two of his cervical vertebrae. We're hoping to get him stable, stronger, then go back in... maybe tomorrow morning. I only do veins and arteries. If he's ready, the orthopedic surgery team will start tomorrow morning."

"Thank you, doctor," said Jacob's father Sam Lipson.

"John," Dr. Drayson said. "We're lucky. He's in great shape, healthy and strong."

"I heard you're the best in the business... The nurse said you weren't working today. I... just thanks. He's..."

Jacob heard his father weep.

"We love Jacob, Mr. Lipson. I'll do everything I can."

"Thank you, John."

~~~~~~~~~

"He's awake."

He opened his eyes to Valerie's red, puffy eyes about an inch from his face. Her nose was bright red and swollen. Out of the corner of his eye, he saw the blur of someone moving away from the bed.

"Your mascara's running," he whispered.

"You stupid jerk," Valerie said. She didn't bother to stem the flow the tears that dropped from her eyes and nose. "This was supposed to be MY drama, MY crisis. MY life is in crisis buddy, not yours."

Jacob tried to laugh. He managed a vague groan.

"Where are my paparazzi?" he whispered.

"Outside. The police escorted us, and a billion photographers, to Denver Health."

"Will I make the cover of People magazine?"

Through her tears, Valerie laughed at his imitation of her early actress days.

"Do you think this outfit makes me look fat?"

He tried to move his right arm to pat his stomach but felt a ripping, burning pain.

The monitors blared.

Everything went dark.

~~~~~~~~~

"Jill."

"I'm here," she said.

He felt movement then saw her face. Her eyes were red from crying and her face a little gaunt from worry. She leaned over to kiss his cheek.

"I wanted to tell you that I'll marry you."

"Really?"

"Well, you asked on Saturday night and I never gave you an answer."

"I remember," he mumbled.

"I figure if you're willing to take a beating, save my Katy's life, and are amazing in bed..."

"Amazing?"

"Well... We don't want to add ego adjustment to your next surgery." Jill worked to keep a cheery voice. She was determined to be light and flippant when she spoke with him. "I'll say... pretty good. Now don't interrupt. I've been practicing. Where was I?"

"Amazing in bed," he said.

"Yes. I figure if you're willing to take a beating, save my Katy's life and are... pretty good..."

Jacob smiled.

"...in bed, then I should marry you before you ride off on some horse."

"Horse? I don't have any pony bags."

"I'd say like a knight in shining armor but that ego adjustment is so costly."

He smiled. She brushed her lips across his in a quick kiss.

"Jill?" Jacob asked.

"Yes, Jacob."

"Would you mind if we got married tomorrow? Maybe save some excitement for our third non-date?"

"Well, I want a really big diamond. I'm willing to give you a few days, but only a few."

"Val has your diamonds. Just ask her..."

Everything went dark.

~~~~~~~~

TUESDAY MORNING, 10 AM

Mike stopped the Mustang at the edge of the grass. The perfect lawn was broken by a few monuments. Sam Lipson sat on a bench near a blooming rose hedge. He was reading the Rocky Mountain News out loud to Celia's grave.

"Are you sure you're up for this?" he asked.

"My brother almost died because he did the right thing," Valerie said. "I need to do the right thing. I need to speak with my father."

Mike's big hand stroked her delicate cheek. Her beautiful face was pale and drawn from her night at Jacob's bedside. For the first time in a decade, she allowed herself to be photographed in her distraught, rumpled condition. Today, Valerie Lipson didn't give a crap what anyone thought or said about 'Just Val.' He kissed her lips.

"I'll be right here," he said.

She held him tight then whispered in his ear, "I love you so very much, Michael Roper."

He smiled.

Valerie slipped out of the car. Leaning in, she took a bouquet of a dozen white roses from Mike. With her shoulders squared, she walked forward across the lawn. Her father looked up to see her and jumped to his feet in surprise.

"What is it? What's happened? Is Jake...?"

"Jake's in surgery. Everything was going well when I left. Dr. Drayson said they found a metal shard, probably from the pipe wrench, next to his heart. They think that's causing the heart attacks. The cardiac team removed the metal. The cardiac surgeon is optimistic that Jake's heart is not damaged. We won't know for certain until he's active again."

Sam Lipson visibly sagged with relief.

"The orthopedic surgeons have another couple hours. Jill and Delphie will call the moment they know anything."

"I was reading your mother the funnies."

"You can finish," she said.

"That's all right," Sam said. "She likes them..."

"Uninterrupted, start to finish," Valerie said in unison with him.

"Some things never change." He smiled.

"I need to speak to you about..." Valerie's face clouded. She wasn't sure how to even start the conversation. Shoving a picture frame at her father, she said, "Jake keeps telling me to look at this picture. What... what does he want me to see?"

"What do you see?" he asked and passed the photo back.

"I see you," Valerie spit the words, "and your... new perfect family."

Sam laughed.

"Why... why is that funny?"

"You can be so stubborn," he said. "That's why I laughed. It's right in front of you and you don't see it. Why is that, Valerie?"

"What am I supposed to see?"

"You and Jake look remarkably alike," Sam said.

"We look like our mother." Valerie flipped her hair at him.

"Celia was fair skinned. She had light brown hair until the very end of her life," Sam said. "You don't have fair skin or light brown hair. Do you?"

"What are you saying? We're African-American?" Valerie spit at him.

"My family has been in the West since long before there was a United States. We're mutts. Dark hair, darker skin, hazelish eyes... African-American, Native-American, Spanish," Sam Lipson shrugged. "The Lipson's pass their features to their children."

Valerie curled her lip at her father. She jerked the photograph to her eyes. Four tiny little blonde bitches... with their tiny blonde whore mother. Trevor's wicked fiancé and her bitty sister stood next to their mother while her father's... What? They looked like... She pulled the photo next to her eye

"Your mother wanted..."

"How dare you blame your slutty behavior on my mother! She was devastated by you!"

"Was she?" Sam asked. "Are you sure?"

Valerie threw the photograph at her father's feet. Crossing her arms over her heart, she started to walk off.

"I promised Celia that I'd only tell you kids when you asked."

Valerie swung around to look at him.

"Jake asked about six month's after Celia died. But you... What's it been nine years? You were at the lawyers today. You walked in on us the night before you mother died. And still, you don't ask the question. Just ask me."

"Fine. Why did you betray my mother?"

"I've never betrayed your mother. Never. Not one time in the lifetime of knowing her. She was the very best thing in my life and I miss her like a hole in the very center of me."

"How can you say that? She gets ill and you're off... With that horrible woman... and... I thought you had a vasectomy?"

"I did," Sam said. He smiled at the question. Valerie was finally ready for the truth. "It's the only time Celia was truly angry with me. She wanted babies so badly but there are reasons she's the last of the Marlowes. She was lucky to survive carrying Jake. She was determined to have more children. I... I didn't want to lose her so I had it done."

Valerie looked down at the bouquet of roses in her hand. She remembered the fight. It was the only time she ever remembered her parents screaming at each other. They fought for days. She was five or maybe six years old. Jake was a little more than a year old.

"Then how did you get your secretary pregnant?"

"I didn't," Sam said.

Valerie shook her head. She almost left again when she realized what she needed to know.

"Dad, what happened?"

"Finally," Sam said. "Thanks for that."

He held out his hands and she gave him the roses. They walked together to Celia's grave. He placed the roses in a flower holder near the bottom of her grave. Letting out a breath, he turned to her.

"Celia was sick for a long, long time. She fought the cancer for a decade or more. She wanted so much to live." Sam smiled remembering. "We kept it from you kids because... Well... because raising you was... important to us. When we knew that fighting wasn't an option anymore, she..."

He stopped talking for a moment. His expression reflected his love and frustration for his Celia.

"Oh your mother... She always thought the best of everyone. If someone was awful, she would say that they didn't know any better."

They said together, "With loving support they will blossom." They laughed.

"Tiffanie's boyfriend was in and out of prison. She was just pregnant with Briana when he violated parole and was sent back to Canyon City. Your mother felt that if I married her, said that the baby was mine, I would save Tiffanie... and her children."

"But why would Mom do that?"

"Why do you think?" Sam asked.

"Can't you just answer the question?"

"Who did your mother love more than anyone in this world?"

"You."

"More than me and more than Jake."

"No one. Jake was her favorite."

"God damn it Valerie. You know that's not true."

At that moment, patience left Sam Lipson. The last twenty hours left him raw, exhausted and unwilling to play into anyone's bullshit.

"Me." Valerie whispered.

"Exactly."

"But this destroyed me. I..."

"Your mother knew things," Sam said.

"Like Jake and Delphie."

"More like Jake. Long term visions, big picture stuff. Life was a chess board to Celia. While all our friends went into building houses, we switched to underground utility. Celia knew the Californians would come to Colorado and build cheaper than anyone else. Everyone we knew went out of business except us. Delphie is good at the next six months and specifics in the next day or hour."

"Mom knew about Mike," Valerie said.

"And your baby," Sam said. "She knew I wouldn't make it... six months without her. With her death, my death, the baby, and Mike... She didn't think you'd survive."

"I barely survived as it is."

"Exactly," Sam said. "The only thing that would keep me going was having people depend on me. And I do love babies. I didn't care about living without her but..."

Sam face shifted to a kind of quiet love. His eyes filled.

"She believed your anger... at me... would pull you through all of the loss." He put his hand on her shoulder. Valerie looked up into his face. "She was right."

"Oh Dad." Valerie reached up and her father hugged.

While she cried into his shoulder, he said, "It was so worth it, Val. So completely worth it."

"Val! Val!" Mike yelled from the car. He ran across the grass to them. "Jake's dead."

~~~~~~~~~

"So that's it?" Jacob asked.

Celia laughed.

CHAPTER SEVENTEEN
CARDS ON THE TABLE
THURSDAY MORNING, 4 A.M.

Jill stood with her hand on the employee exit at Pete's Kitchen. Her feet, still oozing from the lacerations of the glass, ached in her waitress shoes. She shuffled through her regular Wednesday night shift with skinned knees and tattered feet. Pete finally sent her home with instructions not to come back until she was well. With work over, her mind turned to her lists.

"You Ok, Jill?" Pete asked.

"Yeah, I'm just... overwhelmed."

"Of course," he said. The elderly man patted her shoulder in a gesture of support. "You need to take care of yourself."

Jill nodded.

"You'll let us know if you need anything?" he asked.

"Thank you," Jill said.

When Pete returned to tracking down more hash browns, Jill returned to making a list in her head. She needed clothing for Katy. Wait. Where was her journal? At the Castle. Yep, Castle. Maybe she'd do a load... or forty loads... of laundry. When was the last time she washed her hair? Yesterday. Clean underwear was a must. Trash collection was... Friday. Better get the trash out.

Jill looked at her wrist watch. Three hours. Pressing open the door, Jill began the short walk to her apartment.

The last forty-eight hours had been... hell. She might always have trouble lining up all the events. When the cardiac team came out of surgery, they told Jill that Jacob had "popped a bleeder." Both Delphie and Jill heard them say that Jacob was dead. She called Mike to tell him then collapsed in tears of grief and regret.

By the time Mike, Valerie and Jacob's father arrived, Dr. Drayson came out to say a bone shard had been lodged in the subclavian artery, wherever that was. The shard kept Jacob from healing. Dr. Drayson was not only able to suture the artery, he also felt like Jacob would recover in "short order."

And sure enough, Jacob went from being critical to serious condition in a couple hours. He was moved into a private room this... yesterday morning. Jill called an hour ago and Valerie said the nurse told her they would start decreasing his medication in...

Jill looked at her watch. Two hours and forty-nine minutes. She stopped walking to stare at her watch. Was it really only Thursday? She'd known Jacob less than a week. For a moment, images from Katy's reaction to the bee sting to her ex-boss with the straight pipe wrench lofted over his head threatened to send her into blank emptiness.

Not today.

She blew out her breath and starting walking again. Shaking her head, she turned down Fourteenth Avenue.

"Hi Jill." Trevor stepped from the shadows into the light of a street lamp.

Startled, Jill jumped and yelped.

"Trevor! What are YOU doing here?"

"I wanted to see you," he said. He fell in step beside her. "I've been thinking about things."

Jill stopped walking.

"What things? You know I have a restraining..."

"I love you, Jill. You were right. You are my soul mate. We belong together."

"It's an interesting week to decide that," Jill said. She kept walking toward her apartment building.

"We were a family—you and me and our Katy..."

"Until you fucked it up," Jill said.

"I was manipulated, Jill. We both were. I... I was so focused on doing what was right for us, for Katy, I didn't realize I lost the most important thing in my life - you."

Jill stopped walking and squinted her eyes at Trevor.

"I want to get this straight. You thought by divorcing me, taking all of our money, MY money, stealing our only vehicle, a vehicle I bought and paid for I might add, and getting some rich girl pregnant was what was best for US? For Katy?"

"When you say it like that..."

Trevor's voice raised in irritation. Jill shook her head and returned to walking. Trevor noticeably softened.

"Oh Jill, you cut me to the core when you're so cold."

Jill raised her eyebrows and turned into the apartment building.

"Jill," Trevor put his hand on her arm. "Stop. Just listen to me."

Jill turned to face him.

"We were manipulated by these rich people. They used us..." Trevor's hand caressed Jill's arm. "People like that can never understand what we have."

Trevor leaned in. His lips brushed her lips. With her mouth an inch from his, she said, "So you're not getting married on Sunday?"

Trevor jerked back.

"That's what I thought," Jill said. "If you'll excuse me, my dog Scooter needs to be walked."

"Scooter! Oh my God Jill! Where did you find Scooter?"

"Don't even start with me. I saw the papers. A Mr. Trevor McGuinsey turned in him into the Dumb Friend's League."

Trevor grabbed her arm before she stepped into the building.

"Don't let them do this to us, Jill. We belong together. I still love you with every cell in my body, every fiber in my being, every thought in my head, and every action in my life."

Jill visibly sagged.

"Please," Trevor said.

She felt his hand move along her rear. Under his pressure, her hips shifted toward him. While her mind returned to her lists, he kissed her then slipped his hands under her shirt. He flicked open her bra and moved to cup her breasts.

Her weary mind whispered, 'This will be over soon enough.'

For the first time, Jill heard what her mind had repeated every time Trevor touched her. Horrified by the thought, Jill jerked to the present.

And found that...

She was standing on the sidewalk like a Colfax crack whore, while her ex-husband busied himself on her body. She took a step back. She wrenched his hands from under her shirt.

"Get off me."

"You can't just lead me on!" His voice was a terse whisper.

Jill couldn't help herself. She laughed.

Trevor slapped her hard across the face.

"Stupid worthless whore, how dare you?"

Trevor grabbed her arms and jerked her toward him. She banged against his hip. He was rock hard and ready. He mashed his lips onto hers.

At that moment, she knew.

He was going to have her no matter what.

Jill wrenched her arms from him. Using her elbow to push him off her, she bolted into the building. Racing up the stairs, she reached her door when he slammed her face forward into the wood. He caught her when she bounced off the door. With one hand over her mouth, he unbuttoned her pants. His finger nails raked their way to her soft flesh. While he jerked her pants down, and his own, Jill worked to get her key into the lock. Trevor was so lost in his lust he didn't realize what she was doing.

Somehow, she managed to get the door open.

Scooter flew at Trevor. His bark brought Sarah from the living room couch. While Sarah lunged and barked, Scooter snapped at Trevor. Trevor screamed in pain and fury. He lunged at Scooter, but Sarah blocked his way.

When Trevor turned, he saw the hallway lined with neighbors. Jill's next door neighbor Mr. Wilson rushed Trevor with his baseball bat. Terrified, Trevor ran for the stairs. Scooter and Sarah chased him from the apartment building.

Everyone stood in stunned silence. Before anyone could say anything, Mike poked his head into the hallway from the stairs. Whistling for Scooter and Sarah, Mike sauntered toward Jill's apartment. The dogs trotted up the stairs in answer Mike's whistle. Mike looked from Jill to Mr. Wilson. He put a hand on Mr. Wilson's baseball bat.

"Mr. Wilson?"

"Nice to see you, Michael."

With a nod, Mr. Wilson returned to his apartment.

"Trevor?" Mike slipped his jacket and tied it around Jill's waist to cover her bare behind, torn jeans and underwear.

Jill nodded.

"You Ok? Spaced out?"

"No," Jill said. "I'm here."

"Huh," Mike said.

He guided her into the apartment. Settling her on the couch, he went to get her a glass of water. When he returned, she was writing out her list on a pad of paper.

"For someone who was almost raped, you seem very... together," Mike said.

"Raped? Oh, yeah, I guess so." Jill flushed. "I should change. Ah, crap my feet are bleeding."

Getting up from the couch, she went into her bathroom. Mike helped her re-bandage her feet then she went into her bedroom to change.

"Do you ever think things happen for a reason?" Jill asked from the bedroom.

Mike stood in her bedroom door.

"Sure."

"I stayed with Trevor, married him even, because I thought he would never leave me. I wanted something permanent so I would never ever be alone. "

"Like after Mom and Dad died?"

Jill's eyes welled with tears. She pulled a t-shirt over her head. Before she could pull on another pair of jeans, Mike pointed out the scratches on Jill's lower back where Trevor's fingernails had torn her flesh. She turned to give him a soft smile.

Speaking in a whisper, she said, "I knew he cheated but I thought he needed me too much to ever leave. He was so demanding—I need this book, pay for my school, I want this car, make my dinner, fuck me now... I..."

Mike hugged his little sister.

"Then he left and took everything. Just like that. He's gone. And... I didn't die or fall apart or starve or... Every terror I lived with since I was nine years old, every single one, never happened. None of them. I... I realize that I'm a lot stronger than I thought."

"You're one of the strongest people I've ever met," Mike said.

Jill smiled.

"So Wonder Woman, are we moving all this stuff to your apartment at the Castle?" Mike asked. He gestured around the apartment.

"Not today."

~~~~~~~~~

The first thing Jacob noticed was the silence. Not quite alert and not quite unconscious, he scanned his immediate environment for sound. Nothing. He felt tiny fingers pressing his eyelids apart.

"Katy," Jacob whispered.

"I knew you were in there," Katy said.

He opened his eyes and found her face about an inch from his face. He attempted a smile. Katy patted his cheek.

"I'm not supposed to be here."

"Where's here?"

"Psshft. Mommy says this is called a 'hospital.' That means a house for sick people. I was in a hospital but I STILL don't remember being sick."

Jacob smiled and the little girl laughed.

"I wanted to know if you would be my Daddy," Katy said. "No one will tell me so I thought I would just ask you myself."

"I'd be honored to be your Daddy," Jacob said.

"No matter what?"

"No matter what. Pinky swear?"

Katy held out her pinky and they shook pinkies.

"Katherine Marlowe Roper!" Jill scolded from the doorway of the room. "What are you doing here?"

"But Mommy! I didn't touch any of the white gauze!"

Katy seemed to fly through the air when Jill lifted her from the bed.

"Hi," Jill said.

Holding Katy in her arms, she leaned over to kiss him. His left hand cupped her face while his thumb caressed her bruised cheek. His concerned eyes asked the question but Jill shook her head. Her eyes flitted to Katy. Jacob smiled.

"We haven't seen you in a while."

"Where am I?" Jacob asked.

"You have a private room. It's funny because there's been a whole bunch of people here—your family, my family, people from work, the police, your entire hockey team. This is the first time you've been alone. Well, not quite alone." Jill looked at her daughter. "You are in big trouble, Little Missy. I've been looking for you everywhere."

"Oh," Jacob said. "Don't be too mad. She's very sweet."

"He's going to be my Daddy," Katy said.

"KATY!"

"We pinky swore," Jacob said. "Plus she's a Marlowe."

"In honor of Celia M... Oh." Jill blushed. "Sorry. You don't have to..."

"Oh honey..." Jacob's energy evaporated. He closed his eyes then opened them. "I want to be her Daddy. Sometimes... things... defy..." He let out a breath. "Explanation."

She thought he was unconscious again when his eyes popped open. His eyes shifted to look at Jill then said, "Are we engaged?"

"Do you see a large diamond?" Jill held up her left hand as a joke but he was already out.

"Are you going to MARRY my Daddy?" Katy asked. "Well that's PERFECT!"

Katy clapped her hands together and Jill laughed.

~~~~~~~~~

THURSDAY NIGHT, 7 P.M.

Mike looked down the Castle's dining room table at his brother, Steve and Steve's wife, Leslie. They were as silent as Megan, Tim and Candy on the other side of the table. Jill was at the hospital for her first official "date" with Jacob. Delphie was entertaining Megan's kids and Katy in one of the sitting areas. The clinking of silverware echoed in the formal dining room.

Valerie slipped her hand into Mike's. He turned to look at her. She had lost weight this week. Tonight, her beautiful black hair was held back with a simple band. Her face was makeup free. When she smiled, he felt the same heart constricting feeling he had felt the first time she smiled at him.

"Ok," Steve said. "Since no one's going to do it, I'm going to. Frankly, I'm sick to vomit of the secrets in this family. Mike and Val invited us here for dinner and we're acting like church mice."

"What secrets?" Candy asked. Her dark eyes blazed a 'shut up' to her brother.

"YOUR secrets," Steve said.

Candy bristled.

"Meg's secrets." Megan's head jerked up to look at Steve.

"Hell, my own secrets," Steve said. "Fuck, did you know how abusive Trevor was? Anyone?"

Every head shook from side to side.

"Trevor almost raped her and Jill was like same shit different day," Mike said. "OUR baby sister sat in Walgreen's praying for her child's life because that fucker wouldn't let her go to the hospital. Why? Because *she* couldn't afford it. It makes me furious."

"Me too," Megan said. "I... I had no idea."

"We are all we have. Our parents are gone. We don't have grandparents. No more secrets," Steve said. "It's time to put it all out there on the table."

"We'll start," Leslie said. "We can't get pregnant. I have endometriosis and... we'll..."

Everyone's head turned to look at Leslie.

"We're good candidates for IVF. We're healthy, don't drink or smoke. The doctor thinks we'll be successful but..." Steve stopped talking. He looked at Leslie then nodded. "We can't afford it. We wanted to ask if maybe..."

"We'll help," Valerie said. "If you prefer to borrow the money, we can do that as well."

"I make good commissions on my painting and Val's contract was extended for another year," Mike said.

"You're not driving anymore?" Candy asked.

"I only drove so I could drive Val when she was in town," Mike said. "See there's a secret."

"We could be together and no one would know," Valerie said.

"We'd love to help you guys have a baby," Mike said. "Just if that's all right with you."

"Thanks," Leslie said.

"We're not married," Tim said.

Megan's eyes went wide and she shook her head.

"We got pregnant before we got married, then didn't want to..." Tim caught Megan's look and stopped talking. Megan's face was bright red.

"Ah shit. Who cares?" Mike asked.

Megan's red ashamed face turned to her little brother. Mike's warm smile brought tears to her eyes.

"You guys were so young and I got pregnant and..."

"You and Tim raised us," Steve said. "I don't give a crap. I can't imagine Jill cares."

"Jill knows," Tim said. "I told her when Trevor divorced her."

"I'm gay," Candy spit out in the middle of the conversation.

When everyone turned to look at her, she seemed to dissolve into the chair. Steve kicked her under the table.

"Tell them or I will," he said.

"I've been dating a girl for... a long time."

"She lives with her girlfriend Jazmyne," Steve said. "Has for the last four years. Jazmyne is a firefighter and a terrific person."

"I'm going to hell." Candy's face dropped with sorrow.

"Well, we'll be there to keep you company," Tim said. "Are you happy? Do you love her?"

Candy nodded.

"Then we're very happy for you," Megan said. "We just wanted you to be happy."

"Mike broke my nose," Steve said. "Remember I went to Hollywood the summer after college? I was on this tour of the stars houses when I saw Mike and some girl walking down a hill. I mean, I hadn't seen or heard from Mike in two years. Then there he was! So, I followed them. They cut into the backyard of this house. I..."

"He caught us in a delicate position," Valerie said. "In our own backyard, but delicate none the less. Mike hit him on a reflex."

"You DID get a new nose," Candy said. "I KNEW it!"

"Yeah," Steve said. "Valerie arranged for the surgery."

"I could have killed him. I..." Mike said. "I went to treatment about a week later. I have a secret."

"Your secret studio is in the carriage house of this house," Candy said. "We all knew that. We thought it was because you were friends with Jake."

Mike looked from face to face and everyone nodded.

"We also know about you're the artist who painted the 'unknown Denver artist painting' at the Denver Art Museum," Tim said. "Well, we guessed. Now that I've met Val... It's her isn't it?"

Valerie nodded.

"I gave it to a friend who said it was too good to be owned by a single person," Mike nodded toward the ceiling. Everyone looked up to the clouds, blue sky and sun that adorned the dining room ceiling. "I've done a bunch of the work here too. I'll show you around when we finish dinner. I actually have another secret."

Valerie's head turned to look at him. Her eyes puzzled. Mike slipped his hand into his pocket.

"Jake paid a guy to find this for you," Mike said. "He 'just figured' you'd like it back some day."

He opened his hand and there lay Valerie's original diamond engagement ring. Valerie screamed. Covering her mouth with her hands, her eyes welled with tears. His eyes held the question again. She nodded. He slipped the diamond solitaire on to her hand.

"Thao at the Art of Gold cleaned it up and fixed it. She said we could update it but I thought you'd want to..."

Valerie kissed him quiet.

CHAPTER EIGHTEEN
DETAILS! WE NEED DETAILS!
FRIDAY MORNING, 8: 07 A.M.

"Sorry I'm late," Jill said. She scooted into the booth next to Sandy at Snooze. Every Friday for the last two years, she'd met Sandy, Heather and Tanesha for breakfast at Snooze. "I had to take Katy to school. She's still a little sick so she's slooooowwwww."

"Jill!?!" The waitress asked. "Are you all right? Oh my God! I saw the news..."

"Hi Chantel," Jill nodded. "Yeah, I'm okay. Thanks."

"I...," the waitress started speaking, then realized the women were staring at her.

"Sorry, I can't really talk about it," Jill smiled.

The waitress made a sympathetic face and touched Jill's arm. "I'll just bring some coffee."

"Thanks Chantel."

"Hey, we're buying your breakfast," Tanesha said. "So you can actually eat this time."

"It's a bribe," Heather said.

"Bribe?" Jill asked. The waitress set a cup of coffee and a glass of water in front of Jill. "Thanks."

"You can't talk about Monday, right?" Heather asked.

"Criminal proceeding and all," Jill said.

"We want every single detail about Sunday night with His Hotness," Tanesha said.

"And your date last night," Sandy added.

"Oohh a date with His Hotness!" Tanesha said.

"We want to know what really happened on Monday, but..."

"Sorry," Jill said.

"You can talk about the edges. The paper said Jacob came..."

Sandy trailed off as the owner of Snooze, Jon Schlegel, came up the table. A tall thin man, he had to bend over to set a Pineapple Upside Down pancake in front of Jill.

"Hey Jill, this is our way of saying that we hope you're okay."

"Thanks Jon. With a little luck, everything will work out." Jill pushed the plate sized pancake to the middle of the table. "We'll share it."

"Well, good luck," Jon said. "I wanted you to know that you're always welcome to work here."

"Thanks Jon," Jill said. "My feet are pretty messed up. I can't work anywhere for a while. Even Pete sent me home."

"Just so you know," he said.

The moment Jon turned his back, the women dug into the pancake with gusto.

"How did you have a date with Jake Marlowe last night?" Heather asked. "Isn't he like in the hospital?"

"Mm'hmm" Jill swallowed a bite of delicious pancake. "He stopped taking pain meds mid-day so he could talk to me. He had someone from Sasa Sushi bring dinner for me. He had..."

"Cereal," the women said in unison.

"Exactly. Captain Crunch. He wanted me to try sushi since I haven't had it before. He had a bottle of sparkling rice wine for me... um, Sake? I think it's called. It was really good... nice."

"I told you," Sandy said. "Sasa is fabulous. Did you have the chocolate lava cake?"

"Yep, we shared one." Jill blushed.

"And?" Heather prodded

"He's in a hospital. We just talked," Jill said. "The nurse put Jake to sleep around ten and I went to the Castle to get Katy."

"Uh huh," Tanesha said. "And blushing girl, what did you and His Hotness talk about?"

"Sex."

Heather and Tanesha screamed with laughter.

"Details! We need details!" Sandy said.

~~~~~~~~~

"I'm sorry, Jake. I wish I had better news."

Dr. Lionel Smuyth had been Jacob's orthopedic surgeon since he fixed Jacob's knee in high school. Jacob asked him to come to review his situation and help him determine options.

"Your entire shoulder girdle is held together with more metal than bone. Your shoulder blade is... Well, time will tell."

"What does that mean, Lionel?" Jacob asked.

"Long term?" Dr. Smuyth went back to the x-rays. He held up x-ray after x-ray then reviewed the MRIs. "I'd replace the head of your humorus. When your bone fills in, you'll need surgery to reattach all of these tendons. The surgery notes say they found all the tendons and tucked them away. They may be available when you're ready."

"How long before I can work?"

Dr. Smuyth's eyebrows shot up at Jacob's question. His eyes were kind but Jacob's stomach dropped when Dr. Smuyth's usual bright smile fell. The doctor picked up Jacob's right hand.

"Tell me what you feel," Dr. Smuyth said.

He ran a capped ball point pen over Jacob's hand.

"I can feel that," Jacob said.

Dr. Smuyth shook his head.

"You have sensation, Jacob. And that's really a miracle."

"You've never sugar coated anything for me, Lionel," Jacob said. "What is going on?"

"You're having a neck fusion tomorrow."

"Lionel."

"I don't feel confident in the innervation in your arm," Dr. Smuyth said. "I won't say, 'never' but you have a long way to go before you'll swing a hammer with that arm."

"Long way?"

"I'm not going to give you a doctor hex, Jake. Don't ask me for dates, times, and exactly what will happen. We have to take this one step at a time. You have two broken transverse processes in your neck. Two!" Dr. Smuyth shook his head like he couldn't believe the question or conversation. "Tomorrow your neck will be fused. If everything goes well, and by some miracle you take it easy, you should be able to go home on Monday or Tuesday. Then it will be six weeks, at least, before your neck heals. Your bone may have filled in enough that we can replace the head of your humerus and reattach your ligaments. Then, maybe, you'll be able to start rebuilding strength in that arm. But..."

"That's six months from now?"

"At least. Every step depends on the success of the last step. Any infection, slow healing, bad guesses, not to mention surgeon foul up..." Dr. Smuyth returned to look at the x-rays. "This is a vicious injury, Jake. You're lucky to be alive."

"I'm not ungrateful, Lionel. I know how lucky I am."

Jacob closed his eyes for a moment trying to formulate the thought or question in his mind.

"You're saying that these injuries... just like that... I'm not going to be normal again."

"Yes, I'm sorry," Dr. Smuyth said. "I'd tell you that you still have use of your left arm. You're still very young. I can also tell you to never say never. I've seen amazing things happen with hard work and a positive attitude. But you know all of that."

The rest of Dr. Smuyth's visit was lost on Jacob. From the moment the doctor said, 'you know all of that,' Jacob worked to get through it.

When the doctor patted his left shoulder and walked from the room, Jacob took a full breath.

And broke down.

The thoughts flew through his head: he'd wasted the last four years babysitting his father; he threw away his last chance to do the work he loved; he would never be a carpenter again; he'd have to sit back now; he'd sit on the sidelines like a sad fuck while other guys played hockey, ran or lifted weights; he was almost free of his Lipson Construction albatross; NOW he's incapacitated; how could this happen? While he cried, his mind spewed catastrophe after drama after 'my life is over' scenario.

Out of nowhere, he heard Celia's voice: "Why haven't you stepped into your wisdom?"

Wiping his face and nose on the sheet, he blew out a breath and cleared his mind. Closing his eyes, he stretched his being. Not quite sure of what he was doing, he remembered Delphie's childhood instruction—clear your mind of thought, create an open space, breathe, let the images come...

The image of Jill walking across hardwood floors came to his mind. Her naked body was covered with goose bumps and her nipples erect. The beeswax candle she carried shook side to side with her shivers. The candle light reflected off the square cut diamond on her left ring finger. Catching his look, and lust for her, she tipped her head sideways and smiled.

"Jake?"

"Hey Molly." Jacob opened his eyes to his concerned bookkeeper. "Is it eight thirty?"

"Yes. Are you Ok? Should I get the nurse?"

"I'm okay. Thanks," Jacob said. "There's something you could do for me."

~~~~~~~~~

Aden Norsen slowed his SUV to the curb at a small bungalow near Old Towne Aurora. Getting out of the driver's seat, he went to the back hatch for his kids' backpacks and suitcases.

His children were supposed to spend two months with their mom in the summer. She reminded him of their legal arrangement just last night. Of course, her "visitation" only happened when she was in town, when she felt like having them, and when whatever else that was more important than her children was over. This year, Nuala wanted their kids today.

Of course, if this visit went the way of every other visit, the kids would get on Nuala's nerves in a couple of days. She'd "tough it out" for a couple of weeks then the phone would ring. Aden would take them home. His home. Their home in Park Hill. Even though he KNEW this visit would be like all the others, he always hoped things would be different.

"Bye, bye Daddy," his ten year old daughter, Noelle said. She hugged him then took her backpack and suitcase from him. "I'll call you tonight."

"Bye Dad," his twelve year old son, Nash, said. He hugged Aden. "See you tonight?"

"Soccer practice. I'll be there," Aden said. He gave Nash his backpack, suitcase and skateboard. "You'll..."

Nash smiled a half smile, "I'll call."

Noelle was halfway up the driveway when she turned and ran back. She threw her arms around Aden. Too cool to initiate the hug, Nash wrapped himself around Noelle and Aden.

"Love you so very much," Aden said.

Standing with his arms around his precious babies, he prayed for their safety. Every year, he walked away with a knot in the pit of his stomach. Every year, he brought two silent children home. Every year, he sat with them night after night while they cried their hearts out. Aden let out a breath and let go. The God that brought these beautiful creatures to his life will care for them.

Nash picked up Noelle's suitcase. Noelle carried Nash's skateboard and the children began their walk toward their mother's front door. As they approached, Nuala opened the front door. With a lit cigarette dangling from her lips, and an infant on her hip, Nuala was all class in her stained tank top and no bra. She raised an arm to wave at Aden.

Working not to flinch at Nuala's hairy armpit and flopping breasts, Aden smiled. He watched his babies greet their mother then turn into the house. He made it back into the driver's seat before his emotion—rage, sadness, helplessness, shame—caught up with him. Swatting the tears from his eyes, he turned down Colfax toward Denver.

He was due in Jake's hospital room at ten.

Stopping at a traffic light, Aden marveled at how life worked out. He never planned on having kids. In fact, he never thought he liked kids. But when his crazy, wild girlfriend got pregnant, he did the right thing and married her. In a desperate attempt to keep them off the streets, he started as a day laborer for Lipson Construction.

Lipson was good for him. Nuala was not. Fourteen months and another baby later, she was gone.

But Lipson stuck. He worked his way up one job at a time, one year at a time, to become a site manager. He loved being a site manager. He thought he'd retire as a site manager.

Four years and three months ago, Jake appeared at the job site. Aden had worked at Lipson almost ten years. He had seen Jake around the sites, but hadn't spoken to the owner's son before. After all, Jake was a carpenter, a college boy, not an underground man. He wasn't even a Lipson. Aden swaggered over to talk to the kid.

"I need a good man to help me out," Jake said. "Interested?"

"Hire an assistant." Aden said. "I don't mean to be rude, but I've got to get back. We're expecting..."

Aden stopped talking when Jake laughed. Aden shook his head at the kid and started to walk back toward the site trailer.

"You'd get to set your schedule."

Aden spun around to look at Jake. He was about to walk away when he realized what that kind of freedom would mean for his children's lives. He could finally coach a soccer team, participate in Noelle's art classes... and... He squinted his eyes at Jake.

"What do you want?"

"I told you. I need a good man to help me out. I'm sure money's not important to you but the job comes with a fifteen-hundred dollar raise."

"A year?" Aden asked

"A month." Jake smiled.

Aden did the math in his head. Fifteen hundred dollars was a chunk of change but less than a third of what he was making. How serious was this kid?

"Two thousand," Aden said. "And annual raises. This doesn't cap my salary."

"Done."

And, as they say, the rest was history.

He'd worked for about six months before he realized Jake was grooming him, Aden Norsen, to take over Lipson Construction. Jake made him finish college and forced him through an MBA program. Scumbag, loser, dropout Aden Norsen was an MBA.

The thought still made Aden laugh.

Pulling up to the Detroit Street workshop, Aden made his way through the tunnels to the Castle. He tapped on the kitchen door and was met by Delphie. Delphie gave him a small box and a hug.

"They'll be all right?" Aden asked.

"They'll be home tomorrow," Delphie said.

"Tomorrow?"

"Tomorrow night late."

"Thanks." Aden hugged her again.

"Enjoy yourself today!"

Delphie raised an eyebrow then closed the door on his face. Aden made an irritated face at the door. Delphie always told him just enough to relieve his anxiety and peak his curiosity. She saved the full story for later, after it was all over, as a kind of 'I told you so.'

Anyway, he planned to work today then drink himself to sleep tonight. That's what he did every time he left the kids at Nuala's house. In fact, he already told Jake he was going to be hung over tomorrow. Laying in that hospital bed, wrapped in gauze, and sprouting tubes like hair, Jacob Marlowe laughed at him.

Aden tucked the box into his pocket and went through the tunnels to the workshop. Back in the car, he worked his way down Colfax to Colorado Blvd. He had just enough time to run a couple errands before getting to Jake's room.

~~~~~~~~~

Valerie waved from the side door of the Castle. Her publicist, Jennifer Lowe, weaved through the paparazzi with expert ease. Valerie hugged her publicist. Jen pulled back to give Valerie a long look.

"I don't know about this whole marriage thing, but you look great," Jen said. "A little thin. How's your brother?"

"Better, thanks. Yeah, I've lost weight this week," Valerie said. "But I feel good. Really good."

"You're sure you want to go out in public with this guy?" Jen asked.

"My husband?" Valerie asked. "Yes. I want him to be a part of my life. I thought we could introduce him to everyone at a party next week? Maybe Friday?"

"What about Wes? He's sure acting like he wants you back something awful."

"Awful is the word." Valerie shook her head. "That's all over. Plus he texted me to say he has a new 'girl.'" Valerie imitated Wes's voice, "No hysterics, Val. I can't wait for you forever."

Jen shook her head. "Will you..."

"I'm exactly where I want to be" Valerie said.

"Ok, let's take a look at this guy," Jen said.

"My..."

"Right, your husband," Jen said. Under her breath she added, "You're going to have to say that a million times."

"He's painting in his studio out back," Valerie said. "I have to call him."

Mike answered immediately and said he would be right over.

"I love this house, Val," Jen said. "It's very... gothic modern. Is this his house?"

"My mother bought it before her death. Mike and my brother fixed it up. Of course, Mike did the murals, ceilings and detail work," Valerie said.

"He's very talented."

"He is. I'm here probably six months out of the year. A week here... a week there. We have our own private apartment, plus all of this."

Mike came in from the kitchen wiping his hands on a rag. Seeing Val, his face lit up in a bright smile.

"When did you get back?"

As if drawn by a magnet, Valerie fit under the arm he wrapped around her. He kissed her head.

"Jen wanted to meet you," Valerie said.

Jen had to wipe the stunned look from her face. Mike was almost the exact opposite of any of Val's other men. He was big, muscular, and very hairy. He looked like the kind of person you'd find at the end of a hockey stick or maybe on top of a John Deere. He was not the kind of man you'd find standing next to a movie star. Jen shook her head.

"He's not going to work," Jen said.

"What?" Mike asked. "Why?"

"We need to get Ramon," Jen said.

Valerie nodded.

~~~~~~~~~

Turning right, Aden parked in the lot behind Denver Health. On the elevator to Jake's room, he went through the list of things they needed to accomplish. With Ashforth's swinging straight pipe wrench, Lipson Construction ceased to function. Every job site closed. Everyone–employees and clients–held their collective breath in hopes that Jacob would survive.

They had to restart Lipson Construction.

Today.

Then he'd get drunk.

On Jack Daniels? No, maybe Johnny Walker. One night a year, Aden allowed himself a serious drunk. Of course, every year for the last four, Jake happened to have some emergency on the night of his planned drunk. Tonight, Jake was in the hospital. Four years of sobriety would be broken tonight.

"Hey Molly," Aden said. "Jake."

"How are you?" Jake asked. Molly gave Aden a hug on her way out of the room.

"I'm... all right," Aden said. "See you Molly."

"How did it go?" Jake asked.

"It sucked. It always sucks," Aden said. "Delphie says they'll be home tomorrow night."

"You need to renegotiate that custody."

"Tell me something I don't know," Aden said. "I just keep hoping she'll go away."

"That's not likely," Jake said. "Did you get it?"

"Yep, when does the illustrious Jill get here?" Aden asked.

"She and a friend are stopping by," Jake said.

"Should we get started?" Aden asked. "Or wait for them to come and go?"

"Let's see what we can get done," Jake said.

Aden began setting up their laptop computers. He was almost done when the door to the room opened. Turning to catch a first look at Jacob's Jill, he gasped. The door slammed shut.

"That's the girl," Aden whispered.

~~~~~~~~

"We start at Nordstrom's and we'll work our way to Macy's." Sandy outlined their shopping plan on the elevator up to Jacob's room. "After all, you need all new clothing for your new lifestyle."

"What about my feet?"

"What about your feet?" Sandy asked. "You can get a personal shopper!"

Jill laughed.

"Personally, I think I deserve a few pairs of shoes myself. You know, best friend tax. Can't you hear Jimmy Choo saying come and get me!?" Sandy said. "It's a Platinum American Express card?"

"I'm going to pay him back!" Jill exclaimed. "It's just for Katy… her meds…"

"But he told you to take it shopping today?" Sandy asked. Stepping off the elevator, she followed Jill to Jacob's room. "Do I have to watch you pay him back because I like the details but I'm not really…"

Sandy pushed the door open. Standing in the doorway, she saw a man kneeling by an electrical plug. When he looked up, she gasped. Sandy grabbed Jill and pulled her from the room. Sandy slammed closed the door.

"What?" Jill asked.

"That's the guy."

CHAPTER NINETEEN
SO I'M ASKING...

"Maybe you can stop going to every hair stylist in the city," Jacob said.

"I... I... I..."

"Go."

"But..."

"Go!" As Aden ran toward the door, Jacob yelled, "Just leave the..."

Aden stopped at the door and threw the box to Jacob. Aden ran past a stunned girl standing at the door.

"Jill?" Aden asked as he passed.

The girl nodded.

"Aden. Go on in. He's waiting for you."

Just as Aden rounded the nurses' station, he heard the elevator bell ring. With a burst of speed, he slipped through the closing elevator doors.

~~~~~~~~~

"Hi," Jill said.

Jacob scooted over in the bed. Jill sat down next to him. She leaned toward him, closed her eyes, and was swept away, again, by his lips. Each delicate kiss led to a deeper kiss. The motion of his lips brought a well of warmth that rose through her core. If she thought it possible, Jill would swear she had kiss orgasms. Breaking off the kiss was like coming to the end of a great ride at Disneyland. He left her willing to wait in a long, long line for the chance to take the ride again.

"I have something for you," Jacob said.

His left hand stroked her hair. The bruise on her cheekbone was turning purple and a little yellow. He kissed her bruised cheek.

"I can't really get on bended knee, but the moment I can, I will."

Jill jerked back from him. She puzzled at his statement. Shaking her head slightly, she said, "What?"

"Shh," Jacob said. "I've practiced."

"You... I... I mean..."

Jacob sighed. Jill wasn't going to make this easy for him. He put his fingertips over her sputtering mouth.

"Will you marry me?"

Jacob removed his fingertips from her mouth. Jill's face broke in to a huge blushing smile.

"Really? I mean, I know that I said that I would marry you... and you asked at Pete's but..." Jill's words came in a flood. "You haven't even known me a week. And we've only had sex once and you don't know... I mean, I suck in bed... and I have a child and..."

Jacob flopped back on the bed. Jill laughed at the exasperated look on his face.

"Well what about the sex thing?" Jill asked. "I really don't know anything and..."

"I think people learn from each other. I don't know anything, not one thing, about really pleasing you," Jacob said. "But I'm more than ready to spend a lifetime learning from you."

Jill blushed and looked at her hands.

"So what do you say?" Jacob asked.

At that moment, the nurse propped opened the door to Jacob's room. Two male attendants followed the nurse into the room. Moving quickly, the nurse began unhooking Jacob from the machines by his bed. Jill stood from the bed.

"What's going on?" Jacob asked.

"There's an opening in the surgical suite. The doctor that was here this morning?"

"Smuyth?"

"He put you on an unofficial waiting list," the nurse shrugged. "They'll do your fusion today."

The attendants pushed the bed away from the wall.

"Right this moment?" Jacob asked.

"It was a last minute cancellation. The scheduled patient spiked a fever," the nurse said. "You'll be out this evening sometime. I'm sure you two can talk then."

Rolling toward the door, Jacob retrieved the box from its hiding place under the covers. He tossed it to Jill. She caught it.

"I love you, Jill. Go shopping. I'll see you tonight. Tell Aden to check his Blackberry."

The room door closed and Jill looked at the box in her hand. She opened the tattered old box to find a plush ring box. Biting her lip, she couldn't decide what to do.

Should she wait for Jacob?

Should she just open it?

ARG!

~~~~~~~~

The closing elevator doors clipped Aden's shirt then bounced open again. Sandy's head jerked up when he rushed into the elevator. Her stunned face switched to annoyance.

"Are you stalking me now?" Sandy asked. She pressed the Lobby button over and over again until the elevator doors closed again.

"Stalking?" Aden asked. "I... Listen, I've looked all over the city for you. I've been to every hairstylist Jake or I could find."

Sandy raised an eyebrow and smirked. "You came to MY salon."

Aden nodded.

"Ok, you don't want to talk to me. I get that. But I... I'd like to understand. Jake says people tell you what's going on if you ask. So I'm asking."

Sandy crossed her arms over her chest and shook her head.

"We worked out together for six years. Same machines. Same weights. Same time. We talked... a lot... every day... for years. Then the one time I asked you out, you never came back to the gym."

"Oh I go, just not when you're there."

"What did I do?" Aden asked. "I asked you out. You said you'd like to go out with me. You said you'd been waiting for me to ask for a long time. Then you changed your number or gave me a fake or... I thought you liked me."

"Hmmfpt."

"Well I liked you... like you."

The elevator bounced when it hit the ground floor. The doors slid open.

Sandy tilted her head to the side. She sneered, then said, "But you love your WIFE? Is that it?"

Aden grabbed her arm when she pressed past him. Sandy glowered at him.

"Will you hear me out?"

Knowing she had to wait for Jill anyway, Sandy shrugged. She would never admit it, but she had missed him. She'd always looked forward to seeing him at the gym. Even now, when she KNEW he wasn't there, she still looked for his car in the parking lot.

Holding her arm tight, he guided them through the hospital to a shady spot just outside the door.

"I'm not married," Aden said. "I was married... a long time ago. But I haven't been married in ten years. I haven't even dated in... eight or nine years. Why do you think I am married?"

"Why should I believe you?"

"We can go upstairs and ask Jake," Aden said.

"Right like a guy isn't going to lie for his buddy."

"Jacob Marlowe is my boss, and my friend. We aren't buddies. Plus, Jacob Marlowe doesn't lie. He just doesn't."

"Oh," Sandy said. "I... I thought you were a biker."

"A biker?"

"Because of your tattoos," Sandy said.

"Oh," Aden flushed. His arms, neck and back had been covered with tattoos. Thanks to laser technology, his adolescent gestures at identity were almost gone. "No, I work for Jake. I'm his assistant."

"Jill and I went to high school with his assistant."

"Molly?"

Sandy nodded her head.

"Molly is Jake's bookkeeper for his rehabilitation business. I work for Lipson. Jake has me and an other assistant, Blane."

"Oh," Sandy said.

"Why did you think I was married?"

"I went into the locker room and this girl told me line and verse about you, your wife, your kids, and all this stuff. I..."

"Tall? Thin? White blonde hair?" Aden asked.

"Very pretty. A lot prettier than me," Sandy said.

"Lexi."

"Right. Lexi."

"I call her Lexi Luther because she's like my arch-nemesis," Aden said. "Okay. Well that makes more sense. Thanks."

Aden and Sandy stood facing each other. The uncomfortable silence stretched.

"Are you married?"

"No," Aden said. "I was married. She left when our daughter was a couple months old. We weren't actually divorced until four years ago. I kind of hoped she would disappear but... Jake made me file."

"Jake's had a big impact on you," Sandy said.

"You could say that," Aden replied. "I have two kids. They live with me most of the time. Would you like to see their pictures?"

Sandy nodded. Aden opened his wallet and pulled out his favorite picture of Nash and Noelle.

"I dropped them at their Mom's house before I came here. I... They're my life."

"Why would Lexi say all that stuff?"

"Oh," Aden sighed. "Because I fucked up. After Nuala left, that's my ex-wife, I wasn't in a great place. I was still... drinking... and I was going to be a rock star. Mostly, I worked during the days and spent the nights at clubs. I didn't know what it even meant to have kids... I thought women took care of all of that. Real evolved, huh. I thought if I got another woman right away, I could keep living the way I was... you know, not have to change. Lexi and I... got together and ... It didn't go well."

"What happened?" Sandy asked.

"I can't imagine you want to hear all of this crap," Aden said.

"Actually..." Sandy said. She dared to look at his face for the first time. "I do want to hear about it. My dad left my mom when I was a couple months old... and I have a particular interest in stories just like this... stories like mine."

Aden sighed.

"Lexi moved in right away. But Noelle, my daughter, never liked her. She cried until I got home from work. I was at work one day when Lexi called to say she had moved out. Fuck me and fuck my stupid kids. I..." Aden shook his head. "It was totally my fault. I just had no idea of what I was doing. What happened with you?"

"My mom got jobs to support us. It was hard on her... really hard... like it's been for Jill. She met my step-dad when I was eight or nine." Sandy smiled. "He was Catholic, so we all converted. And, he was a really great guy. He was my Dad."

"Was?"

"He smoked... He was older than Mom by fifteen years or so. He died a couple years ago. Lung cancer. So, you can see that I want to know what happened with you and your kids."

"I was such an idiot. People at work leave their dogs in the car so I thought I'd leave the kids in the car. They mostly sleep anyway. I would see them on my breaks."

"WHAT?"

"I know," Aden said. "I told you I was an idiot."

"What happened?"

"I went on my first break and I saw this woman by the car. She was singing to Noelle and rocking her side to side. My son, Nash, was sitting on the hood of the car eating a candy bar. When I got close, she looked up and said, 'She's really just lonely. How about if I take them today?' I was like, 'What?'" Aden laughed. "That was Jake's mom, Celia. Big Sam Lipson came up behind me. He looked at me, then Celia. He just laughed. They started a daycare for Lipson employees the next day and you know what? A hundred kids showed up that day and a hundred more the following Monday. Nobody had day care for their kids. No accidents, that's what Celia said. 'It's no accident Sam invited me to lunch today.' I... Yeah."

~~~~~~~~~

"Oooh Val, what plow did you find him behind?" Ramon said. A slight Asian man, Ramon's exaggerated inflection and silk, leopard print caftan announced "GAY HOLLYWOOD STYLIST" like a neon sign. "He's absolutely Neanderthal dreamy. Look at all that hair!"

"I met him skiing on Copper Mountain," Valerie said. "I was twelve."

"Oooh," the man said. "Well, he's a big boy now."

He reached to squeeze Mike's leg, and Mike slapped his hand away. When Ramon lifted Mike's shirt to ogled his flat stomach, Mike stepped back.

"You must take your clothing off," the man lisped.

"No," Mike said.

Mike backed away. Ramon took a step toward him. Mike stalked out the back door toward his studio. He heard Ramon and Valerie laugh the entire way across the garden.

~~~~~~~~~

Sandy and Aden stood together in close companionable silence. Sandy shifted from foot to foot. Her familiar draw to Aden made her even more uncomfortable. She was about to leave when she saw Jill step of the hospital elevator.

"Thanks for talking to me," Aden said. "I better get back up there."

"There's Jill," Sandy said. "Hey. I thought I'd have to pry you away."

"They took Jacob to get his neck surgery today. He told me to go shopping. I... I think I should stay here but..."

"Ah shit," Aden said.

"Jacob said to tell you to check your Blackberry," Jill said. "I packed up the computers."

Jill gave Aden his computer bag. Aden dug out his Blackberry from the front pocket.

"Excuse me," Aden said. He stepped away from Jill and Sandy to read his daily list from Jacob.

'Heya Aden,

Here's your list:

1. Take the girls shopping.
2. Tell them about Val's party next week. Make sure they both get something... nice. ;)
3. Have fun tonight.

Oh, and the sites? They ready to start again tomorrow morning so don't have too much fun tonight. You'll need to cover for me tomorrow.

-- J'

Aden curled his lip. Even in the hospital, Jacob Marlowe managed to disrupt Aden's drinking plans.

The next email was from Blane, their assistant, with confirmation from every site manager that the sites would start up tomorrow morning at 5 AM.

The last email from Jacob said, 'Get the ring box back from Jill.'

Shaking his head, Aden wandered to Sandy and Jill. Jill was holding the box out to Sandy.

"May I have that?" Aden asked.

"But… but…"

Aden opened the ring box to show Jill that it was empty. He raised an eyebrow and laughed at her shocked face.

"You play with the Marlowe, you've got to expect a little intrigue."

"But he asked me and… I…"

"Did you say yes?" Aden asked.

"I…"

"When you're ready to say 'yes,' there will be a ring in this box. At least I hope so."

Aden made an 'It's my ass if it's not' face. Jill and Sandy laughed. He bowed slightly in his best butler imitation.

"Mr. Jacob has asked me to take you ladies shopping. He would like me to invite you to a fete at the Castle hosted by Miss Valerie in a week's time."

"What?" Sandy asked.

"Val's having a party with all her Hollywood friends. She wants to celebrate Jake's survival and introduce Mike to her friends. Jake wanted to invite Jill as his date. He thought Jill would feel more comfortable if her friends were there."

"Oh… We would mix with Hollywood people… But…" Jill bit the inside of her lip.

"Good thing you're taking us shopping," Sandy said. "You buying?"

"Mr. Jacob," Aden said.

"Great. Jill? Will you call Tanesha and Heather?"

While Jill dialed her cell phone, Sandy looked at Aden.

"How old are you?"

"38. You?"

"26."

"Is that a problem?"

Sandy shook her head. "I'm really sorry. I should have asked, but…"

"I understand," Aden said.

"Do you still want to…?"

"I have to coach soccer at 5 but I'm otherwise free today. You?"

"I work from two to eight but…"

"Perfect," Aden said. "What if we shop this morning and I'll take you to dinner tonight?"

Sandy blushed, smiled, then nodded.

~~~~~~~~~

"Honey, please," Valerie pleaded. "I want you to share all of my life. That means you have to look the part."

Mike looked at her then sagged. He followed her to the main level of the house. A severe matronly woman stood in the middle of the main Castle living room. The complete opposite of the flamboyant Ramon, she arched a penciled eyebrow at Mike then shook her head.

"Neeooo." She annunciated her 'no' as if she was Peppy Le Pew.

Mike raised his eyebrows at her. Not sure of what to do, he held his hand out to the woman, "I'm Mike."

The woman looked at Mike's paint stained hand and crossed her arms.

"You cannot take this… this… creature out in public," the woman said.

"What?" Valerie asked. "Why?"

"He is… too old, too hairy and too…" The woman made a disgusted face.

"But Wes is 67 years old. Mike's only 32 years old," Valerie said.

"Wesford takes care of his skin. What products do you use on your face?" the woman asked.

"Um." Mike felt like he was answering a trick question. "My face?"

"You see, completely unworkable." The woman sneered at Mike. Looking at Val, she said, "Why is it that you left Wes? He was the perfect companion for you. Tall, thin like you are… not so… beefy hillbilly…"

"Sounds like you don't need me anymore," Mike said. "Val, honey, I'm going back to my studio. Nice to meet you, ma'am."

The woman's harping voice drifted through the kitchen. Standing at the garden door, Mike had his fill . Turning in place, he stormed back to the living room. The woman waved her finger in Val's face while Valerie wept.

"Get out of my house," he said to the woman. "You have no right to come in here and say anything—to me or to my wife. You certainly don't know me. You can't know Val if you talk to her like this."

He picked up the woman's bag and threw it out the side Castle door. He held the door and pointed for her to go.

The woman looked from Valerie to Mike.

"You have ruined your career," she said.

"I don't care," Valerie said. "Please leave."

With a smug I-told-you-so look, the woman marched out of the door. Mike scooped up Valerie and held her until she stopped crying.

"We'll figure something out," he whispered into her hair.

"I don't care if I ever act again," she said.

"Oh honey, we don't live like that. You love acting. You can do what you love. We just have to figure out how to make it happen."

Valerie nodded and wiped her tears.

"Who's next?" Mike said.

"I have a facial appointment. I thought I'd leave you with her but… I forgot how awful she can be… "

Mike held her face between his big hands. His eyes caressed her beautiful face then he kissed her lips.

"I love you, Val. Whatever you need is fine. You like that Ramon guy.. um, person. Why don't we talk to him tonight?"

Valerie gave him a watery smile then nodded. He walked her through the tunnels to her Mustang. Valerie clung to him before getting in the car. He waited until she was down the street before he went back to the house.

Laughing, he made his way back to his studio. Then panic set in.

He'd waited a life time to be with Val. What if he wasn't right for her life? He was going to lose Valerie because he was too hairy-beefy-hillbilly. There was no way to fix any of those things.

Right?

CHAPTER TWENTY
HE SAID, 'NO MATTER WHAT'

Jill thought she knew everything there was to know about Sandy. They had been best friends since Sandy converted to Catholicism and Jill made it home from Costa Rica. They shared every trial, every tribulation and every triumph.

But Jill had never seen Sandy in love, or even in like, for that matter. In fact, Jill was certain Sandy would never let any man get close to her. Certainly, not after what her 'real' Dad did to her on his weekends.

Standing in front of a dressing room mirror at Nordstrom's, Jill felt a stab of intense jealousy. Sandy and that cutie, Aden, had flirted and chatted the entire way to the mall. They weren't ignoring her. They were just consumed with each other.

As fast as Jill's jealousy came, it disappeared leaving her strong desire for Sandy's happiness in it's wake. Like Galadriel in that Ring movie, Jill felt like she had passed a test–The Girlfriend Jealousy Test.

Jill wanted Sandy to be happy. Period.

She squinted to herself in the mirror. She had to talk to Aden. But what should she say?

Should she tell him about Sandy's prick father? No.

She could tell him Sandy was only promiscuous to keep people away. Yeah, that's not going to work. But if she didn't tell him, Sandy would push it, sleep with him then dump him like she did every other man. Crap. Jill wrinkled her nose in the mirror.

Coming out of the dressing room, she saw Aden shake his head at Sandy. He gave her another skirt. Sandy wagged her eyebrows at Jill when she went into the dressing room. This was Jill's chance.

"You like Sandy a lot," Jill said. She sat next to him.

Aden's head jerked to look at Jill.

"Is it that obvious?"

"Yeah." Jill smiled at Aden. "Go really slow."

Jill said it in such a low voice that she wasn't sure Aden even heard her. Aden made no indication he heard anything. Instead, he stood to greet Sandy as she came from the dressing room. Jill joined him. Together they encouraged Sandy to get something a little more Hollywood and a little less Hollywood Boulevard.

Sandy laughed then pulled Jill into the dressing room with her.

"Well, what do you think?" Sandy asked.

"About the skirt?"

"Aden. He's the guy from the gym that I..."

"I remember." Jill took the skirt from Sandy and put it on an hanger. "I think he's great! I've told you that for years and years. Did you find out about his wife?"

"He's divorced. Like you told me, it was just some jealous girl," Sandy said. She pulled her jeans up. "You don't think he's too old for me?"

"I've never thought he was too old for you, Sandy," Jill said. "I liked him when you talked about working out with him. Now that I've met him, I really like him. He's smart and funny and cute. I love his smile and he smiles at you...a lot."

"What would Tanesha and Heather say?"

"They'll say what they always say," Jill said.

Together they said, "How big is his dick?" They laughed.

Sandy picked up her purse then impulsively hugged Jill.

"Thanks," Sandy said.

"Just go for it," Jill said. "You've always been really happy around him. You seem really happy today. Why not just enjoy that?"

Sandy nodded.

Watching Sandy greet Aden, Jill smiled to herself. Her little plan worked.

Sandy let Aden hold her hand when they walked through the mall. Sandy even did the unheard of–let him buy them coffee at Starbucks. Sandy never let a man buy something for her. Period.

When Aden dropped them at Denver Health, Sandy asked if he might take her to work. While Jill waved, Sandy made funny faces out the passenger window of his SUV. Smiling, Jill went into the hospital to see if Jacob was out of surgery.

Maybe both Sandy and Jill could find love. Jill beamed with delight.

Love.

Yeah.

~~~~~~~~~

Mike was in a complete panic. Pacing back and forth in the Castle kitchen, his mind worked overtime to convince him that he was not right for Val. He was too ugly! Not Hollywood enough! Too hairy! Those stylists knew the truth. Valerie couldn't be seen in public with him. Sure they'd spent a lot of time together over the years. But it was always in private, away from the camera. Who wanted to be married to someone they couldn't be seen in public with??

With his panic, his rage grew.

Why had he even tried? How could he ever believe she would be his partner? His wife? Who did he think he was? He wasn't famous! He wasn't a star or a producer or a model or anything but a fucked up traumatized asshole. Jerking open the liquor cabinet, he reached for a bottle of whiskey. With his hand on the bottle, he saw the phone number he wrote on the cabinet for moments just like these.

"Yeah."

"I need..."

"Where are you?" she asked.

"Castle," Mike said.

"We just got back. Meet us at the workshop. We can't deal with the photographers," she said. "Get going, Michael. We're going to lunch."

Mike sighed.

Alex Hargreaves's voice always meant freedom and safety. Help was on the way. He wasn't alone. Mike's panic seeped from his pores. Alex would save him.

Again.

Mike almost skipped through the tunnels. He paced the workshop for five full minutes before Alex Hargreaves's Jeep CJ screeched to a stop on Detroit street. Alex, John Drayson, and a couple other guys piled out of the Jeep.

"Annie's for lunch?" Alex asked. She hugged him then kissed his cheek. "How's Jake?"

"He's in surgery. He should be out in an hour or so," Mike said. He pulled the workshop door closed. "But he should be home in a couple days."

"That's great news," John said.

The men greeted him with hugs and pats on the back. Mike fell in beside them for the short walk to Annie's Café.

He was going to be all right.

~~~~~~~~~

"Hi." Jill leaned over Jacob's bed in the Recovery Room.

"Hi. How did you get in here?" Jacob asked.

"I told the nurse I was your wife."

"We got married? Did I miss our wedding night too?"

Jill laughed.

"Was I amazing?" Jacob asked.

"I hope so," Jill said.

~~~~~~~~~

"Chocolate chip?" Delphie asked.

"Yes! Yes! Yes! Can we make brownies?!? Mommy likes brownies and I like brownies and I bet my Jacob likes brownies and I bet my new Auntie..."

Katy stopped talking. Her face scrunched up in puzzlement.

"Valerie?"

"Right, Valerie, likes brownies and I can bring some to Aunt Meg's house tonight. I go to Aunt Meg's house every, every, every Friday night. THIS time, I'll bring brownies!"

Delphie lifted Katy onto the counter in the main kitchen of the Castle. Delphie retrieved Katy from school early so they could spend some time together.

"I thought you wanted cookies," Delphie said.

"Aren't brownies a kind of cookie?" Katy asked. She took a sipper cup of milk from Delphie.

Delphie nodded her head at Katy's logic. Moving around the kitchen, Delphie pulled all the ingredients for brownies from the cupboards and refrigerator.

"Would you like to crack the eggs?"

"Yes! Yes! Yes!" Katy clapped her hands and bounced on the counter. "I NEVER get to really cook. They say I'm too little but I'm FOUR. FOUR is not too little to do anything."

Delphie held Katy's hand and they cracked an egg together. Katy squealed with delight when the liquid dropped into the bowl.

"I wanted to ask you about being four," Delphie said. She gave another brown egg to Katy. "Together?"

Katy bashed the egg against the bowl. The egg crushed in her hand.

"Ooh not so hard," Delphie said. Using a dishtowel, Delphie wiped the egg from the girl's hand.

"I'm sorry!" Katy's dark eyes filled with tears. "Did I ruin the brownies??"

"No honey," Delphie said.

"Oh good." Katy held her hand out for another egg and Delphie laughed.

"Yes, just like that. Tap, tap, tap," Delphie said. "You're three years old."

"I AM NOT! I AM FOUR!" Katy shouted. Her lip vibrated and tears dropped from her eyes. "I'm no baby! Three year olds are BABIES. I'm a BIG girl."

"Katherine, you can only be what you are."

"NO! Don't say that! NO! NO! NO! I'm FOUR."

Delphie raised her eyebrows at the little girl. While Katy worked through her tantrum, Delphie set up the blender. She plugged it in next to Katy.

"Would you like to blend?"

"Yes." The storm of emotion left Katy's face bright red. "Are you mad at me?"

"No, honey. I don't understand why four is better than three," Delphie said.

"It just is."

"Hold it steady." With on hand on the blender and one arm around the child, Delphie reassured the child. Katy leaned into Delphie's warmth.

"I had a Daddy..." Katy whispered.

While tears dropped from Katy's eyes, Delphie's hand moved softly over Katy's back.

"He didn't love me... I tried to be really, really good but he didn't even like me... even one bit. He was always mad... at me."

Delphie turned off the blender. Keeping her arm around the little girl, she dug in the bag for a handful of chocolate chips. She opened her hand to the crying girl. Katy took one chip after another until Delphie's hand was empty.

"He didn't want stupid baby like me. He made Mommy so sad. She cried forever." Katy shifted away from Delphie. She whispered, "and it was all my fault."

Delphie held Katy in a tight hug.

"I woke up in that place... that hospital place? And I thought Mommy left me too."

"Your Mommy will never ever leave you."

"But she might if she finds out I'm bad."

"Oh honey, how are you bad?"

"I'm a needy, whiney, stupid baby." Katy's voice was barely over a whisper.

At her statement, Delphie heard a snort then felt movement behind her. Delphie stepped aside to let Jill hold Katy. While Delphie finished preparing the brownies, Jill and Katy cried and whispered back and forth. Delphie was about to leave the kitchen when Jill stepped away from Katy.

"She'd like to ask you something," Jill said.

Katy's hand twirled in her hair. She whispered into Jill's ear.

"Ask her, Katy-baby," Jill said. "She won't lie to you."

"Do you think I'm a needy, whiney, stupid baby?" Katy asked.

"I think you are a beautiful, funny, smart girl. It's a pleasure to know you," Delphie said. "But I also think you're three years old."

"But do you think I'm a needy..."

"No Katherine. You are not a needy, whiney, stupid baby."

Katy's face scrunched up as if she was thinking about something hard or complicated.

"Mommy says sometimes people don't know what they're saying. She said my old Daddy wasn't telling the truth when he said that about me," Katy said. "Do you think my Jacob wasn't telling the truth when he said he would be my Daddy?"

Delphie laughed. The timer rang for the brownies and she pulled the pan from the oven. She tossed several handfuls of chocolate chips on top of the hot brownies. Holding another handful of chips out to Katy, Delphie said, "I've known your Jacob a long, long time. I've never known Jacob to say something he didn't mean."

"He said, 'No matter what.' And we pinky swore. Does 'No matter what' mean that when I'm a needy, whiney, stupid baby he will STILL be my Daddy?"

"No matter what," Delphie said. "I think that's true for all of us."

Delphie made a movement with her hand. Valerie came into the kitchen from the sitting room where she had been secretly listening.

"I'll be your Auntie forever," Valerie said.

"I'll be your Mommy all of my life," Jill said.

"And I'll be your Delphie."

Katy nodded her head.

"Ok, I'll be three."

~~~~~~~~~

He hadn't meant to kiss her. But she leaned in and... Aden could barely breathe. Desire pumped through him like he was fifteen again. With effort, he stepped back. Jill said go slow but oh my god...

"I'm sorry," he said. "Tomorrow is a very big day for me. And..."

"What is it?" Sandy said.

"I can't have anything in my life right now that's not one-hundred percent," Aden said.

He took her hand and led her from under the bright porch light to the porch steps.

"What do you mean?" Sandy asked. She sat next to him on the step.

"There's not one thing I'd like more than to.. be.. with you... tonight." Aden fumbled for words. "That kiss was... incredible."

Sandy blushed. She took a few slow breaths to slow her panic filled heart. "Why don't we go inside?"

"Because... I... I can't," he said.

"We don't have to do anything. I mean Jill and Jacob just slept in the same bed. We could..."

"I don't have that kind of self control," Aden said. "No, Sandy. I can't do that."

"Why is tomorrow such a big day?" Sandy asked.

"Tomorrow is the first day I will act as the head of Lipson Construction. If I didn't know better, Jacob set this up to get me out there."

"Head of Lipson Construction? I thought you were an assistant."

"I'm supposed to take over the running of Lipson Construction in

January," Aden said.

"Oh," Sandy said. Her heart sank. He was saying she wasn't good enough for him. "I can see why you don't want to..."

"I want to. You have no idea how much I want to."

Sandy turned so she could look at his face. Her eyes reviewed the shape of his brow, his eyes and the set of his mouth. There was no lie in Aden Norsen's face.

"What's going on?" Sandy asked.

"I'd like to date you, see if we work—you and I - and go slow. As much as I wish I did, I don't have Jacob's skill at figuring the future. I have to go one tiny step at a time."

"Date?"

"Yeah. Date… exclusively. Like I hoped you might be my date to Valerie's party next week," Aden said. "And I wondered if you were available for dinner tomorrow night."

"You want to date," Sandy said. "Me?"

"I'm not much of a catch," Aden said. "I have two small kids and I work a lot. You're young. You should enjoy your unfettered time."

"Porn? Prostitutes?"

"I got over porn decades ago," Aden said. "I've never paid any woman for sex. Before you ask, I'm only attracted to women."

"Diseases?"

"They check us every year at Employee Health. I'm clean. No diabetes either. You?"

Sandy shook her head. She didn't make her usual 'just boy crazy' joke.

"Other girlfriends?"

"Not in years," Aden said. "I have two small kids. I'm their only parent. And I work a lot."

"Date?"

"Exclusively."

"Me?"

"Yes, Sandy." Aden flushed. Humiliated, he was about to get up when, for no reason at all, he said, "Dinner tomorrow? I'll be exhausted. It's my long day."

"Saturday is my long day too," Sandy said. "I'd like to see your house. Before I decide, I'd like to see your house."

"I'll make dinner. Can I pick you up?"

"I get off at six," Sandy said.

"I'll pick you up at work."

"Great."

Smiling and blushing, they stood in front of each other. Aden kissed

Sandy's cheek and went to his car. Sandy stood on the porch waving until he was out of sight. Turning into her building, she took the stairs two at a time to her apartment. When her black and while cat Cleo gave her a scolding, she started laughing. She laughed as she fed Cleo and changed for bed. Staring at the ceiling, she absolutely beamed.

Aden wanted to date… her… exclusively!

CHAPTER TWENTY-ONE
WHERE YOU BELONG
SATURDAY MORNING, 3:30 AM

Jill spun the empty ceramic mug on the table in the main Castle kitchen. Not wanting to bother anyone, she sat alone in the dark. Without work, or Katy, Jill felt lost. Mike and Valerie had even taken Sarah and Scooter to the fishing cabin overnight.

And Jacob was out of the picture. The nurse caught him working yesterday afternoon and called the doctor. They sedated him until Sunday just to keep him still long enough to heal.

For the first time in her life, Jill just had Jill to think about.

"But Jill is so boring," she said.

"Is she?" a male voice said from behind her.

Jill turned to see a man come into the kitchen. He retrieved a mug from the cabinet and poured himself a cup of coffee.

"You're Celia's hot boyfriend. That's what she called you. Her 'hot boyfriend,'" Jill said. "I used to see you guys walking when I got off work."

"We walked you home a number of times," he said. "I'm Sam. Sam Lipson. We passed in the hospital but with emotions high, I imagine you don't remember much."

He held his hand out for her to shake. Jill shook his hand.

"You're Jacob's father."

"Valerie's too," he said. "It's nice to see you again. Celia was in so much pain those last months. The only thing that helped was walking. We'd walk for hours. Celia was always excited to walk you home. You brought her a lot of joy that year."

He held up the coffee pot and Jill nodded. He filled her cup then sat down next to her.

"You don't seem very happy," he said. "I can explain all the complications but my guess is that you aren't sitting in the dark here wondering about my life."

"Oh." Jill nodded. "Yeah."

"What's wrong, Jill?"

Jill looked at the man sitting next to her. His eyes held the same patient receptive quality she found so attractive in Jacob.

"It's been a tough week," she said.

"You mean your normal doesn't include your child almost dying, losing your job, injuring yourself and seeing your boyfriend attacked?" Sam laughed.

"What boyfriend?" Jill asked.

"Well that too," Sam said. "I bet last week this time you were in a very different place."

Jill nodded. She glanced at Sam. He easily summed up how she felt.

"I'm not working. And have no idea when I'll work again. Katy's gone. I don't cook or clean for myself here. I can't go home because Trevor's stalking the apartment until he gets *married* to some other girl and leaves for his *honeymoon* tomorrow. I'm supposedly engaged to this guy that I don't even know. My best-friend is appropriately caught up in her own world." Jill stopped talking as abruptly as she started. After a few moments of silence, she took a breath. "I can't even work out!"

"Why don't you come with me today?" Sam asked. "I spend Saturdays going from site to site. You could come along with me. You'd learn a little bit about our business. Maybe you won't feel so strange."

"Is there a lot of walking? I tried to shop and couldn't really do that."

"No," Sam said. "Do you need to rest?"

Jill shook her head, "I think I've slept more this week than I have all of my life."

"I need to say good bye to Ruth. Why don't I meet you here in ten minutes?"

"Oh, that's why you're here… you and Delphie?"

"I live here," Sam said. "I have a room on the ground floor. We've just missed each other this week. But, to answer your question, Delphie and I are seeing each other. We have for the last few years."

"What about your wife and kids?"

"Surely, you know that my children live at the Castle, Jill. As for Tiffanie? My marriage-in-name-only will end soon. Thank God."

Sam looked toward the door where Delphie stood in her bathrobe. He stood to hold her. They were still talking when Jill returned from Jacob's apartment where she and Katy were staying. Delphie hugged Jill then went back to her apartment.

Because Valerie made a big show of leaving for the mountains, the paparazzi had retreated from the Castle. Sam and Jill went to his Lipson Construction truck parked in the driveway.

"Ruth thinks you should go ahead with your plan for the walls," Sam said.

Jill blushed. "How did she know I was doing that?"

Sam laughed.

"She thinks, and I agree, you will feel more at home when you make it homey," Sam said.

"That's assuming this will be my home."

"It's odd for you and I. Val too. We fight against accepting what's right in front of us. But be honest Jill. Don't you feel like this is exactly where you belong?"

In answer to his question, Jill buckled her seatbelt.

"I'm glad you came along today. Saturday is my favorite day. We start with breakfast at four. Aden and Blane will meet us at the Gyro Palace. Although, now that you and Jacob are an item, we can go back to Pete's Kitchen. Jacob could never handle a workday after seeing you."

"He really likes me?"

"He's crazy about you, Jill."

Jill smiled.

"You're right. I feel like I belong. But…"

"But?"

"I'm not sure why."

"Welcome to my world," Sam laughed.

~~~~~~~~~

SATURDAY AFTERNOON, 3 PM

"Who are you?" Mike asked.

He walked into the kitchen where a short, slim blonde woman was riffling through the cupboards. The woman made a disgusted sound and began tossing box after box of cereal in a five gallon trashcan.

"What are you doing?" Mike grabbed box after box of cereal.

"I'm cleaning the junk out of this kitchen. You must be Mike."

Mike set the cereal on the table to grab more boxes from the trashcan.

"STOP." Mike yelled.

The woman looked up at him with a bright smile.

"Like your cereal do you? Well, it's not very good for you."

The woman grabbed a box of cereal that Mike was holding. They tugged the box back and forth between them.

"Who are you?" Mike asked.

"Oh, I'm Valerie Waters," she said. "Val calls me 'Waters.' I'm her trainer."

"And you know who I am?" Mike asked.

"You're Lipson's husband," Waters said.

"How do you know that?"

"I figured it out. I mean come on. Lipson comes home from her 'Colorado retreats' all dreamy and happy. No amount of yoga does what a good man can do for your stress levels. Plus, she told me about you a long time ago."

"What's all this 'Who is Valerie's husband' crap then?" Mike asked.

"I don't know. I didn't know there was any," Waters said. She moved toward the stack of cereal boxes on the table, but Mike blocked her way. She put her hands on her hips and said, "This is not even food. Why are you protecting it?"

"Jacob eats cereal. He likes it. I like it too. We eat it together," Mike said.

"Oh. I'm so sorry. I've never met Jake but I know what a great guy he is." The little woman stood on her toes to give Mike a quick hug. "Should I put it back?"

"We don't eat too much. We eat other healthy stuff too. We just like cereal."

"Does Lipson eat it?" Waters said.

"I don't," Valerie said. "I eat only wholesome food prescribed by my awesome trainer. Hi!"

The women hugged.

"Mike, you know Valerie Waters. She's the one who is responsible for..."

Valerie turned around and pointed to her high firm rear end. Mike raised his eyebrows in appreciation. Valerie Waters laughed.

"Waters is here to help me get ready for Friday," Valerie said.

"You're thin," Waters said. "We have work to do."

"Wait. If everyone knows about me," Mike said. He looked at Valerie and she smiled. "Why is Wes so upset?"

"UGH! Wesford. He's totally another story," Waters said. "He's always known that Lipson was married."

"I told you that," Valerie said.

"Then why..."

"Drama. Hollywood. I don't know," Waters said. "I like him, Lipson. I like him a lot."

"Oh good. I'm planning on keeping him," Valerie said.

"Now, where's the gym?" Waters asked.

"Basement," Mike and Valerie said in unison.

"Bye, bye hot husband," Waters waved her hand. "We have work to do."

"Bye," Mike said to the women's backs as they retreated to the basement. "I have an appointment..."

Knowing they didn't hear him, he shrugged, picked up a set of keys and left for the garage.

~~~~~~~~

"Oh," Jill said. She was sitting in the passenger seat of Big Sam's work truck.

"Oh?" Sam asked.

"Well, I just realized why people say Jacob is gay."

"Because of Blane."

"They look a lot alike. Is Blane your son?"

"No," Sam said. "We think he's either my brother's son or my Dad's son. My brother died of AIDS in the late 1980s. Even as an old guy, my father was fairly promiscuous. He died right after my brother. Blane was dropped at a hospital when he was about three months old. They never found his parents so he spent most of his life in foster care."

"Did you do DNA?"

"Yes," Sam said. "Celia insisted on it when she found him. She wanted him to know that we were his family."

"He's younger than Jacob," Jill said.

"By a few years," Sam said.

"Why does he look so old?" Jill asked.

"He has AIDS," Sam said.

"Oh, that's why..."

"Exactly."

~~~~~~~~~

"What do you mean I have to undress?" Mike asked.

"How can I wax you with your clothing on?" Jessie Dillard asked. A small woman with long golden hair and a bright smile, she said, "Alex? Are you staying here?"

"Yeah, I'll stay," Alex Hargreaves said. "I've seen him buck naked before."

"But... you see... I..." Mike sputtered.

"I'll let you two work this out," Jessie said. Standing with the door half open, she said, "I'll be right back."

Alex and Mike watched her pull the door closed.

"I don't know about this," Mike said. His eyes flicked toward the door.

"You want to fit into Val's Hollywood world don't you?" Alex asked. "How many men said you should get waxed?"

"Everyone I asked."

"Did they say it would kill you?"

"No," Mike said. "But it might."

Alex plopped down in the armchair in the corner.

"Strip."

She pulled out the handgun she always wore at her sacrum and pointed it at him.

"Strip."

"You won't shoot me."

"Wanna bet?" Alex asked.

Mike sneered at her then took off his clothing. Alex pointed to the sheeted table and he lay down. She threw a towel at him to cover his genitals. There was a tap at the door.

"Shooting people?" Jessie asked.

"Oh sorry," Alex holstered her handgun.

"What are we doing?" Jessie asked. She looked over Mike's body. "Can you sit up?"

Mike sat up.

"What do you think?" Alex asked.

"The unibrow has to go. You're seeing Michael Moore?"

"Next week."

"I'll clean up the eyebrows but leave something for Mr. Moore to do. We should take off all the hair from his shoulders, back and butt," Jessie said. She lifted the towel. "I think we can leave his chest hair. Arm hair too. There's not too much of it. It's just long. You'll trim it?"

"Sure," Alex said.

"Why do I have to do this?" Mike asked.

"You don't," Jessie said. "You'll look better on television and in photos. The hair presses your clothing off your skin."

"Oh," Mike said. He lay back on the table.

"We'll get rid of this hair too." Jessie touched his public hair.

"What?" Mike sat up again. "Why?"

"You'll see," Alex said. "Go ahead, Jessie. Do what you think is best."

Mike sat up and rotated his legs to the edge of the table.

"You know Val has never complained. It's not like we've EVER had any..."

Alex pointed her gun at Mike again. He dropped back to the table.

"I'm just saying," Mike added in his defense.

Jessie laughed.

~~~~~~~~~

Jill pulled the Lexus SUV up to Megan's house. Before she could fully stop the car, Katy flew out of the front door. She hopped up and down until Jill got out of the SUV.

"MOMMY!!"

And Jill knew she was right where she belonged.

~~~~~~~~~

"Hi," Valerie said. She ruffled Mike's hair. "I wondered what happened to you."

After Jessie, Mike received his first professional haircut from George at Luxe Salon. George clipped, trimmed and shaved until Mike's hair hung in curls just below his chin. Alex then took him back to her house where he stood on the deck and had his remaining body hair trimmed. Alex dropped him at the workshop to shower.

"No, I mean it," Valerie thread her hands around his neck. Her finger slipped under his shirt. She sighed into him. "What happened to you?"

"I asked some friends for help," Mike said.

Valerie pulled off his shirt. Her fingers played with his trimmed chest hair. He had to grab her hands to stop her from taking his pants off in the middle of the main Castle kitchen.

"We're supposed to meet with some designer."

"Ramon already picked out three dresses for me. I don't need another dress."

"It's for me," Mike said. Breaking off from a kiss, he said, "Mostly. They want..."

Valerie kissed him. He stepped back.

"Oh," Valerie said. "Ramon already picked out something for you too. Who's the designer?"

"Um ... Sorry, Alex told me but I forgot. She wants to ask you if you'd like to be a spokesmodel for some clothing thing they have coming out. She hoped to talk to you while they were in town. They live in Paris."

Valerie shrugged then kissed Mike.

"You'll talk to her," Mike said.

"I like meeting new people," Valerie said. "When are we meeting them?"

"Tomorrow morning early."

Valerie dropped his pants.

"Oh Mike..."

She dragged him into the sitting room.

~~~~~~~~~

SATURDAY, 9 P.M.

Sandy leaned her head against the rolled towel Aden slipped behind her head. In the warm safety of the hot tub, he rubbed her feet one at a time. If she wasn't so full, she would be completely limp.

Over the course of the day, her resistance to dating Aden had waned. Of course, a dozen white roses waiting on her doorstep, a large bouquet of spring flowers waiting for her at her station, AND her favorite lunch delivered from Pasquini's—Caesar salad with chicken and no dressing—helped. He picked her up from work in a Saab sedan which led to the 'Is this your car?' conversation that made him laugh. And after all of that, he made her favorite dinner—cheeseburgers with homemade French Fries.

Turns out, Aden had paid attention all those years at the gym.

But for Sandy, the flowers and food wouldn't matter if he hadn't been so attentive. He listened to her stories about clients and laughed at her jokes. He charmed her by talking about his worries about taking over Lipson Construction.

And he'd wanted to go out with her almost as long as she wanted to go out with him. All those years that she thought he wasn't interested, he was just going to school and raising his kids. In fact, he thought SHE wasn't interested.

Just the thought made her smile.

Outside of a little kissing, he hadn't mauled her or expected some payback for his attention. At least he didn't act like he wanted payback. He had been a complete gentleman. He even insisted they wear t-shirts and shorts in the hot tub.

When he brought up birth control, they had the most mature conversation Sandy had ever had about birth control. Condoms? He had 'no problem' wearing them. Even after he learned she was on the Depo shot! It was up to her.

Only Jill would be crazy enough to think about love. Love was something that happened to people whose hearts weren't permanently broken. Love didn't happen to people like Sandy.

Still.

Watching the summer stars, Sandy felt a definite… like for Aden. She nodded at the stars. She definitely liked Aden. When he sat next to her, she rested her head on his shoulder.

"I spend every Saturday night right here," he said. "The kids go to a sports camp on Saturdays so they're in bed early. I sit right here. Just me and the stars."

"What a great way to end the day," Sandy said.

"I'm glad you're here," he said.

"Me too," Sandy said. "Do you know the names of the stars?"

"Names? Yes, Sandy, we're on first name basis. See that star?"

He pointed to the star right above his head.

"Uh huh."

"That's Frank. He thinks you're the most beautiful creature he's ever laid eyes on."

"Frank's a little forward."

"He's trying to get in your pants," Aden said.

Sandy giggled.

"You can never trust a star. Take Fred here."

"Which one's Fred?" Sandy asked

"Right over there. He's a shy guy. Much more discrete than Frank. Still, his girl…"

"Francine?"

"How did you know?!" Aden said. "Francine says Fred's a bit of a swinger. Likes the boys and the girls. LOTS of boys and LOTS of girls. Even Frank says..."

"Excuse me."

Two Denver Police officers came in the gate to Aden's backyard. Aden popped to his feet.

"Are you Aden Norsen?"

CHAPTER TWENTY-TWO
THE FAMILIAR DANCE

"Yes."

"Would you mind stepping out of the hot tub, sir?"

Sandy stood when Aden hopped out of the hot tub. She watched the police say something to Aden. His mouth dropped open and his face blanched white. He shook his head back and forth.

Before they could tell her not to, Sandy got out of the hot tub to call Jill. Jill's cell phone rang once... and ADEN WAS IN HANDCUFFS!!

Rang twice... and Jill pushed opened the glass sliding door from the house. In two steps, Jill encircled her best friend in a hug.

"You can hang up," Jill said.

Terrified and humiliated, Sandy clung to Jill.

"I don't know what happened. He was just telling me funny stories... How did you get here so fast?"

"I live with a psychic who has Aden's house key," Jill said. "Let's go inside."

Dripping wet, Sandy shivered. Jill led her to the nearest bathroom for a towel. Jill wrapped her in a warm towel.

"Stay here," Jill said. She took another towel and left.

Sandy stood in the bathroom shivering from the shock. Just like every other experience in Sandy's life, her moment of blissful happiness was shattered by something awful.

She wanted to cry.

She wanted to scream.

Instead, she felt the familiar sinking numbness. The image of Aden in handcuffs bounced around her brain. Once again, life confirmed that she did not deserve to be happy.

"They want to search the house," Jill said. "Did you guys drink tonight?"

"No, he can't drink. He's an alcoholic."

"Great," Jill said. "Why don't we make some hot chocolate? Aden's in the backyard. I gave him a towel but I bet he's cold."

"He's not arrested?"

"Not yet," Jill said. "They're checking the house for drugs."

"Drugs?"

"They want us to stay in one area of the house. I told them we'd be in the kitchen."

Jill helped Sandy dress in her clothing. Taking Sandy's arm, she led her into the kitchen.

"Now what do I do?" Jill asked.

Sandy shook her head at Jill and Jill stepped aside.

The kitchen was a place of comfort for Sandy. Ever since they were kids, Sandy made hot chocolate for Jill when they were upset. While the police worked their way through the house with dogs, Sandy's mind turned to the step by step process of cooking. Her anxiety unwound and her confidence returned in the normalcy of making hot chocolate for Jill. She even whipped up a pan of brownies. The police were still working when Jill and Sandy went to the backyard with mugs of hot chocolate and a plate of fresh brownies.

Jill opened the sliding door to the back door for Sandy to go through. Aden's back was to the door while he talked to Sam. Feeling their movement, Aden turned. He was so delighted to see Sandy that he rushed to her. Sandy blushed at his unrestrained delight. Jill took the brownies from Sandy. Aden lifted her off the ground in a hug.

"Hi, I'm Sam Lipson," he said to Sandy after Aden released her. "I love brownies. Do you mind? Delphie made some today. They disappeared with Katy before I could have even one."

Sandy nodded her head. Sam took a brownie off the plate.

"What happened?" Sandy asked.

"They raided Nuala's house," Aden said. "I guess there was some drug something… making drugs… something… I don't know. They found Noelle and Nash locked in a closet. Nuala said I was her drug supplier. Well, they ran my record and… I'm so sorry this happened to you. I… I'm sorry."

"They were just going to arrest you?"

"That's what happens," Aden said. "I have a record for drug dealing and violent behavior. They restrain first, ask questions later. Luckily, Big Sam came by."

"Aden left his phone at a site. I picked it up on my way to the rehearsal dinner," Sam Lipson said. "I thought I would drop it by on my way home."

Sandy would have believed Mr. Lipson's story if Jill hadn't laughed when he said it.

"Is that what you told them?" Jill asked.

"Uh huh, you were supposed to meet me here," Sam said.

Jill shook her head at him and he smiled.

"You wanted a full update from the rehearsal dinner."

"Trevor's rehearsal dinner?"

"You were at the engagement party," Sam nodded and Jill laughed.

"How did Mr. Lipson help?" Sandy asked Aden.

"Please call me Sam."

"They do drug testing at Lipson," Aden said. "My last arrest was twelve years ago... the year I started working at Lipson. When Jake took over, he insisted on hair follicle testing every employee. We have a zero drug tolerance policy. Everyone knows that about Lipson. Big Sam offered to provide all those records."

"We'll probably have to, but..." Sam's voice trailed off when a policewoman came out the sliding glass door.

A little boy pressed passed the policewoman followed by a little girl. They threw themselves at Aden. Aden held them both in a tight embrace.

Watching Aden with his kids, Sandy felt a strange pang in her heart. The children were crying and talking at the same time. These people, the two children and their father, seemed like three pieces to a whole. They just fit together.

The Police stopped to speak to Aden and Big Sam before leaving. They didn't find drugs. Yes, Aden would be available for questioning. No, he wasn't going anywhere. His children hung on him the entire time. When the police cleared out, Aden took Noelle and Nash to their rooms.

Jill and Sandy set to work. The Park Hill bungalow had been turned upside down by the Denver Police. Together, the women righted the furniture, straightened what was amiss and swept up what was broken. By the time, Sam came for Jill, the house was in order.

"I'm going to leave my car," Jill said. Sandy's attention jerked to Jill. "You can go home whenever you want."

"I'll go with you. I'm sure Aden would like to be with his kids," Sandy started.

Jill shook her head then hugged Sandy.

"I think he'll need your special help," Jill said in Sandy's ear. "You know what it's like to come home from an awful experience. You could really help. I bet Aden will need you when the kids get to bed."

Jill gave Sandy the Lexus keys.

"Your car?"

"Yeah, I just found that out. I guess Jacob bought it for me for our non-date." Jill hugged Sandy again. "I'm going with Sam. Love you Sandy."

Sandy stood at the front door to Aden's house and waved. When she closed the door, Aden came running from the back of the house. Seeing Sandy, he slid across the hardwood floors to a stop.

"Will you stay? The kids are exhausted. Noelle's already asleep. Nash should be out in a moment. I could really use... a friend."

Sandy nodded.

"Good." Aden kissed her. "Thanks."

~~~~~~~~~

On the living room couch of Aden's Park Hill bungalow, with her leg tucked up under her, Sandy felt a part of her unwind or melt. Her soul listened to this man talk about his life. His eyes and mind turned to her with an open caring she'd never imagined coming from a man. She craved more—more connection, more warmth, more of Aden Norsen. With her head on his shoulder, she fell asleep on the couch. He woke her then insisted she stay in his guest bedroom.

Sandy came out of the small guest bathroom to find Aden asleep on the twin guest bed. He'd waited for her to say good night. His eyes opened the moment she was close.

In a rush of emotion, he reached for her. After six years of longing, his simple gesture sparked a blaze inside her. She was swept away by her own passion for this man.

Lips pressed, hips merged and they joined in a dance of sensation. Her fingertips burned with the plush texture of his skin. Her body responded at the nip of his teeth against her nipples, her neck and her ears. Her mouth pulled kiss after kiss from his lips. Each pulse brought deeper waves of connection. Fast and slow, on top and under him, she felt only her fervor for this man.

Their final blaze of glory brought up Sandy's long held pain. While his lips kissed her face and eyes, she wept. His arms held her tight through the passing of nameless pain and sadness.

When the storm passed, Sandy attacked. She pulled and pressed at him. She bit at his body and allowed her fingernails to rake at his flesh. Aden matched her with sheer animal passion. In this pure, honest physicality, Sandy's soul opened to him. Her hands above her head, her body conquered, she called him to join her. Without hesitation, he followed her into oblivion.

Sandy's very being joined his to dance among the familiar stars. Around and around they waltzed until, one breath at a time, they rejoined their bodies on the cramped bed in the guest room of his Park Hill bungalow. They fell spent to the bed. Wrapped around each other, they slept.

~~~~~~~~~

Mike had asked, but Valerie didn't want to go out. In fact, Valerie didn't want to leave the bed. She wanted to be tickled, cuddled and loved. He got up at some point and brought Brie, strawberries and champagne back to bed. With her head in his lap, he fed her the fruit and cheese. Looking into her hazel eyes, he saw her love for him shining back. Around midnight, they migrated to the large bathtub.

"It's been a week," Mike said.

He slipped her hair over her shoulder to use a sponge on her back. She lay back into his lap. He kissed her lips and she smiled.

"Are you... Do you... I mean..." Mike scrunched his eyebrows together. Valerie's thumb smoothed out the crease between his eyebrows.

"There's only one time in my life that I've felt this right... complete."

"In Monterey?"

"In Monterey."

He pulled her between his knees. She tucked her arms over his knees then leaned back against his chest.

"Are you going to start..."

"Our usual argument?" Valerie finished his statement. "You always start our usual argument."

"I do? How?"

"'You're just going to leave again,'" Valerie imitated his voice. "'You may as well just go.' Or, my personal favorite, 'If he's that great, why don't you just marry him?'"

"Ouch," Mike said. "Wes?"

"The other two were just for the press," Valerie said. "Yes, Wes."

Mike stared at the wavy glass block window to the Castle garden. The moon hadn't reached them yet. The distant street lights reflected off the glass creating a wispy dance of light. He sighed.

"Sorry. You went on and on and on and on about him."

"I did?" Valerie asked. "Really?"

"He was smart and sophisticated and went to all the cool parties and knew everyone and wore designer clothing and produced the best films and... I figured you were already fucking him so... Were you?"

"Not until you told me to leave," she said.

She didn't dare look at his face because she knew the pain she would see there. She wasn't proud of herself or her actions. She and Mike danced this dance so long that she wasn't really sure what were her decisions and what were his. Did he make her sleep with Wes? No. But he told her to. Or did he?

She sighed.

"What's wrong?" Mike asked.

"Oh, I was thinking about us."

"What about us? Are you leaving again?"

She hit his leg with her hand and he laughed. She tipped her head up to kiss the underside of his chin.

"I..." Valerie started.

She shook her head. The thoughts bounced around her head like ping pong balls until a single image floated to the surface–Mike's back as he left for basic training.

"I stood at the door for three hours hoping you would come back. You'd change your mind and work for my Dad. I was sure you'd never, ever, ever leave me."

Hoping she would continue, Mike let the silence lag. She almost never talked about herself, and never talked about this time in their life. She took a breath the let it out before saying anything else.

"I met the mailman at the door every day for three months. And when your random and rare letters came, I'd sit in my room for a day, at least, and read them over and over again. I was sure you'd be home in time to take me to prom or homecoming or... see me graduate. When you finally came home, you were so grown up, mature. You'd traveled all over the world. I could almost taste the women on you. I was just some stupid little small town high school girl and you were a man."

"Val, I..." Mike started then stopped. This was her turn, her story. He could wait. He kissed the top of her head. Leaning back, he stretched his long arms to reach her brush on the marble counter. She almost purred when he began brushing her hair. "I want to hear what you have to say."

"When I went to UCLA, I was going to find someone else... someone who'd stay... with me. But I never did."

Valerie sighed.

"I'm sorry," he whispered. "I was trying to be good enough for you... for you."

"Push, pull, push, pull, push, pull."

Valerie jerked around in the bathtub so fast that the hairbrush flew out of Mike's hand.

"Tell me this." Her index finger jabbed his chest. "Who have you loved? Who? Who? Tell me. WHO?"

"I've only ever loved you, Val."

"THEN WHY DID YOU LEAVE ME?"

Her eyes blazed her anger and pain. He saw her, at sixteen, standing at the door waiting all those hours. He saw her clutching his half-assed letters. He saw her face the last time they made love before he left for basic training. And the betrayal on that same face when he returned from his first tour. He'd changed. She hadn't.

He left and didn't come back until long after she stopped waiting for him.

In that moment, her finger bruising his chest, he saw every twist and turn of their relationship. His big hand covered her hand and finger. He raised her hand to his lips then kissed it.

"I left because of me and me only. I came back because of you. I'll never leave again, Valerie and..." Mike stopped talking. His eyes caressed her face.

"I'm sorry."

"Please finish."

"I will fight every day to stay right here… by your side…"

Their eyes held. She leaned forward and their lips touched. Sighing, she leaned against his chest.

"But if you want to be with Wes, fine. Hell, torture has its privileges. I can tolerate almost anything every once in a while, as long as I don't have to fuck him."

Valerie smiled and shook her head. This was one of the things she loved about Mike. He could diffuse any situation with a tangential reference to something absurd.

"He can have you on Wednesday nights."

"Wednesday?"

"While I play hockey. Our team switched from Saturdays to Wednesdays."

"Hockey?"

"Yeah, he can spend a couple hours while I'm at hockey if that's what you want but…"

Valerie kissed him quiet.

"But when we're in tournament…"

"Stop," she said. "I don't want to be with Wes. I only want you. I love you."

He kissed her lips.

"Please don't leave me again," she whispered.

"Never by choice."

"Never by choice," had she repeated his vow.

Mike retrieved the hair brush from across the room. Turning on the hot water to warm the tub, he kissed her head and returned to brushing her hair.

"So no more hockey tournaments?"

"Now Val, be reasonable…"

CHAPTER TWENTY-THREE
WHAT WAS THAT?
Sunday morning, 6:30 AM

Jill tapped on Mike and Val's door. When no one answered, she knocked. Naked, Mike jerked open the door just as her hand moved to pounded on it. She thumped him on the sternum.

"Sorry."

Mike nodded and swung the door closed.

"WAIT," Jill said. She held the door open with her foot. "There's a bunch of people here for you. They're in the kitchen. They came through the tunnels. Alex said she knew the codes because she set them up?"

"Alex?"

"It's Alex Hargreaves and her twin Max and a bunch of people speaking french..."

"OH CRAP. Val! You have to get up!"

Mike moved into the hallway.

"Clothing?" Jill asked.

"Right," he said.

He went back into the apartment. Jill stood in the doorway until he came out pushing Valerie in front of him. Valerie was wearing one of his dress shirts and his boxer shorts. Her hair was tied in a loose knot. In this unguarded moment, Valerie was stunningly beautiful. Mike pulled a t-shirt over his head as they started down the hall.

"Pants?" Jill asked.

"Oh crap. Keep her here."

Mike jogged back into the apartment for a pair of jeans.

"Why are they here, Mike?" Valerie said.

The sleeves to his dress shirt hung over her hands. She rubbed her large hazel eyes with the shirt's cuffs. The moment he was near her, she clung to him. He lifted her into his arms.

"Sorry, we just fell asleep," Mike said. "She's like this when she doesn't sleep. She'll snap out of it when she sees people."

Jill grinned when she heard them kissing behind her. Jill jogged down the stairs to give them some privacy. When she entered the main kitchen, Alex was making coffee. Jill could see a crowd of people laughing and talking in the main Castle living area.

"Are they awake?" Alex asked.

"Barely. They are a little..."

Alex raised her eyebrows. She nodded her head toward the stairwell where Mike held Valerie in his arms. Mike was clearly trying to talk Valerie into meeting their guests; Valerie was only interested in kissing him.

"They're always like that," Alex said.

"I never knew there was a 'they,'" Jill said.

"They have all this drama about whether they are together or not. But get them in the same room?"

Jill nodded.

"ROPER." Alex commanded.

Mike's head jerked up. Alex pointed toward the Castle living room. He carried Valerie through the kitchen and into the living room.

Valerie squealed.

Jill stepped out of the way so Valerie could run past her. Valerie took the stairs two at a time. Valerie's footstep pounded overhead. Wham. Their apartment door slammed closed.

"What was that?" Jill asked.

Mike poked his head into the kitchen. He looked at Jill then Alex.

"She's a little excited," Mike said.

Alex and Jill laughed.

~~~~~~~~~

Aden woke alone on the cramped twin guest bed.

And certain he had never felt so very alone.

Jill told him to go slow. He had tried to go slow. But last night...

He fucked up.

Standing from the bed, he stretched his sore body then smirked. The guest bathroom mirror reflected the unmistakable marks of passion created by Sandy's teeth and nails.

And his heart ached with loss.

Sandy was gone, probably forever.

How could one man experience so much wonder and so much loss at the same time?

Hearing the water run, he remembered that the kids were home. He slipped downstairs to his bedroom, showered and dressed then went to find the kids. They weren't in their rooms. Standing in the hallway, he heard Nash's voice then Noelle's voice coming from the kitchen. He went down the hall to find them.

"Oh, don't worry, Sandy, we know all about sex," Noelle said. "I haven't had any sex. I don't think Nash has had any sex either."

"Nope," Nash said. "But we saw a bunch this weekend."

"Yeah," Noelle said. "I didn't like it. It wasn't like Daddy said it was."

"What do you mean?" Sandy asked.

"Well, Daddy says that sex is how adults play with each other. Like Nash plays soccer and I play gymnastics."

"It didn't look very fun," Nash said.

"Why did you see sex?" Sandy asked.

"Because Nuala was doing drugs and having sex with men," Nash said. "I told her we couldn't be around drugs. But she just laughed at me."

"What do you mean?" Sandy asked.

"Daddy says we have addict parents," Noelle said. "Do you know what an addict is?"

"Sure do."

"Dad says because we have addict parents, we are more sensitive to drugs and alcohol. We can't be around it," Nash said. "That's why I locked us in the closet."

"That was a very smart and brave thing to do, Nash," Sandy said.

"My brother was amazing," Noelle said. "You should have seen him. He wouldn't let them take me or..."

"Take you?"

"Into the other room," Noelle said. "They wanted to have sex with me. But I told them that I was NOT a grown up and I did NOT want to play with them. Then Nash locked us in the closet."

Aden's heart seized with rage. No wonder Nuala was so adamant that she wanted the kids this weekend. Nuala's party plans included his daughter. He rushed forward to comfort his kids but stopped in his tracks. Sandy's neutral kindness was helping the kids. He paced back and forth to cool his rage.

"That's why you called the police?" Sandy asked.

"Yeah," Nash said. "Dad gave me a phone and told me to call him if I needed him. I was going to call but then I hoped he was with you... on a date. Dad said he was going to see you when we talked. So I called the police."

"I think you both are very brave," Sandy said. "Muffin?"

Aden heard the kids move forward. Blowing out the last of his rage, he walked forward into the kitchen. Noelle sitting on a bar stool at the kitchen median while Nash was sitting in front of the kitchen computer. They were both eating muffins.

"DADDY!!" Noelle said.

She jumped off the stool to hug Aden. Nash joined them.

"We were just talking to Sandy," Noelle said. "We like her a lot. Plus, she made blueberry muffins. Don't they smell great? She made coffee too. Do you want some? I can get it."

Aden kissed Noelle's head, then Nash's.

"It's great to have you here" Aden said. "I need to steal Sandy from you."

"Ok Daddy," Noelle said. "She has to go anyway. But she said she would come back to see us."

"Can we go to the splash fountain today?" Nash asked.

"And the zoo?" Noelle asked.

"You bet."

Taking Sandy's hand, Aden led her into his basement bedroom. He wrapped her in his arms and she giggled.

"Last night was..."

"Incredible," Sandy said. "Yeah."

He brushed her lips with his lips.

"I thought you'd gone... that I'd blown it... that..."

Sandy put her finger over his lips.

"I heard Noelle crying. She was standing in the hall looking for you. She didn't want to disturb you... us... She seemed to know who I was—which was weird..."

"We don't have a lot of secrets around here."

Sandy smiled.

"I'm glad. I told her I would make her some blueberry muffins. She woke Nash. We talked. That's all that happened. They had an awful time at their Mom's."

"Sounded like you're really good with kids."

"I took care of my little sister and brother a lot." Sandy shrugged. "I think the kids need you. Can you take Monday off?"

"I can but keeping to the schedule helps them feel more normal than hanging around with me."

"Jill's baby Katy is like that."

He tugged her toward him and she rested her head on this chest.

"I have to get going," Sandy said. "I meet Jill for breakfast and church every week. We're hanging out today. Val said she would let us go through her old dresses since we didn't find anything at the mall. Plus, it's the one week anniversary of the non-date. Delphie told Katy she would make a cake."

"Quite a week."

Sandy stepped back a bit to look at him. "Thanks for... last night."

"When do I get to see you again?"

"Call me."

"Sandy... what did you decide?"

"About?"

"Dating exclusively."

"After last night?" Sandy smiled. "Oh yeah."

~~~~~~~~

"I'm Frederic," a young man said in heavily accented English.

"Nice to meet you Frederic. I'm Mike."

"Yes. I need you to take your clothing off."

"Why?" Mike asked.

"I have to see what your body looks like in order to make sure we get something that looks right...um... right for you." The man touched his arm. "I can't tell with this on."

"But..." Mike said.

The young man cocked his head and laughed. He said something in French and they all laughed.

"Why don't you hit the shower?" Alex asked. She pointed to his unbuttoned 501s.

"He's not coming into my shower," Mike said.

"You're such a homophobe," Alex said. "Chill out. I've had to take my clothes off in front of everyone too. Scared them with my scars. Frederic? You want him in underwear."

The young man said something in French. Everyone laughed.

"Do you have any briefs?" Alex said. "He won't like your boxers."

Mike looked at Alex then nodded.

"Great. Wear those," Alex said. She whispered to him, "They're very particular about undergarments. They usually just buy mine but they know my sizes and stuff."

Mike nodded to Alex and started walking toward the kitchen. When he turned into the stairwell, he found Valerie peeking around a corner. Valerie was dressed with full make up and her hair was curled. She looked every bit the movie star.

"Do you know who that is?" Valerie whispered. "That's Claire Martins. She's a world famous designer. Designs for the Queen and... No one in Hollywood has worn her dresses... and they've tried. I..."

Mike shrugged.

"I mean real 'A-list' stars have begged to wear her gowns. Remember the vintage Dior gown Reese wore? Her stylist camped out in Paris for a week to see if he could get a Martins gown. He found the other gown while he was killing time between begging. He thought that beautiful dress was a good second. A second to a Claire Martins gown! And..."

"She wants to talk to you, Val."

"Where are you going?" Valerie asked.

"Alex said shower. Just following orders." Mike shrugged. "Honey, just go talk to them."

He gave her a little push toward the living room.

Valerie stood in the doorway to the main Castle living room watching Mike's guests. Alex and Max were clearly a part of this little group. Claire Martins had a long black braid down her back and was carrying a baby in a bjorn across her chest. There was a young man stretched out on the couch. They seemed so happy together...and so French. Val's heart raced with panic.

"Hey Val."

Max saw her from across the room. She couldn't escape now. She raised her hand to say 'hello.'

"This is my dear friend, Claire," Alex said. She came over to give Valerie a hug. Leaning in, she said, "She speaks English but she's impossible to understand when she's excited. Do you speak French?"

Valerie shook her head.

"No problem, I'll translate," Alex said. "Claire brought a few dresses for you to look at. I guess you're having a party next week?"

Valerie nodded her head.

Alex puzzled at Val's timidity then shrugged, "Claire has a line of clothing coming out in the fall. She wanted to know if you might take a look. She thinks the clothing will look great on you."

Valerie nodded. Smoothing her hair, Valerie glanced at Claire just as Claire's baby peeked over at her. Val's heart melted. Her anxiety slipped away in the dark eyes of the six month old baby.

"Meet Gerard," Claire said. "Would you like to hold him?"

"I... I'm a little baby crazy right now," Valerie said.

"I've always been baby crazy," Claire said. "Why don't you hold Gerard and I will take some measurements? Ok?"

Valerie nodded. She took the baby from Claire. Enraptured by the warm bundle in her arms, she didn't notice Claire buzzing around her.

When Mike returned to the Castle living room, Valerie was singing to the baby. His heart stood still at the sight. She looked up at him and smiled.

His Val.

He jerked back to the present when the young man touched him. Frederic was holding a couple pieces of fabric up to him.

"What are you doing?" Mike asked.

"I need to know what colors work on you and get your measurements," Frederic said. "Don't worry man, you're not my type."

"You're not gay? I mean, I don't care if you're gay, I just don't want..."

"My girlfriend would hate it if I was gay," Frederic said.

"How come you do this?" Mike asked.

"We don't choose our gifts," Frederic laughed. "My mother is a great designer. You'll see when your wife tries the off the rack. Maman also brought a couple of her gowns."

Mike nodded his head as if he understood. He mostly hoped the young man would stop touching him. Mike didn't like to be touched very much. In fact, outside of a quick hug from people close to him, the only person who touched him was Val.

"What are you comfortable wearing?" Frederic asked.

"Jeans, t-shirts."

"Your legs are too big for these Levis," Frederic said. "They can't fit well."

"They don't. But I like them."

Frederic shook his head, "Bring me what you have."

Mike went off to the apartment for his jeans. When he returned, Valerie was wearing a brown pencil skirt with a jacket. The brown was just a shade lighter than her dark hair. She was so beautiful that he had to stop to catch his breath.

"Wow."

"Wait until you see the gowns," Frederic said. "This is our first attempt at an off the rack line. It's nice. Yes?"

"Yes," Mike said. "What does that mean? 'Off the rack?'"

"It's a line that can be sold off a rack in a store," Frederic said. "My father retired and needed something to do. This was his idea. So, we're trying women's clothing in the fall and men's in the spring. Maman wants to create children's clothing as well."

Mike nodded again as if he understood.

"These are the jeans?" Frederic asked. "Can you put them on?"

One after another Mike put on his jeans while Frederic watched. Finally, he shook his head. He said something in French and Max came over.

"He wants to know if we can get you some other jeans," Max said to Mike. "Where did you get these?"

Mike shrugged. "What's wrong with them?"

"They're too small," Max said.

"They fit the waist," Mike said. "I just deal with the leg thing."

"That's why they rip right here." Max pointed to rips near the crotch of each of Mike's jeans. "I'll keep a list. We already have undergarments. Jeans are easy. Levis?"

"Yeah. But they can't be too big. They fall off me."

Speaking very slowly, Max said, "Frederic will tailor them. That's what he does."

"Oh," Mike said. "Sorry this is all..."

Mike stopped talking when Valerie turned around in the gown. He put his hand over his heart certain it had stopped beating. Valerie caught his look and smiled.

Max tapped his arm.

"Frederic brought a tux for you. He had to guess at the size. He thinks it's too small. Do you have a tux you wear when you drive?"

Mike nodded. Frederic made a motion with his hand.

"We'd go back there but you were..." He said a word in French.

"Frightened," Max translated.

"Oh, come on," he said.

One by one, Mike tried on his clothing while Frederic shook his head and spoke in French to Max. To Mike's surprise, Frederic liked some of his favorite shirts and pants. Before he could figure a pattern, they had exhausted his closet.

When they returned to the living room, Valerie wore a pant suit. Claire spoke in very rapid French which Alex was translating. Valerie looked over at him in desperation. He slipped his arm over her shoulder.

"What's going on?" he asked.

"Claire just asked Val to be her exclusive media representative," Alex said.

"Exclusive... What?" Mike asked.

"That's spokesmodel to you! I think Val's a little overwhelmed. She looks great in the clothing. But there's a Ramon...?"

"You look so much better than in anything he's put you in," Mike said. "Let's ask Jen. She's still in town right?"

Valerie nodded, "She's setting up Oprah."

"Oprah?" Claire said. She nodded. "That would be very good for us. This line is not expensive but well-made. For the every day woman who wants to look..."

"Classy," Alex finished Claire's sentence. "Where's Jill? Claire thought Jill would be perfect too but she disappeared."

"She went back upstairs," Mike said. "She's painting and wanted to finish the trim before Mass."

Alex and Claire spoke in rapid fire French for a moment.

"Can you get Jill, Mike? We think she would look great, too."

At the mention of Jill, Valerie lit up.

"We could both be spokesmodels?" Valerie asked.

"Two exclusive media representatives?" Alex frowned.

"Oui," Claire said as if it was obvious.

While Valerie hesitated to hurt someone's feelings, in this case Ramon's tender designer feelings, she loved to spread good fortune. And Valerie loved Jill. Mike smiled at the change in her and kissed her nose.

"Call Jen and I'll get Jill."
Valerie nodded.

CHAPTER TWENTY-FOUR
HOW MUCH I NEED TO KNOW

Jill had just finished the last of the bathroom trim when Mike came up the stairs. According to Mike, some people wanted to see her wear some French clothing. Jill washed the paint off her hands and ran a brush through her hair. She was certain she would get down there and they would say something like, 'Oh paint-in-your-hair girl? Yeah. We didn't mean you.'

But Jill would do anything for Mike.

And he had asked, so she followed him down the long stairs from Jacob's apartment. Sandy knocked on the side door just as she got to the bottom of the stairs.

"I lost track of the time. I'm sorry," Jill said to Mike. He held her in place so she couldn't retreat upstairs. "Sandy's here to pick me up for breakfast."

Sandy took one look at Jill's nervous flutter, and asked, "What's going on?"

Mike nudged Jill into the Castle living room.

"We want to see how Jill looks in some clothing," Alex said. "Claire thinks she'll be perfect as a spokesmodel with Val."

"I apologize," Jill blushed. "I lost track of time. We go to breakfast..."

"I'd offer to make breakfast but you can ask Mike," Alex said. "You don't want to eat what I might make."

"I'll make it," Sandy said. "I'd like to."

"Let's make breakfast together," Delphie said from the kitchen door.

"You're so much prettier than me, Sandy. Why don't you be the spokesmodel?" Jill asked.

"No way," Sandy said. "I've had enough pictures taken of me to last a lifetime. Plus, they want you."

"Come on Sandy," Delphie said. "Let's see what we can come up with."

"We're doing this early so everyone can get to Mass," Mike said. "I'll call Meg. If we eat here, you can try on some stuff and have breakfast and get to Mass."

"Come on Jill. It's pretty fun," Valerie said.

Valerie took Jill's hand and led her over to a stack of clothing. Every time Jill looked up there were more people in the Castle living room. Of course, Megan, Tim, and Steve went to school with the Hargreaves. And the Hargreaves seemed to multiply in front of her. Alex and Max were joined by their brother Colin, and sisters, Erin and Samantha. Even Candy knew the

Hargreaves. Then the spouses, boyfriends and children arrived.

The usually silent Castle was filling with noisy, talking-all-at-once Catholic siblings, spouses, children and even more people from France.

Jill thought her sanity would be restored when Katy arrived. On the heels of Katy's arrival, Claire Martins' husband and other children arrived. It was love at first sight for Katy and Claire's five year old, Camille. Katy only wanted to be with Camille. The little girls played together in a corner of the room.

And Jill tried on clothing.

Claire would take a measurement or say she liked one thing or another. This woman remained convinced that Jill was going to model for her. But Jill's high school French only went so far. From what she could make out, they were going to pay her to wear these beautiful clothes.

And pay Katy. Claire Martins wanted Katy to join Camille in modeling their children's line.

Having had enough of the noise and chaos, Jill made her escape. She set down the last of the outfits, checked on Katy, then slipped through a hidden stairwell to Jacob's apartment. She was almost to the top when she heard someone behind her. Turning, she saw Alex Hargreaves looking up the stairs at her.

"Escaping?" Alex asked.

Jill nodded.

"Can we come?"

Max's identical face appeared over Alex's shoulder.

Jill laughed. "There's only cereal up here. I think they're having breakfast in a minute."

"Is there coffee?" Alex asked

Jill nodded. Max pulled the door closed.

"You don't want to be out there with all of…" Jill started.

"We don't." The twins responded in unison.

Jill waved and they followed her up the stairs. Alex set to work on coffee while Jill and Max set up cereal on Jacob's table. Jill had spent most of her life intimidated by the rich and powerful Hargreaves, in general, and independent Alex, in particular. In the twin's funny company, Jill began to feel a little more normal. They even helped her finish painting the apartment. In fact, they insisted on helping her.

Sitting in Sunday Mass, Jill felt as if she was a totally different person than she was last week. Last week, she felt like little mousey, trampled on Jill. This week, she felt as if she was exactly where she was supposed to be.

She just wasn't sure where that was.

~~~~~~~~

"You're not going to Mass," Sam said.

Valerie was standing in the middle of the Castle living room. Her eyes flitted back and forth from a stack of beautiful clothing to the gorgeous hanging gowns. She was trying to decide what she wanted to try on next when her father came in.

"I've avoided it for all these years. I'd hate to break my record."

"When does Jake wake up?"

"Three or four o'clock. Jill called this morning and he was still out."

"They're releasing him today?"

"That's what the doctor says. We'll know more when he wakes up."

Sam nodded. He sat down on one of the couches.

"Wedding today," he said.

"Why do you bother?" Valerie asked.

Looking over at her, he sighed. He shook his head and picked a chocolate brown sweater tunic from the pile. Valerie took the sweater from him then pulled it on.

"That's very nice," Sam said. "It's a good color on you."

Valerie looked at herself in the full length mirror Mike brought from their apartment. She rotated back and forth in the mirror then sneered at herself.

"Since we talked, I've debated with myself about how much I need to know about you and your… wife."

"Tiffanie."

"Her."

"And?"

When Valerie flipped around to him, Sam chuckled to himself. Valerie's face mirrored Celia's 'you're-in-big-trouble-Mister' face.

"I agreed with your mother's plan but I didn't really think it through," Sam said.

They said together: "Typical man." They laughed.

"She was so sick, Val. Not even Jake realized how sick she was. And she was adamant. She wanted out of that pretentious house. She wanted to finally live in Central Denver. We'd owned this house for…"

"You owned this house?"

"Own. Yes. We bought it right before you graduated from high school," Sam said. "Celia loved this house and wanted to find a place Delphie could live and walk to work. Delphie never had two pennies to rub together. So we bought it. We were going to move but were afraid it would be too much for you at college and Jake in high school.

"She got so sick so fast. It was like walking off a cliff. After almost a decade, all of a sudden she wasn't going to survive the year."

Sam's eyes welled. He shook his head and looked away. Valerie busied herself with trying on another outfit while he regained his composure.

"I did whatever she wanted. Sell the house. Done. Get a divorce to split up the company. Done. Marry Tiffanie. Done. But leave Celia's side? Not a chance. We moved in here together. I worked to reformulate the company. She wanted me to transform the company from single owner to a board of directors and... I worked fourteen or fifteen hour days... Not even Jake knew I was here every night. Then she died and...

"I woke up one day about two years later and... Jake was at college. I didn't remember taking him. You were an actress. And I was married to Tiffanie."

Valerie sat next to her father. She held out her hand and Sam took it.

"We had this arrangement for Briana. Tiffanie would drop her off at the office almost every night. You've met Briana? She's really a wonderful little girl. I don't know how I did it but I was Briana's Daddy. Tiffanie and I had lunch three times a week or so. We'd talk about finances. She set up society functions, nights at the Country Club, stuff like that. Just like when she was my secretary, I did what she told me to do then returned to the Castle at night."

"It was your photos that finally woke me to my life," Sam said.

"My photos?" Valerie asked. "But..."

"I was approached by someone saying they had naked photos of you. I paid... a lot of money for them. Originals. When I saw them, I knew what they were. I called Patrick Hargreaves. You know Alex and Max's Dad? I knew he was in the military before he was a Senator. I figured he'd know what to do."

Valerie nodded her head.

"He confirmed that Mike was missing. He took the photos saying he'd look into it," Sam said. "The next time I had lunch with Tiffanie, we decided that I would move in. We would try it as a married couple. Everyone believed my trophy wife and I were happily married."

"And?"

"It didn't go very well. I had loved your mother for more than half my life. I couldn't imagine even sleeping in the same bed with another woman. I moved into one of the spare bedrooms in Tiffanie's show home."

Sam fell silent. Not sure what to do, Valerie changed into another outfit. She was zipping the skirt when Sam said:

"I thought about killing myself every moment of every day."

Valerie gasped.

"My children were gone. My Celia was gone. I... I don't know how long we went on like that. One night, Tiffanie came in and... "

"She was pregnant already," Delphie said. She came into the living room from the kitchen. Her crossed arms and pierced lips betrayed her indignation. "She wanted to pretend that Becky was Sam's child. But Sam can't... and..."

"That didn't go very well either," Sam said. "I moved back here the next day."

"God I hate that woman. I just..."

"Delphinium, please. For me. Let's not do that today," Sam said. "I just have one more day."

"Sorry Sam." Delphie smiled.

"Would you mind telling Val the rest? I have to find my tux."

"I had it cleaned," Delphie said. "It's in your closet."

"And the shirt?"

"Of course."

Sam smiled his 'Thanks.'

"You have to find the cuff links yourself. I couldn't find them."

"The cuff links? It's going to be a long day."

"Why don't you shower? I'll tell Val the rest."

Sam nodded. He was half way out of the room when Valerie said, "Dad?"

Sam turned and Valerie ran into his arms. They held each other and cried. After a moment, Sam kissed her cheek then went down the hall to his room.

"He lives in the Birch room, the one Celia died in. He's happiest there, I think," Delphie said.

"Is it hard for you?" Valerie asked.

"That Sam is hung up on Celia?"

Valerie nodded.

"I'm hung up on Celia. No, it's not hard." Delphie smiled slightly. "After all these years of knowing him, it's nice to have a deeper relationship. Does it bother you?"

"No, I used to say to Mike that I didn't know why he was with Tiffanie and not you."

Delphie smiled, "Would you like to hear the rest of this?"

"I think I need to," Valerie said.

Delphie nodded her head toward the couch. They sat next to each other.

"For whatever reason, we still don't know why, your naked photos arrived in the mail the day after he moved out. So Sam leaves the house and the next day the photos arrive. They were in a brown envelope addressed to Sam. We were told that a clerk sent them without realizing what they were. Well, the envelope was intercepted by..."

"The step-whore." Valerie's lip curled.

"Exactly. So this thing happens with Tiffanie. Sam moves out and plans to divorce her when he finds out she's pregnant with Becky. The photos are stolen, which he doesn't know anything about until they show up in the press. Then she..."

"The step-whore."

"Yes, honey. I wish you wouldn't call her that. It's not good for you to hold so much anger."

"It's what she is," Valerie said.

"Let's not argue. Your step-sister had just graduated from high school. Sam offered her a job. Like everyone who starts at Lipson, she worked the roads."

"Work the roads until we see if you fit. If you fit, the roads will show you where you fit." Valerie repeated a Lipson Construction motto.

"Exactly, except she didn't like it much. She told everyone that she owned the company. She... Anyway, Sam flew to Maine and asked Jake to buy the rest of Lipson. I think Sam planned to sell the company then kill himself. Jake and Sam argued for... days. The third day into it, Jake called me. I flew to Maine."

"You flew? In a plane?"

"Yes. Like all psychics, plane trips are hard on me but Jake was desperate. Sam and I weren't, well, together then. I think Jake didn't know what else to do. Sam was a mess... a complete mess." Delphie sighed. "I had no idea he was so bad."

"Please tell me what happened," Valerie said. "I've asked Jake and he won't tell me."

"I don't really know what happened between them. I was able to convince Sam it was all right to trust Jake. That was my part."

"Dad didn't trust Jake?" Valerie's voice reflected her disbelief. Sam and Jake were always two peas in a pod.

"Sam wasn't really himself." Delphie shook her head at the memory. "The upshot was that Jake bought the company. He made you buy some of it."

"He tricked me into buying four percent," Valerie said. She imitated Jake's voice, "Please Val! I have to borrow some money. I need to get this property and I can't afford it." Valerie returned to her own voice. "All bullshit."

"I'm not surprised. He was on a tear. His way or forget it. Sam was such a wreck he couldn't see that Jake's way was really the best."

"What did Jake do?"

"For starters, he put an end to the bullshit. Your step-sister was escorted off Lipson grounds. The lawyers went after the publications that published your photos. Money was no object. The publications couldn't prove it was you and they didn't have releases. I don't know how much it cost, but Jake won reparations from everyone who published the photos. Blocked from these two avenues of cash, your step-sister started selling your details to the press. Jake pulled no punches. She was arrested and spent time in jail until she took a plea bargain. I think she's still on probation."

"Wow."

"Jake was done with the entire mess. He bought the fishing cabin in Dexter and made Sam live there. That was another round of... Well, Sam was at the cabin a week before he came to his senses. Sam needed to fish, breathe fresh air, and live in peace. He was all but destroyed by all this... turmoil."

"But Tiffanie was pregnant and..." Valerie said

"He wouldn't divorce her," Delphie finished.

They sat contemplating Sam Lipson for a moment.

"It's not really Becky's fault that her mother is..." Delphie sighed. "That's pretty much it. Jake came home. This place was literally falling down. Sam was in Dexter and I was camped out here. Mike showed up the day after Jake came back to Denver. Jake and Mike went to work on the Castle. By the time your step-sister was out of jail, and Becky was born, the Castle was almost livable. Sam returned from his sabbatical ready to start living again."

"Why didn't Tiffanie divorce Dad?"

"Jake worried that Tiffanie would use a divorce to destroy Sam. Sam was very fragile. More public drama would have ruined him. So Jake set up those trusts. If Tiffanie files for divorce, she voids everything. He and Tiffanie are meeting on Monday to sign the divorce papers Jake set up four years ago."

"Why is Dad going to the wedding?"

"He promised he would. Your father keeps his word. It's important to him." Delphie shrugged. "Since Becky and all of that, Tiffanie has been on her best behavior. She knows she screwed up. I personally think she's horrified by the monster her daughter has become."

"I'm horrified at what her daughter has become," Valerie said.

"Your publicist will be here in a few minutes," Delphie said. "She's at Starbucks with some little person."

"Thanks," Valerie said. "Why do you think the step-whore went after Trevor?"

"Birds of a feather? I don't know. She did it with deliberate purpose. I think she wanted to hurt Jake or maybe Sam. But what they did to Jill? To Katy?"

Valerie shuddered.

"Let's just be glad our Jill is free," Delphie said. "I'll get the door."

Delphie was standing next to the door when there was a knock.

"Oooh honey, what ARE you wearing?" Ramon flew across the threshold to Valerie. He squealed. "This is... NO. Don't say it."

"Claire Martins."

"I told you NOT to say it," Ramon twirled around the room until he saw the gowns. He fluttered over to the gowns. "Oh. Oh. Oh."

"She wants me to be the spokesmodel for a new off the rack line. This is..."

"NO! Claire Martins has a new line! You're the look of a Martins line?" Ramon fell on the floor in a mock faint. "I've died and gone to heaven."

"I thought we were dressing the troglodyte," Jen whispered to Val.

"Mike? My husband?"

"Right, your husband."

"They've done that as well," Valerie said. "Or they are going to. Frederic, Claire's son, is working with men. Mike's one of his first men. Did you book Oprah?"

"Thursday," Jen said.

"I think Frederic said Thursday would work. He's creating a special tux for Friday," Valerie said. "You should see Mike. He's been waxed. He even got a hair cut. He's drop dead gorgeous."

Jen fell to the floor in an imitation of Ramon's mock faint. Valerie stood over Jen and Ramon laughing. Jen opened one eye.

"Is this Mike as good in bed as he is coming up with miracles?"

"Yeah," Valerie laughed.

Ramon opened one eye, "Does he have a brother?"

Valerie fell on the floor next to them.

CHAPTER TWENTY-FIVE
A GRADUAL UNVEILING

"Oooh that looks fun," Valerie said. She pointed to a red bite mark above Sandy's left breast.

Valerie, Jill and Sandy were looking at dresses in the second floor of Mike's art studio. The entire floor had been converted to Valerie's designer dress storage. Since Jill was going to wear one of Claire's gowns, Valerie was acting as personal shopper for Sandy. Jill was zipping Sandy into a royal blue silk Dior gown.

"Sandy is dating Aden," Jill said.

"ADEN!" Valerie squealed. "Really!"

"Yeah, why?" Sandy asked. "Am I too fat for this dress?"

"The zipper's jammed," Jill said.

"Mike's fault," Valerie said. "He drives me to all these events then... well..."

She lifted and dropped her eyebrows to indicate how Mike had jammed the zipper. The women laughed.

"I had it cleaned but they didn't un-stick the zipper." Valerie held the fabric so Jill could work loose the zipper.

"Wait. Why did you react like that about Aden?" Sandy asked.

Sandy's natural mistrust had returned full force at church. She already told Jill she was not going to see Aden again. Jill worked to keep her friend open to the possibility of Aden, but was losing the battle.

"He's one of your men."

"Aden?" Valerie was so surprised she stepped back. "I've never been with Aden. I don't know anyone who has."

"So why did you squeal?"

Sandy felt an overwhelming desire to run away, get out of the warm closet of this spoiled rich girl. Before she could run away, Valerie put her hands on Sandy's shoulders and looked into her eyes. While Valerie never had an ounce of psychic capacity, she was very emotionally intuitive. She felt Sandy's aching, frightened heart as if it was her own.

"I squealed because he seems like he would be very fun. I've known him a long, long time. I'm excited for him to find someone great. Mom used to say..."

Valerie clamped her mouth shut. She spun in place and moved into the sea of dresses.

"Oh no you don't." Sandy caught Valerie's wrist. "What did your Mom say?"

Valerie sighed.

"Celia used to say that we had to get Aden ready for when he met his baker," Valerie said. "She thought it was a funny turn of words. I stopped talking because you're a hairdresser, right?"

Sandy nodded.

"Mike and I thought it might be Candy, you know, because she is a pastry chef. But, Candy's gay." Valerie looked away. "I didn't want to tell you because you're not a baker..."

"Sandy's a great baker," Jill said. "She can make anything just by feel. She does it to relax, so didn't want to do it for work.."

"You baked the scones for breakfast?"

Sandy nodded. With her eyes wide, Valerie squealed again.

"YOU'RE THE BAKER?!? Oh Jake will just die!" Valerie looked around the upstairs then shook her head. "Get out of that dress."

"But it's nice," Sandy said. "It fits."

"We're going shopping for something very special, very sexy to seal the Aden deal. That's a man you don't want to get away," Valerie said. "Not that he would. I bet he's smitten. Still, I'm sure Jill will let you wear some of her diamonds."

Valerie clamped her mouth closed again.

"What diamonds?" Jill asked. "Jake said that: 'Val has your diamonds.' I thought he was hallucinating."

Valerie clapped her hands together like Katy did when she was excited.

~~~~~~~~~

Jacob opened his eyes to a silent room. He knew he was in the hospital. He just couldn't remember why. With deliberate care, he wiggled his toes, then his fingers. His right arm felt funny. With his left hand, he felt the gauze on his right shoulder and arm.

Shoulder injury. Okay.

He wracked his mind for details. How did he get here? Hockey? Shooting accident? No, hunting season is in the fall. Judging from the light, it was still summer. Had to be a construction accident.

He should know this.

"So you're awake," the nurse said.

Ah great, Nasty Nurse. Why do I remember her and not why I'm here?

"When will I be released?" Jacob managed.

If Nasty Nurse knew he was foggy, he wouldn't make it home. Every cell in his body wanted to be at the Castle.

"Today," she said.

"It's Sunday?" Jacob guessed.

"Right," the nurse said. "You want me to call someone?"

Jacob calculated. Dad would be at Trevor's wedding. Aden and Blane too. Valerie was in LA faking an engagement to that producer. Delphie doesn't drive.

"Yeah, can you call my friend Mike?"

"What about your girlfriend?" the Nurse sneered.

"My girlfriend?"

The nurse snorted at him.

"I figured as much. That sweet girl's just one of a crowd, eh?" she sneered. "You men are all the same."

"Ok," Jacob said. "Mike's number should be in my file."

"You can call him yourself."

"I don't seem to have my phone."

The nurse curled her lip at him. With her hands on her hips, she seemed to cackle.

"You'll get your phone after the doctor takes a look at you."

The nurse slammed the door behind her.

Girlfriend?

What girlfriend?

~~~~~~~~~

"Ok," Valerie said.

She was in full actress mode. Her audience? Jill and Sandy. They picked up Sam and Mike on their way through the kitchen.

"Is this going to take long? The limo is due here in..."

"Dad!"

Valerie mock glared at Sam and they laughed. Mike held a clipboard in one hand while his other hand ran over Val's round behind. She leaned into him. They were standing near a fireplace in the basement of the Castle.

"How long have you been divorced?" Valerie asked Jill.

"Um... Trevor asked me in January. It was supposed to go through in three months but he screwed up the paperwork. It was a big mess but my lawyer sorted it all out then resubmitted the paperwork. The engagement party was three weeks ago. The divorce was final the next day."

"Six months since Trevor originally filed?" Valerie asked.

"Almost seven," Jill said. "Right?" She looked at Sandy for confirmation.

"Almost seven months," Sandy repeated then added in a mock whisper, "Thank God."

"Mike?"

"It's not exactly right. She's supposed to be divorced for six months but..." Mike looked at Valerie then Sam. "Objections?"

"Sounds fine to me," Sam said.

"Val?"

"I don't care and I know Jake could give a shit."

"Ok, check," Mike said.

Valerie cleared her throat. "Mr. McGuinsey no longer has access to any of your financial records or accounts?"

"Mike set that up," Jill said. "Wait. Mike insisted on that."

"Mike?"

"Check," Mike said.

"Mike will you read the instructions," Valerie said. "See, I'd make a great game show host."

"Maybe when you're ancient and wrinkly." Mike kissed her.

"Wrinkly? Like that's going to happen," Valerie laughed. "Rules."

"Jillian Roper is to inherit my entire diamond collection. However, they are willed in trust."

"What are you talking about?" Jill asked.

"Celia wanted you to have her diamonds, Jill," Sam said. "There are conditions on the gift. That's what they're telling you."

"I can't take her diamonds!" Jill said. "What about Val!? Gosh, you must be so..."

"Excited," Valerie said.

"Let them finish," Sandy said. She whispered to Jill, "We'll sort it out later."

Jill nodded. She and Sandy could work out anything.

"I'll be good," Jill said.

"Basically," Sam said. "Celia willed you her diamonds. But you were only able to know about the inheritance, and receive the diamonds, when you were financially separate from Trevor. Celia was afraid that he would take the diamonds or the money from you."

"What does the trust thing mean?" Jill asked.

"The diamonds aren't allowed to leave the Marlowe family," Mike read. "Jillian Roper can sell the diamonds within the Marlowe family or bequeath them to a Marlowe. However, the diamonds will remain within the Marlowe family."

Jill looked at Sam.

"Val wants to buy some," Sam said. "That's why she's so excited. She's waited nine years to get them."

"Oh," Jill said. "Why would I sell them? Val can have what she wants."

"Nope," Valerie said. "Doesn't work like that. Mike?"

"There's a hand written note here Jill. It says, 'Welcome to the family.'"

"Celia worried that you would feel intimidated by all this money. She wanted to give you a chance to be on a little more even footing."

"Of course, it never occurred to Mom that you and Trevor would be married for so long. She believed you and Jacob would marry and live happily ever after. She wanted to ease the way there," Valerie said. "Don't worry Jill. I'm not jealous."

When Valerie's face lit up, Jill saw Celia's daughter. Pure and simple, Valerie was the kind, generous, open hearted daughter of Celia Marlowe. Jill was so struck by seeing her dead friend in another person that she failed to notice what Valerie was doing until Sandy gasped.

"Pretty, huh? Mike and I set them up for you. We thought we'd give them to you Monday but... Jill?"

Mike caught Jill before she hit the ground in a dead faint. He cradled her head.

"What happened?" Valerie asked.

"She faints when she hasn't eaten," Sandy said. She kneeled down to hold Jill's hand. "Did you see her eat yesterday?"

"She said she was sick to her stomach," Sam said. "She just drank coffee."

"I didn't see her eat today," Sandy said. "She said she ate with Jacob but we'd have to ask him how much she actually ate."

"Does she have an eating disorder?" Valerie asked.

"Yeah, it's called poverty," Sandy said. "If she can't pay, she won't eat. We tried to bribe her into eating Friday morning but outside of a few bites, she wouldn't eat. She's been like that since we were kids."

"Blane said she wasn't eating because she couldn't pay," Sam said. "I just couldn't believe it. I'd buy her anything. I don't care."

"She cares," Sandy said. "I doubt she's eaten much this week. She just had enough money for Katy to eat. She traded for the paint. She painted as a way to pay for her rent this week."

"Oh God," Valerie said.

Mike stood up with Jill in his arms.

"I'll deal with this," he said. He moved out of the basement leaving a guilt stricken group. Standing at the bottom of the basement stairs, he turned, "There isn't anything you can do. My parents were very strict about this kind of thing–no charity. Val can you lock up?"

Mike carried Jill up the stairs as Noelle Norsen, followed by her brother Nash, came down the stairs.

"SANDY! Daddy, Mr. Lipson's down here with Sandy! Hi Sandy! I didn't know YOU would be here!"

"Hi honey," Sandy said. "What's going on?"

Aden jogged down the stairs.

"Blane can't make it," Aden said. "He's having a bad day. He asked if I would go in his place. Delphie's with Katy but she said she would watch the kids. I..."

Aden saw Sandy for the first time. His face flushed with emotion.

"Hi Sandy."

Valerie giggled at his reaction. She put her arm over Sandy's shoulder.

"Wanna go to Trevor's wedding?" Valerie asked Sandy.

"I don't have any thing to wear," Sandy said. She looked from Valerie's delighted face to Aden's blushing face. "Plus he didn't..."

"I'd love it if you would come with me. We're filling in for Jacob," Aden said. "We're just there to pay the bill and support Sam. We won't stay for the reception. Just the wedding."

"Oh, I..."

"Val can get you dressed," Sam said. "Can't you?"

"Of course," Valerie said. "How much time do we have?"

"Twenty minutes at the outside," Sam said. "Aden's tux is here."

Valerie grabbed Sandy's wrist and dragged her through the basement.

"Twenty minutes," Valerie yelled back to the men. "And I get Delphie."

"Wait for me." Noelle ran after them.

Sam looked up to the ceiling when Delphie and Katy cheered overhead.

"Time to get dressed," Sam said. "I wondered why your tux was in my closet. Delphie had it cleaned."

"Of course," Aden said. "You want to come with us, Nash?"

"Sure," Nash said.

"Maybe you could help me find my cuff links."

~~~~~~~~~

"Hi," Mike said to Jill.

He had carried her to Jacob's apartment and laid her on the bed. Jill sat up with a gasp.

"Drink this," Mike said. He held a glass of chocolate milk out to her. "Do it."

Jill took a sip and set it down.

"Drink it."

Jill sighed and drank the milk.

"I can't help it. I feel awful. I don't have a job! I don't have a way to take care of my child! And all this bullshit. I'm going to be some spokesmodel and marry some rich guy I don't even know. The guy I almost got KILLED because I'm too incompetent to even keep a job. And diamonds? I mean come on..."

Mike hugged her to him.

"I'm sorry," Mike said. "I've been so caught up in Val being home I never thought to ask if you had money."

"I'm not your responsibility," Jill said.

"You're my sister, Jill. Yes, you're my responsibility. So is Katy, but I can't imagine you've let her suffer at all."

Jill shook her head.

"Sandy said you painted as a way to pay for your rent. Is that true?"

"I'm no freeloader. It's nice that they let me and Katy stay here but..."

"How did you pay for it?" Mike asked.

"I know the guys at Belcaro Paints. They give me seconds and returns."

"And you give them?"

"I work as a color consultant," Jill said. "It's easy and..."

"JILL! That's what? Your third job?" Mike was so exasperated he could barely speak.

"Fourth. But..."

"When did you eat last?"

"At Pete's on Wednesday. I always eat at Pete's when I work. It's one of the reasons I work there. But Pete won't let me work so... What am I going to do Mike?"

"You're going to let me give you money," he said. "I make really good money, Jill. When your feet are healed, and you take in all that's happened, you'll decide what you want to do."

"I will pay you every penny back," Jill said.

"You will not. I won't let you."

"But..."

"Dad was wrong, Jill. About so many things, just plain wrong. He never would have let me marry Val. Never. Not because she wasn't good for me or didn't love me or even because she isn't even Catholic. He wouldn't let me marry Val because he was afraid. He didn't want us to have friends or make connections here. He was afraid they would get..."

"Discovered," Jill said.

"You remember what happened?"

"I've always remembered what happened. But whenever I talked about what happened, I was told that I was wrong."

Mike hugged Jill again.

"Do you want..."

"I don't want to talk about that now," Jill said.

"When you're ready, I know someone who has all the answers about our parents."

"Ok," Jill said. "I can't deal with it today. Is that all right?"

"Of course. What's going to make this better, Jill?" Mike asked. "If I had known how hard it was to be with Trevor, I would have helped you. I..."

"I know," Jill said. "I couldn't let you help. I mean, I begged Megan to let us get married. One week into it, I wanted to come home. I screwed up.

Then, it was one tiny step at a time into a complete nightmare. I..."

"And now?"

"I don't know." Jill sighed.

Mike nodded.

"What would you eat?"

"You know, I'd love to go to Pete's. I really miss it," Jill said.

"Let's go," he said.

"Do you mind..."

"I know how hard it is to believe, but normal people don't care about paying for a meal or helping out. They want to do it."

"Are you saying you're normal?"

Mike laughed.

~~~~~~~~~

Sandy wasn't sure what to make of Aden. Ever since she flew down the stairs from Val's apartment, he had this weird smile on his face. He was so awkward and odd that she was sure she'd offended him. He just held her hand like a prom date.

But she didn't dare ask him in front of Sam.

Tucked into the blue dress, she was synched, bolstered, pressed and made up to where she looked like... a movie star. She was even wearing a pair of Valerie's Christian Louboutin black pumps. Her toes stretched into the toilet paper Valerie stuffed into the toes. As long as she didn't have to pee, or sneeze, she was in good shape.

Yep, Sandy was prettified.

And Aden was weird.

They dropped Sam in front of the Cathedral of the Immaculate Conception on Colfax. The limo driver turned onto Logan Street before Sandy said something.

"You are acting very strange," Sandy said.

Aden pressed the back of her hand to his pants.

"Oh," Sandy said.

"I'm a little uncomfortable," Aden replied. "No blood flow to the brain."

The limo driver pulled over on Logan Street to let them out.

"I'm not wearing underwear." The driver opened the door for her and she scooted out of the limo. Under her breath, she said, "Can't have panty lines."

"Now, that's just unfair," Aden said.

Sandy giggled. Aden followed her out of the limo. Kissing her on the sidewalk, his hands moved to check the underwear promise. She grabbed his hands.

"You're very beautiful."

She smiled. Hearing the music for the wedding, they hurried down the sidewalk and up the stairs into the Cathedral where Trevor's wedding was about to start.

CHAPTER TWENTY-SIX
THERE IS SOMETHING YOU COULD DO

Sam sighed.

Like the kind, stupid step-father he had become, Sam waited outside the bridal chamber. His eyes drifted over the pews filled with the society people Tiffanie befriended with his money. He wasn't even Catholic. Out of no where, a single thought echoed in his head:

"I'll never see any of these pretentious, stupid people ever again."

Sam beamed. He nodded to Aden and Sandy as they came through the door. They sat in the back pew of the church.

The music started and the wedding party began down the aisle. Trevor waited at the end of the aisle for his bride.

Sam steeled himself for the walk down the aisle.

The door opened a crack. Tiffanie was pushed out of the bridal chamber by small hands with acrylic French tips.

"Sam," Tiffanie said.

"DO. IT. NOW." His step-daughter whispered through the crack in the door.

"Sam, I..."

"She doesn't want to be married to you anymore." The step-whore pushed her mother out of the doorway. Dressed in her wedding finery, her made-up face twisted with hate and anger. "You stupid fuck. You look ridiculous in that tuxedo. Give. Him. The. Papers. Mother. DO. IT. NOW."

"Tiffanie, you don't have to do this," Sam said.

He felt more than saw Aden get up from the pew.

"Yes, she does," the step-whore said. Whipping around, her train flipped into the aisle and the step-whore stood at the end of the aisle.

The wedding crowd stood for the bride.

"I was going to have you walk me down the aisle. But I didn't want an incompetent fool like you to soil my day. This is the start of MY new life."

Her hand pushed at Sam's chest.

"I don't want you to be ANY part of MY life. We don't want anything to do with YOU."

Watching this drama unfold, the crowd began to whisper to each other.

"MOTHER!"

Tiffanie's face held a gentle smile for Sam. She gave him a stack of papers. He opened the divorce papers then shook his head.

"Now get out of this church!" The step-whore said. "TREVOR"

"Tiffanie..."

"It's Ok, Sam," Tiffanie said. "Tell Jacob not to worry about the bill."

"You don't have to do this."

Tiffanie kissed his cheek.

"Sweet Sam," Tiffanie said. "I've never been able to say no to her. Her father, either. It's for the best."

Trevor and his best-man reached for Sam's arms to throw him out of the church. But Aden blocked their way. Trevor moved to hit Aden. Aden shifted. In one easy movement, Aden threw Trevor over his hip. Trevor landed with a thump on the ground. The best-man took one look at Aden and stepped back.

"Trevor!" The step-whore screamed. "Oh my God! Mother! Look what you've done!"

"Come on, Big Sam," Aden said. "We have other things to do today."

The step-whore flew at Sam. Her fists battered his chest. Her acrylic nails reached for Sam's eyes.

"May I?" Sandy asked.

Aden shrugged.

Sandy grabbed the step-whore by her shoulders and threw her off Sam. Leaving Trevor and his bride on the floor of the church vestibule, Sam, Aden and Sandy jogged down the Cathedral steps.

Tiffanie stood at the door and waved good-bye.

The music started inside the church as they walked up Colfax to the parking lot. Sam opened the limo door for Sandy. Aden scooted in behind her. Sam bent to speak to them.

"I'm going to walk a little bit," Sam said.

"Are you all right?" Aden asked. He moved to get out of the limousine. "We can walk with you."

"I feel..." Sam's eyes welled with tears. "My Celia is right here with me. I have my wife... my life... back... I can't explain it. I... I'd like to walk with Celia for a while. Don't worry. I'm fine. Jacob wakes up at four o'clock?"

"Four o'clock. Right."

"I'll be there," Sam said. He laughed. "There is something you could do for me."

"Anything," Aden said.

Sam gave Aden the divorce papers then yanked an ornate wedding ring off his left hand. He smiled then handed the ring to Aden. He took off his bow tie and unbuttoned his shirt. Pulling out a long gold chain, he jerked a worn silver band from the chain. He gave Aden the broken chain and slipped the ring on his left ring finger. Sam's face broke into a huge smile.

He walked off toward Sixteenth Street. Sam waved to them as they drove by.

"Wow," Sandy said. "What are you going to do with that?"

Aden rolled down the window and threw the ornate wedding band out the window. Sandy watched it bounce along the payment until it dropped through a sewer drain.

"Where to?" the limo driver asked.

"My house?" Sandy asked.

"Oh yes."

~~~~~~~~~

"We need to make sure we're there when Jacob wakes up," Delphie said to Valerie.

"What's the big deal?" Valerie asked. "He's been in an out of medication for the last week."

"Medication blocks a psychic's ability. I know it sounds weird but for a true psychic, your ability to intuit is like a third leg. When your intuition is clogged, you don't remember the most basic things. It's like being brain damaged."

"Like when you had your hysterectomy?" Valerie asked. "I'd better call the hospital immediately."

Valerie dialed Denver Health on her cell phone. She waited on hold for Jacob's nurse.

"My hysterectomy? That was not good," Delphie said.

"You couldn't remember your name," Valerie said. "You kept asking me how I grew up so fast. You thought I was twelve. It was hilarious."

"Yes, it was," Delphie said. "All of that medication is going to catch up to Jacob. You know how intense your brother can be."

Valerie held up a finger. Talking back and forth, she thanked the nurse then hung up the phone.

"He's awake and with the doctor now. The nurse said he will be released at four o'clock. Something about medication half life… something."

"We'd better be there."

Valerie nodded.

~~~~~~~~~

"Oh my God," Aden said.

He fell onto the bed. Sandy laughed and rolled onto her side. He caressed her naked shoulder.

"Sorry about the dress," he said.

"The zipper was stuck when I tried it on. It's just re-stuck."

"Re-stuck? That sounds very fun."

He helped her out of the rest of the dress then slipped on top of her. She lifted her head to kiss his lips. His eyes gently moved across her face.

"I love you, Sandy."

Sandy's entire body reacted in horror. She pushed him off her. Her body vibrated with emotion but she was too upset to speak.

"What?"

She threw his shoe at him, then another.

"LIAR!"

"What happened?"

"GET OUT OF MY HOUSE!"

Aden ducked to avoid a half full champagne glass that flew across the room at him. Sandy balled up his tuxedo and undergarments. Stomping to the door, she threw his clothing outside her apartment door.

"HOW DARE YOU!"

"Sandy, wait. Sandy."

Naked, Aden scrambled toward her. When he was close enough, she battered him with her fists. Her face contracted in pain. Her hair fell wild on her shoulders. Her entire body was red with fury.

One at a time, Aden caught her fists. She jerked her hands away. But he held them firm.

"I'm sorry I frightened you."

Sandy jerked her hands away from him. Aden held them firm. Seeing that it was fruitless, she bit her lip and glowered at him.

"I'll let go of your hands if you stop hitting," Aden said. "Can you stop hitting?"

She looked away from him. Without warning, Sandy fell to her knees. Her mind and body were overwhelmed with agony. She moved so fast that she pulled Aden down on top of her. Aden wrapped himself around her crumpled form. He rocked her back and forth while she cried.

"Please go," Sandy whispered between sobs.

"No," Aden said. "I won't leave you like this. I won't do it."

"Please."

"No. Don't ask again."

She dared to look into his face. In the torrent of tears, her make up had smeared down her cheeks. The pain in her eyes was almost unbearable to Aden.

"Why did you say that? About me?"

"I've loved you for a long time, Sandy. It's why I didn't ask you out sooner. I felt too strongly about you."

"How can you SAY that? You don't know me at all and..."

"Shh..." He wrapped her in his arms until her tears slowed. "Let's just get through this. What would help?"

"Baking," They said together.

"Why don't you make some cookies?" Aden kissed her cheeks.

Sandy nodded.

"I need to clean up," she said. "What about your kids?"

"They love Delphie and the Castle. We've stayed in one of the apartments before. I'm sure we can stay there again." Aden scratched his head. "I canceled their camp for next week because I thought they'd be with Nuala. We'd probably end up staying at the Castle anyway so I can work and take care of them."

Sandy nodded.

"I'll call while you clean up."

He helped her to her feet then walked with her to the bathroom. He turned on the shower then helped her step in. Under the warm water, Sandy cried her heart out.

~~~~~~~~~

After stuffing Jill full of pancakes, eggs, bacon and sausage, Mike took her to his bank ATM. He gave her three hundred dollars from his account and another three hundred dollars from Valerie's account. He would have taken the maximum from their joint account as well but Jill was freaked out about six hundred dollars. They yelled back and forth at each other with all the heat and intensity of close siblings.

Finally, Jill said very simply, "Thank you. I really need this money."

And Mike laughed.

Mike knew Jill was excited to see Jacob again so he let her out at his artist's studio. He was parking the car at the workshop when he received a call from Jacob.

Without giving it another thought, Mike drove to Denver Health. Wearing a sling and a neck brace, Jacob waited for him just inside the doors. Mike ran to the passenger door to help Jacob into the Bronco.

"Pissed off?" Mike asked.

"Very," Jacob said. "Sorry to bug you for a ride."

"Not a problem," Mike said. "Everyone thought you were waking up at four."

"What am I supposed to do? Wait around until I evolve?" Jacob bristled at his interaction with the Nasty Nurse. "And who the fuck is everyone?"

They drove in silence down Speer Boulevard to Fourteenth Street. They stopped at the traffic light at Logan.

"Guess that's Jill's soul mate," Jacob said. He pointed down Logan to the bride and groom coming out of the Cathedral of the Immaculate Conception on Colfax. "God, Jill must be devastated."

"She didn't say anything." Mike shrugged.

"What's she going to say?" Jacob hit the dashboard then groaned. "Fuck."

"Careful, lover boy," Mike said. "You don't want to go back to the hospital."

"Where are you going?" Jacob asked when Mike drove past Race St.

"Workshop? The Mayor hasn't figured a way to get rid of the paparazzi," Mike said.

Jacob frowned at Mike. He had no idea what Mike was talking about but was too angry to find out. Mike pulled into the workshop. He helped Jacob out of the Bronco.

"Did you get your prescriptions?"

"Ah FUCK!" Jacob exclaimed. "I have to get those filled."

"I can get them if you..."

"I haven't used my drug insurance. I have to go. Fuck!"

"Come on. You probably need condoms anyway."

"What?"

Mike laughed.

~~~~~~~~~

Ever since Jacob said he would be Katy's Daddy, Katy insisted on taking her nap in his big armchair. For the last few days, Jill dragged the armchair near the door of the bathroom. Katy slept like a stone in Jacob's chair while Jill took a bath in his huge bathtub.

Jill was excited to see Jacob today.

She washed her hair then let it air dry while she soaked in the tub. Even though she knew Jacob probably was too sick for real intimacy, she carefully shaved her legs. She tried to relax but her heart raced with the idea of Jacob coming home.

Frustrated at her own impatience, she remembered that Jacob had told her that she could use his iPOD. Maybe some music would help her settle down. Jill wandered around the apartment until she found the tiny music player.

Flopping naked on the bed, she tried to figure out how the player worked. Pressing play all, she stuck the ear buds in her ears.

Jacob liked the same music!

Maybe it wasn't so crazy to be engaged to a guy she didn't know.

She smiled.

~~~~~~~~~

"I think Katy's napping," Mike said.

They worked their way through the tunnels.

"Okay."

Mike opened the door to the kitchen.

"You're really acting strange," Mike said.

"Sorry man, I just need to be home. Catch you later?" Jacob asked.

"Sure."

Jacob made his way up the back stairwell to his apartment. He noticed the warm pumpkin color on the walls. He'd always dreamed that Jill would decorate his living space the way she had fixed up that hole she lived in. Looking at the walls, he sighed.

Like he ever had a chance with Jill. Mike must have had some time on his hands.

Fuck. Why can a cretin like Trevor get, and keep, a girl as amazing as Jill?

At least he was finally home. Shaking his head at his own temper, he flipped open his apartment door. Another night wondering what the fuck was wrong with him.

He noticed the soft yellow walls first. Then the little girl curled up in his favorite arm chair. He blinked.

That's Katy.

Taking a step into the room, he saw her.

Jill.

Her feet swung back and forth. Her round behind rose off the bed like a brilliant half moon. He heard his blood pump in his ears. He wasn't sure why she hadn't noticed him.

And he didn't care why she was there.

In two swift steps, he moved across the floor. He had to touch her. He had to make sure she was real and not just some dumb fantasy.

Standing just behind her feet, he watched her behind rise and lower with her swinging feet. He stretched his right hand and stroked the side of her foot.

Jill rolled over with his touch. She pulled the iPOD earbuds from her ears. With the smile on her face, his memory returned. She jumped up from the bed to hold him.

"I thought you were a dream," he said.

She tilted her head and smiled at him. "Let me get dressed."

"Please don't."

"You need to lay down," she said.

"Would you mind helping me?"

Jill helped him out of his clothing. He refused a t-shirt or underwear. She helped him into bed then slipped in next to him. Laying on her side, her hand stroked his chest.

"Seems like you have something on your mind," she said.

"Since the moment I saw your beautiful behind on my bed," he said. "I just don't think I can..."

"I asked the doctor. He said it wouldn't hurt you."

Her hand stroked his thighs.

"This has to be a dream."

Reaching, she grabbed a condom from the bed side table drawer. She slipped on top of him.

"Where did those come from?" he asked.

"I was hoping..." She slipped the condom on him.

"Now I know this is a dream."

"What would convince you?" she asked.

She wrapped herself around him. Very gently, very slowly, they built in intensity. Their lips were locked when Jill began to release against him. Unable to resist her pull, he followed in a solid burst. Jill rolled to the bed.

"Convinced?"

"I've died and gone to heaven."

~~~~~~~~~

"Aden," Sandy said. "Before we go..."

Standing in the entryway of her apartment, Aden turned to look at her. She held up a plate of warm chocolate chip cookies.

"Do you think these cookies are enough?" Sandy asked.

"Val said they ordered dinner. It's just a little family dinner to welcome Jacob home. Did you pack some overnight things?"

Sandy nodded. Aden took the cookies from her so she could put on her jacket and get her purse. She took the plate of cookies back from him. He unlocked the door and started to open it.

"Aden?"

"Yes honey."

"Thank you for staying with me. I... I'm sorry... for everything."

Aden took the cookies from her and set them on the entry table. He slipped his arms around her. His eyes scanned her face.

"I won't say it again until you're ready to hear it. But you need to know that what I said was true for me."

"But..." Sandy started.

"And, I am sorry I frightened you."

Sandy nodded. She kissed his lips and hugged him. He moved back to the door.

"Aden?"

He turned to look at her.

"I love you too."

He beamed at her.

"Don't say anything, Ok?" Sandy moved passed him. His hand stroked her behind as she passed. She turned to look at him. "Please?"

He nodded and followed her down the stairs to the waiting taxi.

~~~~~~~~~

MONDAY MORNING, 3 AM

"Jill," Jacob whispered.

"Yes Jacob."

Jill rolled onto her side. She kissed his face.

"Where's Katy?"

"She's asleep in her crib, remember? Mike brought it from the apartment," Jill said. "Why?"

"I think I need some convincing."

Jill giggled.

Denver Cereal continues at DenverCereal.com